BRAZOS
SCOUT

Also by Don Worcester
The War in the Nueces Strip

Don Worcester

BRAZOS SCOUT

A DOUBLE D WESTERN
DOUBLEDAY
New York London Toronto Sydney Auckland

A Double D Western
PUBLISHED BY DOUBLEDAY
a division of Bantam Doubleday Dell Publishing Group, Inc.
666 Fifth Avenue, New York, New York 10103

Double D Western, Doubleday,
and the portrayal of the letters DD
are trademarks of Doubleday, a division of
Bantam Doubleday Dell Publishing Group, Inc.

Library of Congress Cataloging-in-Publication Data

Worcester, Donald Emmet, 1915–
Brazos scout/Don Worcester.—1st ed.
p. cm.—(A Double D western)
1. Indians of North America—Texas—Wars—Fiction. I. Title.
PS3573.O688B73 1991
813'.54—dc20 91-8152
CIP

ISBN 0-385-41493-5
Copyright © 1991 by Don Worcester
All Rights Reserved
Printed in the United States of America
October 1991
First Edition

To Jeanne Williams, who has done so much for so many

AUTHOR'S NOTE

In order to depict historical figures accurately, I have relied heavily on Kenneth Franklin Neighbours' thoroughly researched study, *Robert Simpson Neighbors and the Texas Frontier, 1836–1859* (Waco: Texian Press, 1975). I am also indebted to Jerry Don Thompson's *Colonel John Robert Baylor: Texas Indian Fighter and Confederate Soldier* (Hillsboro, Texas: Hill Junior College Monograph #5, 1971) and Judith Ann Benner's *Sul Ross, Soldier, Statesman, Educator* (College Station: Texas A & M University Press, 1983).

BRAZOS
SCOUT

ONE

When Major Robert Neighbors asked me to work at the Brazos Indian Agency near Fort Belknap I couldn't say no, much as I hated Indians. He had, after all, taken me in and raised me after redskins killed my folks when I was about five, and he was the only father I'd ever really known. He was a tall man, a couple of inches over six feet, with brown hair and beard. He always wore a black coat. He joked a lot but seldom smiled, and I never once heard him use a cuss word.

He put me with a family in San Antonio when school was in session, and he made me go to church with him whenever he was around on Sunday. The rest of the year I stayed at his ranch, where his Tejano vaqueros taught me to ride and rope and speak Spanish. I loved him like he was my real father, even though he kept telling me I was wrong to hate all Indians.

He'd been on the go a lot while I was growing up; for part of the time he was superintendent of Indians in Texas. The Indians were dying of hunger and disease, he said, and would soon be gone unless something was done to save them. That suited me, but I didn't admit it. Anyway, that was why he persuaded the state legislature to set aside land for the Penateka Comanches on the Clear Fork of the Brazos and for what was left of the other Texas tribes downstream near where the Clear Fork entered the main Brazos.

Most of the time I'd been the Major's only family, but while I was in high school he'd married. After that things were never the same again, or at least that's how it seemed to me.

Not that he treated me different, for he was as kind to me as ever. But now I had to share him, first with a wife he adored, then with a daughter. I never let on how lost and jealous I felt when he got married. He may have suspected it, for at times he was especially thoughtful and let me know I was still his special son. But, I thought bitterly, not of his flesh and blood. I was about five eleven, slender and blond, and didn't even look like him.

Last year he'd insisted that I accompany him to a council with the Caddos, Wacos, and Anadarkos near Fort Belknap to learn where they wanted their reservation. It was the first time I'd seen a lot of Indians and although they seemed to respect the Major, I figured they'd as soon scalp him as talk to him. The Major introduced me to some he said were great warriors, like Anadarko chief José María and Ah-ha-dot of the Wacos. They shook my hand and grunted.

José María had done most of the talking for the Indians, and I had to admit he was a powerful speaker. The whites, he said, had driven them from their farms many times, but they still wanted to be near Fort Belknap for protection from the prairie tribes, meaning Comanches and Kiowas. "I've been caught between whites and Comanches before," he said, "and of those two evils I prefer to be near the whites. At least they usually allowed me to eat part of what I raised, but the Comanches took everything. The whites also made war on us, but if we must die, we prefer to die with full bellies."

"Well, what did you think of them?" the Major asked me afterward.

"I've got to admit what José María and Ah-ha-dot said made sense. I'm just glad I don't have to be around them every day." He looked at me solemnly.

"You wouldn't say that if you knew them better," he told me. "Someday I hope you will." I nodded like I agreed with him, but I was thinking, Not if I can help it.

I finished high school in '55, a year after he'd set up the two reserves. He wrote me to meet him at Fort Belknap and he'd introduce me to some of the cowmen who were beginning to stake out ranches in the area. Maybe one of them would hire me as a cowboy until I was old enough to start a ranch of my own. "Chip," he said when he met me at the fort, "I need you to help George Hill on the lower reserve for a while. He's mighty sick, but he won't leave until his replacement arrives. I'd take over there myself, but I've got to stay with the Comanches until a new agent gets here."

"If you need me, of course I'll do it, but . . ." He stopped me.

"I know what you're thinking, but I'm asking you to try to keep an open mind, and I want you to get to know some Indians. You'll find they're humans same as us, some good, some not so good. Anyway, right now I need your help."

"I'll try to keep an open mind" I promised. I owed him that much and more, but I still wasn't eager. "For how long?"

"Learn all you can from George about the reservation and the different tribes. Captain Shapley Ross will take over as soon as he gets his appointment. You can tell him what he needs to know so George won't have to stay. After Captain Ross gets settled in you can decide whether you want to leave or stay. It'll be a good chance to save money."

"Anything else?"

"Yes. Indians don't cotton to men who talk a lot right off. Many of them know some English, and several speak it well, but they won't let on until they figure you're worth talking to. Just go slow and feel your way. And be careful you don't fall for any of the girls." He flashed a rare smile, so I knew he was teasing.

"Fat chance of me doin' that."

"Don't be so sure."

I figured if they didn't want to talk to me that wouldn't hurt my feelings. I'd met Mr. Hill in San Antonio, where the Major had his headquarters. He was a short, stocky man with a red face and white hair, and seemed good-natured. I knew he'd be a good man to work for. But on an Indian reservation? The Major handed me a note to give him.

Feeling a bit glum I rode to the Brazos Agency, nearly ten miles from Fort Belknap, while the Major returned to the upper reserve on the Clear Fork about thirty miles away. When I got to the agency I saw a number of log buildings and cabins. I stopped at the one I figured must be the agency office, for it had a hitching rack in front of it. Several Indians were squatting in the shade of a Spanish oak, their ponies tied nearby. I dropped my reins over the hitching rack and entered the office through the open door. Mr. Hill was seated at a table, holding a letter with one hand and brushing away flies with the other. I handed him the Major's note.

"Have a seat," he said. "What have you got for me? Oh, it's from the Major." He read it aloud. " 'Put Chip Collins on the payroll at twenty dollars a month and let him do everything he can for you. For heaven's sake, man, spare yourself. Captain Ross will be here to relieve you as soon as he gets his appointment.' "

He laid the note on the table. "Good! I can sure use some help. Aren't you the lad the Major raised?" I nodded. "I thought I recognized you. Guess you've heard I must quit. I don't want to, but if I don't they say I may not last till Christmas. May not anyway." I sure hated to hear him say that.

He pointed to a rough map of the reserve tacked to the wall, and I saw it had the names of a lot of tribes written on it. "That shows the trails and where the villages are," he said. "The Wacos are the closest, right over yonder. It won't take you more than a few days to learn their locations and get acquainted with the chiefs."

"I've already met a couple of them. What's it like, workin' around redskins? I sure wouldn't be here if the Major hadn't asked me," I told him. "Some of 'em killed my folks, you know."

"If this had been your home and a lot of strangers came along and took your land and killed your friends, what would you have done? Do you think bein' white makes everything we do right? Workin' with these people is the most satisfyin' thing I've ever done, even more than bein' secretary of war for the Republic."

I found that hard to believe, but kept it to myself. I looked over the map and was surprised to see how many remnant tribes there were on the reserve, Hasinais and a bunch of other Caddo tribes. By each name was the number of men, women, and children. Some were represented by only a dozen families, others by three or four hundred people. Once the Caddos had outnumbered all of the others, I'd heard, but there weren't all that many left. The map also listed Bidais, Keechies, Tawakonis, Anadarkos, Tonkawas, and more, even Shawnees and Delawares. All told, there seemed to be about a thousand.

"Most have been farmers for centuries," Mr. Hill remarked, "but the Tonkawas have always been hunters. They're about the best scouts and trackers you can find. They were never a large tribe, and though they've always helped the whites against the Comanches, they've gotten little thanks for it. Only about four hundred are left, and they're not all here yet. It's up to us to see they survive. We owe it to 'em."

I wasn't at all sure about that.

"How come there are Delawares and Shawnees here?" I asked. "They aren't Texas Indians."

"Back in '43 when Sam Houston was in his second term as President of the Republic, he wanted to negotiate treaties with the Comanches and other hostiles. He figured the only way to make contact with them was through some reliable Indians, so he asked Butler, the agent in Indian Territory, to send him some. Butler sent John Connor, Jim Shaw, and Shawnee Tom; the others came along with them. Since then they've been indispensable as scouts and guides, and sort of diplomats. They know a lot of other Indian languages; all of the tribes respect 'em, even the Comanches." He paused, like he was having trouble breathing.

"The people here got to work right away clearing fields and plantin' corn and fruit trees," he continued. He didn't say so, but I heard later he'd bought them eight hundred little peach trees with his own money. "They're putting up native houses or cabins and rail fences, so they're off to a good start. In the past when their crops were ripe, white men drove them away and stole the harvest and their land. If they're given a chance you'll see some of the best farms in Texas right here." He paused again to catch his breath.

"The Tonkawas have never done any farming, so we have to teach 'em. They're not stupid by any means and are willing to learn; you'll find them likable people. Most of them know a little Spanish and some speak English, by the way. I wish I could stay a few more years and see them off to a good start." He coughed uncontrollably and his face turned redder. It was easy to see why the Major was worried about him. I shuffled my feet, not knowing what else to do.

"I can get by pretty good in Spanish," I said.

When he was breathing better he led me to a double log cabin and pointed to an army cot. "Yours," he said. "We eat in that cabin yonder by the sutler's warehouse. The privy is under those trees." We walked slowly back to the office, and on the way an Indian dressed like a white man waved to us.

"Who's he?"

"That's Fox, our Caddo express rider. You'll get to know him. He's as reliable as any man in Texas. The fort borrows him now and then to carry dispatches. He can get to any post and back quicker than army express riders."

Back at the office he pointed again to the map. "Spend the rest of the day gettin' to know the reservation, as much of it as you can," he told me. "It's nigh onto forty-six thousand acres, so it'll take a while to learn your way around the whole of it. I'll get you a guide, a lad about your age who knows some English." He walked slowly to the door and beckoned to a slender young Indian who was dressed a lot like me, only he had no hat and wore moccasins instead of boots. He had no gun, but a hunting knife was in a sheath on his belt. His hair was in two long braids that fell over his shoulders. His eyes were keen and the skin on his face was as dark and smooth as saddle leather. I wondered what tribe he was but didn't ask.

"Tosche," Mr. Hill said, "this is Chip. He's goin' to help me. I'll appreciate it if you'll show him the reserve and point out the different tribes and chiefs."

Tosche said nothing. I was ready to shake hands with him but he barely looked at me. He left the office to untie a roan pony that had been hitched to a Spanish oak, then hopped on it bareback. Without looking to see if I was coming, he headed down the trail at a trot. I mounted and followed, wondering if I couldn't do as well by myself. Remembering what the Major said about not talking a lot at first, I said nothing. If I'd talked it would have been to myself or my pony anyway. I hoped Captain Ross was on his way.

In about a mile and a half we came to a cluster of tipis and brush wickiups covered with cow and buffalo hides. Nearby was a small corn-field and patches of beans, melons, and squash. The corn looked sort of discouraged, wilted like it needed a good rain. In the distance I saw a couple of corrals with a few Indian ponies in them.

Tosche stopped his pony. "Tonkawas," he said. "My people. Campo is our chief." I was glad to see he could say that much. A few women were hoeing weeds, while a dozen men lounged in the shade. A girl of sixteen or seventeen came out of a tipi and spoke to Tosche in their language, but she didn't seem to notice me. Her face was oval and her skin was much lighter than his. I had to admit she wasn't bad-looking, at least for a squaw. She wore a loose-fitting blouse and skirt, both of buckskin. The skirt was just wrapped around her, and when she turned to point out something to Tosche I caught a glimpse of one leg clear to the thigh. The blouse didn't hide much when she bent over. I'd never seen such sights before, and even though she was an Indian I couldn't take my eyes off her. Without looking at me she sensed I was gawking at her and turned her back. I felt like she'd hit me in the face with a fresh cow flop.

My face burned as I turned my pony and looked over the cornfield like I was really interested in it, but I stared at the corn without even seeing it. Finally Tosche rode on without a word to me. I felt like letting him go on by himself, but followed. I wanted to ignore the girl but couldn't help glancing at her, and my face got even redder. She gave me a scornful half-smile, like she knew what she'd hit me with. I rode on in silence thinking, If these two are typical Tonkawas I don't want to know any of them, no matter what Mr. Hill said. Just looking at that girl gave me sensations I'd never felt before, at least not so strong. I wanted to wring her neck, but that was only part of it. If I ever got to know Tosche, which didn't seem likely, I might ask him about her. It was a feeling I enjoyed. Damn her.

We visited one village after another. At each Tosche told me the band or tribe and named the chief, but I had trouble remembering them. Once he repeated everything, and I suddenly realized I hadn't heard a word he said, thinking about that fool girl. He looked at me like maybe he thought I was loco. Could be he was right.

Most of the people we saw had much larger cornfields than the Tonkawas, and their corn wasn't wilted. They'd built log cabins or native round houses with roofs of reeds or grass, and they were putting up rail fences to keep stock out of the fields. The men barely glanced at us and went on with whatever they were doing. It was late afternoon when we got back to the Tonkawa camp. Tosche turned off the trail to the agency and left me without a word. I wondered if I was supposed to thank him, but he was gone before I could decide. I figured if I stayed around Indians very long I'd forget how to talk.

A few mornings later, just after sunrise I rode down to the Brazos on my way to take a message to a Caddo chief. Near the river I heard women's voices, and walked my pony quietly through the trees toward the bank. About thirty women and girls were bathing in the river. I knew they were Tonkawas because one was the girl who'd talked to Tosche. I held my breath as I watched her, for I had to admit she was a right pretty sight. I felt guilty spying on them, but I'd never seen a naked woman before and couldn't force myself to leave. I looked around to see if there was any way I could get real close to them without danger of being discovered, but gave it up. When they started to come out and put on their clothes I walked my pony back up the trail before turning and trotting past them like I'd just arrived. I tried to look straight ahead and act like I didn't see them, but I couldn't help a sideways glance at the girl. Our eyes met; she didn't smile, but I had that funny feeling again.

Later Mr. Hill told me that the Tonkawas and the others bathed about every day, not once a week like white folks. That made me wonder why people said Indians were dirty.

Another day Mr. Hill sent me to the Anadarko village to ask Chief José María to come to the agency. I remembered him from when I went with the Major to his council with the Caddos and Anadarkos. José María was short and heavyset and looked to be about fifty, but he was still a great war chief and he'd battled both whites and Comanches many times.

On my way to his village I rode past the Tonkawa camp and looked around, hoping to see the girl. I didn't see her, but Tosche silently joined me. We jogged down the trail and came to a clearing where cattle were grazing. The government had given the Indians three hundred cows and some bulls. Tosche showed a lot more interest in them than he had in cornfields, which he ignored. Now he stopped his pony and pointed to a calf that had a broken mesquite branch caught around its neck. When it tried to nurse, the thorns pricked the cow and she wouldn't stand still. If the calf didn't get rid of that branch it would starve; it already looked weak.

"You ride around to the other side and keep them out of the brush while I rope the little feller," I told Tosche, shaking out a loop in my rawhide lariat. When he was in position I took out after the calf and easily caught both hind legs in my loop. While the cow bawled and the calf bleated, Tosche hopped off his pony and removed the branch. I gave the calf some slack and it stepped out of my lariat and scampered after its mother. We watched until it started nursing, so I knew it would be all right.

"You're a good roper," Tosche said as I coiled my lariat. I knew I wasn't nearly as good as the Tejano vaqueros who'd taught me, but few Anglo cowboys could rope as well as the best vaqueros.

"Do you know how to rope?" He shook his head. "Want to learn?" He almost smiled.

"Yes. I want to work cattle. Tonkawas weren't made to grow corn."

I thought some about it, wondering what I was getting into, and if I'd be wasting my time trying to teach an Indian to use a lariat. Then I figured maybe it was part of my job, whether he could learn or not. "One of these days I'll teach you what I know," I told him. He almost smiled again.

Back at the agency I told Mr. Hill about it. "Go ahead," he said. "Get started right away. We've needed someone to look after the cattle before they stray and get lost or stolen. Teach him all you know about cow work. He can have my old saddle and lariat—I'll never use them again."

The next morning I rode to the Tonkawa camp to get Tosche, but the first person I saw was the girl. Seeing her made me all tingly, as usual, and my mind wandered a bit.

"You want to see Campo?" she asked. I was surprised she knew English. Her voice was soft and pleasant, almost musical.

"No. Tosche." Just then he rode up. I told him what Mr. Hill had said, and for the first time I saw him look real happy. "Let's go get the saddle and lariat," I said, and we loped off to the agency. As we left I glanced at the girl; she was watching us, smiling. I tried to keep my mind off her, but it wasn't easy.

Tosche's pony didn't like it much when the cinch was tightened, but it wasn't long before he got used to it. Having a loop whirled over his head also boogered him at first. I showed Tosche a few things to get him started. I could soon tell by the skillful way he handled the lariat that he'd probably catch on faster than I did. That was a surprise. In fact I resented it a little, but we continued the lessons whenever we could.

"Nothing much afoot today," Mr. Hill remarked one morning after breakfast. "Why don't you and Tosche check on the cattle and push the strays back on their own range."

That suited me, so I saddled up and headed for the Tonkawa village. I saw Tosche and waved to him, then told him what Mr. Hill had said. While he went for his pony I looked around and saw the girl. I remembered what a sight she was when I saw her bathing, and figured I'd like to see her like that again, only real close. Tosche soon returned and we headed for the lower end of the reserve, unfamiliar country to me. A few hours later we had accounted for most of the cattle in that area. "Should be some Tonkawa ponies here," Tosche said. We rode to the top of a hill and looked in all directions, but couldn't spot any. We rode on a few miles, but by midafternoon hadn't seen a single one.

"There's good grass that way," Tosche said, pointing to his left, "and over there." He swung his arm to the right. "Ponies may be at one or the other. You go that way. Meet me here."

I rode on in the direction he indicated, and came across a bunch of fresh pony tracks heading in the same direction, so I followed them. Along the way I noticed the tracks of two shod horses, but thought nothing about it. I was now off the reservation, so it was likely the shod horses belonged to some ranch remuda, though I hadn't heard of anyone living in that area.

The trail led down to a creek, and I followed it a mile or more. The creek turned sharply around a brush-covered ridge and I followed the narrow trail around the bend. About a quarter of a mile away I saw a makeshift horse trap—a crude fence across the mouth of a canyon. Beyond the fence a lot of ponies were grazing. There was no ranch house that I could see.

I figured I'd better get out of there, for it looked like I might have stumbled onto a horse thief setup. I turned my pony and looked up into the barrel of a rifle aimed at my head. A short, stocky man with a black beard was squinting down at me from the ridge. He'd been hiding in the brush.

"Drop your gun belt real careful," he said in a gravelly voice. "My trigger finger's a mite nervous." It couldn't be any more nervous than I was, but I unbuckled the belt and dropped it. "Now turn around and ride real slow," he ordered as he came down from his hideout.

I walked my pony up the canyon toward the horse trap, my back feeling real quivery with that cannon aimed at it. As we neared the fence I saw a lean-to and a couple of blanket rolls off to one side and headed for them. A tall, skinny man was standing by the ashes of a campfire, hands on hips, glaring. I tried to look at him calmly, but fear swelled up in me like I would burst. If I'd stumbled onto a horse thief camp, and it sure as hell looked like I had, I was in big trouble.

"Who you got there, Jake?" the skinny one called.

"Some coyote sneakin' along our trail."

"Get off," he ordered. I dismounted, wondering what they'd do to me. They were two mean-looking hombres; it was easy to see that killing me wouldn't give either of them bad dreams.

"Reckon we'd better plug him and dump him in the crick?" Jake asked, sort of hopefully. The skinny one pondered that, while I held my breath.

"We best tie him up tonight. Red and the others'll be along in the mornin' with more ponies, and he'll want to know what folks are sayin' about Injuns stealin' their stock. You can plug him when Red gets through. You better get back on lookout—he's maybe got friends coming, and it won't be dark for another hour." He turned to me. "How about it? Anyone with you?"

"No. I was just lookin' for some ponies that strayed off the reserve."

"Next time yer ponies stray you best forget 'em," he advised me, "only fer you there ain't goin' to be any next time." He guffawed at his own joke, then bound my hands tightly behind my back. "Set down." I did. He looped a lariat tightly around my feet and tied it to a stump.

"Reckon if you have to pee you'll just have to pee your pants," he said, chuckling to himself.

I tried not to show my fear, but I was sure full of it. My mind was racing like a jackrabbit with coyotes after it as they stirred up the coals and built a fire. I watched the sun sink toward the horizon, wondering if I'd ever see another sunset, then concentrated on how to get loose. I saw where they tied my cow pony to graze, but didn't let them see me looking.

While the bacon was frying the men each had a few turns at a demijohn. "Reckon we oughta plug him now?" Jake asked. "No sense takin' chances. I'd as leave do it now and get it over with."

The skinny one seemed to be thinking it over, while I sat there in a cold sweat, every muscle taut. He took another swig of whiskey and wiped his mouth on the back of his hairy hand. I'd been figuring on working my hands free and being long gone when the one called Red came in the morning.

"Naw," the skinny one said at last. "What's your hurry? He ain't goin' nowheres. Red's figurin' on gettin' some Injuns to help us after this. He'll likely want to know if folks are gettin' suspicious of our friends around here. Leave him be till morning and then you can have your little fun."

"We're gettin' low on grub or we'd offer you a bite," Jake said as he shoveled beans into his mouth. "But don't you fret none. You ain't likely to starve to death. Ain't that right, Skinny?" Both guffawed.

The smell of the bacon was tantalizing, but right then I wasn't thinking about food. They spread their blankets about thirty feet from me. "You stay put, hear?" Jake said. "I'm a real light sleeper, and iffen I hear you rustlin' around I'll likely calculate you ain't sleepin' too good. I got somethin' that'll make you sleep real sound." His lips curled as he patted his pistol.

I waited until I heard them snoring, wondering what Tosche had thought when I didn't show up. He'd figure I'd gotten tired of waiting and left without him, I thought bitterly. I could see him just shrug and go on his way. I tried to work my numb wrists to loosen the rope, but I was careful not to make a sound. I thought of crawling to the fire and putting the rope against a live coal, but I couldn't get my feet loose.

I struggled until I was drenched with sweat and my wrists were raw, but the rope didn't seem to get any looser. I had to rest frequently, though I was frantic to get away. I sure didn't want to be around in the morning.

Near midnight I heard an owl hoot real low. I listened, remembering what I'd heard about Indians signaling each other in the dark around enemy camps. But the one I heard was a real owl, I was sure. No human voice could sound like that. If only Tosche and some Tonkawas were coming to my rescue—my hopes soared for a moment, then I realized that was foolish. Why would they care what happened to me? I struggled desperately to free my bleeding wrists. If I don't get loose pretty quick, I thought, I'll soon see my last sunrise.

A hand gently rested on my shoulder and I flinched like I'd been stuck with a knife. Jake and Skinny still snored in their bedrolls, so it wasn't one of them. It had to be Tosche! He knelt beside me and cut the rope that bound my wrists.

At that moment one of the men stopped snoring, and grumbling to himself threw off his blankets and arose. I put my hands together behind my back, in case he checked, while Tosche moved back a few steps and crouched, knife in hand. I heard the man relieve himself, then walk toward me. I froze, my muscles tense. The man, I think it was Jake, shoved me with his foot to be sure I was still tied, then crawled back in his blankets. I was drenched with sweat.

When both men were snoring again, Tosche cut the rope around my ankles, then gripped my arm and helped me to my feet, for my legs were so numb I could hardly have stood by myself. He led me slowly away from the camp, then saddled my pony and led him quietly out of hearing. I found my gun belt where I'd dropped it, and with fingers that felt like sticks, managed to buckle it around my waist, scarcely able to comprehend that I was free.

"Tosche," I whispered, "you saved my life! They were going to kill me in the morning." I was so relieved to be rescued I was almost blubbering.

"Did you hear me tell you I was coming?" he asked.

"No, all I heard was an owl hoot."

"That was me." I couldn't believe it.

"Wait here," he said, "while I get their ponies." He faded away in the starlight and soon returned leading the men's saddle horses. He handed me the lead ropes. "Now I'll open the gate," he said. "In the morning our ponies will leave."

When he returned we mounted and led the men's horses a few miles then turned them loose and headed for William Marlin's ranch, about eight miles from the agency. It was sunup when we got there and found him drinking coffee. I told him about the horse thieves.

"Let me round up some ranchers," he said. "Help yourselves to some coffee. Can one of you fellers lead us there?"

Tosche looked at me, and nodded. "Let me show them," he said.

"They tied me up pretty tight and said they'd shoot me in the morning," I told Marlin, holding out my skinned wrists. "Tosche cut me loose. He'll take you there while I get fixed up."

Dr. Stern, the agency doctor, put some salve on my wrists. "I think you'll live," he said drily, "but you'd better associate with a different class of people after this. Fill your belly then rest awhile."

I ate then slept till noon. When I awakened I rode to the Tonkawa camp and waited for Tosche. He soon rode up.

"What happened?" I said.

"The ranchers caught those men. Marlin and part of the posse went after the others." He paused. "Those men—" He made a gesture that told the story. The ranchers had strung up Jake and Skinny. "The others got away," Tosche added, "but not with our ponies."

"Tosche," I said, dead serious, "I owe my life to you. I want us to be friends, real friends."

"Brothers," he said.

Back at the agency I thought some about that, wondering what I was doing claiming an Indian as my brother. Then I remembered Jake and Skinny—but for Tosche, by now Jake would have had his little fun. Anyway, having one Indian friend wasn't all that bad—it didn't have to change my feelings about the rest of them. Deep down I was beginning to wonder if maybe the Major was right after all, but I wasn't ready to admit that yet.

One afternoon a week or two later Mr. Hill and I were at the agency office when a stray cow wandered down the road that led to the fort. "That's the Widder Jones' milk cow," Mr. Hill said. "Must have gotten loose. You'd better drive it back and fix the place it got out." He pointed to where I'd find her farm, a little more than a mile away.

I got my pony and drove the critter home. I'd never met the Widder Jones and figured she'd be a little old lady wearing a sunbonnet. But she wasn't real old, maybe in her early thirties. Her brown hair was tied in a knot at the back of her head, and the skin on her neck was real white. The top three buttons on her dress were open and the rest looked like they were barely hanging on to the buttonholes. When she walked ahead of me to open the gate, it looked like her dress must have shrunk around the waist, and watching her walk gave me a funny feeling. She turned her head and saw me staring at her little round rear end, and smiled. Her face was real pretty and she had a nice smile, but I turned red.

"I'll see where she got out and fix it," I stammered.

"Be sure to come to the house when you finish so I can thank you properly." Her voice was low and sweet-sounding.

It didn't take long to fix the fence. I figured I'd best head on back to the agency, but she was standing by the cabin door when I reached the gate.

"Tie your horse and come in," she ordered. "I've got some biscuits and honey ready. You must be tuckered out."

I wasn't a bit tired, but biscuits and honey sure sounded better than the corn pone and molasses we ate at the agency. I tied my pony and followed her into the cabin.

While I was eating, she asked who I was and what I was doing. She perched on a stool opposite me and put both feet on the middle rung, pulling up her skirt a bit as she did. I could see her bare legs halfway to her knees, and I was looking at unfamiliar territory. I'd seen the Tonkawa women at a distance, but not face to face or eye to eye like now. I got so flustered I almost bit my thumb instead of a biscuit. Seeing that white skin really did things to me, and when I stood up I was real embarrassed and hoped she wouldn't think I carried an ear of corn in my pocket. She just smiled and untied the knot in her hair so it tumbled down over her shoulders. For some reason that made me even more quivery. I figured I'd better get out of there fast.

No chance of that. She arose and put her hands on my shoulders. "Chip, you remind me so much of my dear dead husband when he was your age," she said softly, moving her face close to mine and staring into my eyes. She locked her hands behind my head and kissed me hard. "I hope you'll forgive me. You look so much like him I can't help myself. You can't imagine how wonderful it is for me. It makes me feel so good!"

I had to admit I was feeling pretty darn good myself, getting more excited and scared by the minute. I sure didn't want to spoil her pleasure in remembering her husband.

"He always put his arms around me like this," she continued, pulling my arms around her waist. "Then he'd hug me hard." I squeezed her gently, hoping she wouldn't bump into me in the wrong place. "You look stronger than that." She kissed me again and I crushed her. "Ooh," she giggled as she pressed against me. That did it.

She took my hand and led me to the bed in the corner of the cabin.

"Do come see me again soon," she said as I was leaving. "Otherwise I'll have to open the gate and let the cow out so you'll have to bring her back. That would be a waste of precious time, so don't make me do that."

I promised to visit her soon, but right then I was scared and embarrassed and only wanted to get away. I tried not to look guilty when I entered the agency office, but didn't do a very good job of it.

"Have trouble with the cow or the fence?" Mr. Hill asked.

"Both," I lied. "Then I had to eat some biscuits and honey." He smiled, and I wondered what he was thinking.

"What was Mr. Jones like?" I asked.

"He was short and plump and redheaded. Why?"

"Oh, I was just curious."

TWO

Captain Ross didn't arrive until late summer, and by then I was well acquainted with the reservation and knew all of the chiefs. The Captain was a tall man like the Major and also around forty. He looked weather-beaten, like he'd been on the trail a lot. Mr. Hill had told me he was a famous Indian fighter—he'd fought many battles with the Comanches, but also with the Wacos and the Tawakonis and some of the other tribes on the Brazos reserve. I couldn't help wonder how he'd get along with them, knowing that he must hate Indians as much as they hated him. Anyway, the Major had promised I could leave as soon as he was well settled, so I was glad to see him, but not as glad as I'd expected.

"George," he said to Mr. Hill after we'd shaken hands with him, "I want to thank you for helping me get this appointment. I really appreciate it." His pale blue eyes seemed to twinkle when he spoke.

Mr. Hill smiled. "Shapley," he said, "you owe nothin' to me. The Indians got you the appointment through their chiefs. They asked for the tall man who lived down the Brazos and who'd fought them for years and treated them well afterward. He is brave, they said, and brave men aren't mean. The Major and I knew at once who they meant—that's why you're here."

Captain Ross looked pleased. "I'm glad to hear that, but I know you and the Major had a lot to do with it and I want you to know I'm grateful. But I sure hated to hear that you have to quit." I knew right away I'd like working for him, at least for a few months.

The next day I took Captain Ross around the reserve, and our first stop after the Waco village was the Tonkawa camp, where I introduced him to Campo. "Plácido and his people will soon be here," the Captain told him. "The Major expects them within a month. They're down on the Nueces now."

"Bueno," Campo replied.

I looked for Tosche but didn't see him. We'd gotten to be surefire friends after I started teaching him to rope and he saved my life, and I'd hoped he'd join us. I saw the girl, though.

"We're on our way to visit all the villages," I told her. "I hoped Tosche could come with us."

"When Tosche comes I'll tell him his cowboy friend is looking for him," she said softly. I still had that funny feeling whenever I saw her, which wasn't often, and I'd spoken to her only once. I bit my lip so I wouldn't grin like an idiot.

"Thanks," I said, and the Captain and I rode on down the trail.

"Some Indian gals are right pretty," the Captain said, "like that one you were talkin' to. I reckon she has a white father. She's one of the prettiest I've seen." I didn't say anything, but I knew I couldn't take my eyes off her, and I thought a lot about teaching her what I was learning from the Widder. Still, I didn't want to admit she was good-looking. After all, she was an Indian squaw.

"Don't you agree, Chip?" the Captain asked with a twinkle in his eye.

"I reckon so, sir, if you say so. Some folks might call her pretty."

"I'm sure I don't have to tell you they're off limits for us. We're here to help, not add to their troubles."

"Yes, sir. They're safe from me, every darn one of 'em. I'm no Injun lover." He gave me a look that made me feel uncomfortable, like I'd said the wrong thing. Fortunately for me Tosche loped up just then and allowed me to change the subject.

"Captain Ross, this is Tosche. He wants to raise cattle, not corn, so I'm teachin' him what I know about it."

"Good. Cattle take some lookin' after and we need to build up the herd. We can use cowboys for sure."

A few days later Tosche and I rode around the range to check on the cattle. "I've been meanin' to ask you about that girl you talked to, I don't know her name. Is she your sister?"

"Cousin. Her name is Taka. Her father was a white man, her mother a Tonkawa. Both are dead, killed by Comanches. She lives with her aunt and uncle." He paused and I saw the corners of his mouth twitch like he was trying not to smile. "She says you're not bad-looking for a cowboy. Said it's too bad she don' like cowboys." He smiled broadly for half a second, then his face was as impassive as ever.

I was glad and mad at the same time. I'd figured she was pretty good-looking for an Indian and she thought I wasn't bad-looking for a cowboy. That was almost funny. Who cared whether or not she liked cowboys? I sure didn't give a damn, at least that's what I told myself. Then I found myself wondering why she didn't like cowboys.

Then I remembered what Tosche had said about her parents being killed by Comanches. We had one thing in common, I thought; one thing, but that was all. It meant nothing. I should feel sorry for her, I thought, knowing what she must have gone through. But she didn't seem to be the kind you feel sorry for, and anyway she wouldn't want sympathy from a cowboy.

The Captain and I were sitting in the agency office one morning when one of the Delawares told him a Tawakoni man wanted to see him. "Send him in," the Captain said. A few minutes later a huge Indian loomed up in the doorway and just stood there, unsmiling, blocking out the sunlight. I was curious why this unfriendly-looking warrior wanted to see the Captain, figuring he maybe had an old score to settle. I sure hoped not. I'd seen him before at his village but we'd never spoken—he always looked like one who had a big hate for all whites, and now it looked like he was on the prod. The Captain pointed to a stool, but the man ignored him and remained standing, nearly filling the doorway with his huge frame, his dark face looking like it was carved out of brown stone. He was one damn big redskin and looked mean as hell to boot.

"Get up," he said at last. The Captain rose slowly to his feet while the hair on the back of my neck shot up like soldiers when the sergeant yelled, "Attention!" I'd have been on my feet ahead of the Captain. We never carried guns around the agency headquarters. Now I wondered if that was a good idea; my Colt six-gun would have felt pretty comforting on my hip right then. I wasn't sure what I was supposed to do, but if he'd said, "Fly!" I was ready to flap my wings.

"You killed Big Foot," the Tawakoni continued. The Captain nodded slightly, looking the big warrior in the eye, while I held my breath. "Big Foot was my only brother, the bravest man in the country."

"He was that," the Captain said, watching him closely. I'd heard that Indians always killed anyone who shot a relative, and I reckoned he'd claimed that privilege. I was desperately trying to figure out what to do if he jumped the Captain. I'd have to help him, of course, unless he beat me out the back door. But that warrior looked so powerful I figured he could easily throw me through the roof.

"I want you to be my brother now," the Tawakoni warrior said. I exhaled like I'd been holding my breath for ten minutes. I'd heard people say that a sudden feeling of relief had swept over them. Now I sure knew what they meant. I felt as limp as a wet latigo strap.

"I'll be happy to be your brother," the Captain said, and shook his hand.

The Tawakoni took a big mesquite thorn he'd been holding, bunched up the skin over his heart, and ran the thorn through it. He cut the thorn out with his knife, then held the gory thing up so the Great Spirit could witness that he told the truth, I figured.

"Now I want a white man's name," he said. "George Washington."

"George Washington it is," the Captain said. George Washington left us without another word. I had to go out behind a tree for a few minutes. I'd been plenty scared, and my legs were still shaky.

The Major rode over from the Clear Fork to see sutler Charles Barnard, and that afternoon the new Comanche agent, John R. Baylor, arrived. He was a huge man, about an inch taller than the Major, and he must have weighed two hundred and thirty pounds, all muscle. His skin was swarthy but his hair and beard were light and his eyes were dark blue. A man that people noticed right away. He was friendly and easygoing, but also reserved; he seemed completely sure of himself.

With him was a short, shifty-eyed man who spoke with an Irish accent, but he didn't say much. Mr. Baylor introduced him as Ed Cornett. "He's goin' to be my assistant for a while," he explained. Cornett seemed about as opposite to Mr. Baylor as he could be, and I saw nothing in him to admire. "Never judge a man's character by his looks," the Major had told me. In this case he had to be wrong. I wondered why Mr. Baylor had hired him, but that was his affair.

At breakfast next morning the Major said, "Let's visit a few of the villages here to give you an idea of what we want to do with the Comanches."

"Good idea," Mr. Baylor said.

"We'll start with the Tonkawas. Like the Comanches they were nomads, but they're adjusting well to settling down."

When we stopped at the Tonkawa camp, Taka and some of the other women were standing or sitting in the shade of an oak. Cornett stared boldly at them, one after the other, until he saw Taka. "Now there's a squaw I'd like to . . ." The Major's frown stopped him like a kick in the crotch.

"Aw, what's wrong with wantin' to diddle a damn squaw," Cornett mumbled.

"Leave all of the women alone or you won't last long around the Comanches," the Major warned him. Mr. Baylor seemed not to hear any of this.

Cornett said no more but kept on ogling Taka, and I knew what the bastard was thinking. I didn't like him much at first; now I itched to get my hands around his scrawny throat and strangle him. It didn't matter that I'd been thinking the same thing—it was the idea of a seedy crumb like him even touching a pretty girl like Taka. If he ever tried that I'd have his scalp.

Pretty quick we headed for the Clear Fork reserve, while the Captain stayed at the agency. The Major and Baylor rode together, talking about the Comanches, while Cornett and I followed. He looked pretty glum and hardly spoke the whole way, which suited me.

"You the Major's son?" he finally asked.

"Sort of. He raised me after my folks were killed."

He spat and mumbled something I couldn't hear and didn't want to. When we got to the Clear Fork Agency, Delaware Jim Shaw met us. He looked to be about fifty, though with Indians it's hard to tell age. He was the tallest Indian I'd ever seen, taller even than Mr. Baylor.

"Get Ketumse," the Major told him. "I want him to meet his new agent."

Shaw soon returned with a heavyset Comanche who was at least a head shorter. Through Shaw the Major introduced him to Mr. Baylor. I'd always figured it was Comanches who'd killed my folks, though I never knew for sure. Anyway, I stared real hard at Ketumse, wondering if he'd been the one, but if he noticed me he didn't let on. He and Baylor shook hands, then he left us.

"Ketumse is the only Comanche chief who accepts the fact that his people must change their way of life to survive," the Major explained. "He said, 'Give us a country we can call our own, where we can bury our people in quiet, and we'll live there.' He's even willing to learn farming, and he told me other chiefs say they are. He doubts it. Sanaco, who now claims to be head chief of the Penatekas, doesn't much like the idea, but I think he'll come around eventually."

"What does Sanaco say about living on the reserve?" Baylor asked.

"When I first suggested it to him he looked angry. He said, 'You come to our country, make a line around a little piece of it with the things that steal land'—he meant surveying instruments—'and tell us the Great Father will give it to us to live on. He must be crazy. Everyone knows that all the land from the Red River to the Colorado has always been ours. But if the Great Father tells us we have to live on one little part of it, I suppose we will have to live there whether we want to or not.' I'm not sure he'll come in any time soon, but if he sees that Ketumse's people are

well fed and contented while his band is starving half the time, I expect
he'll have no choice but to join them. It's a sorry business in a way,
forcing them to settle down, but in the long run it's our only hope of
saving them."

"At least feeding them is a lot cheaper than fighting them," Baylor said.
"It's too bad more of them aren't here."

"When I set up the reserves last year all of the Penatekas came," the
Major said. "There were about twelve hundred of them. Right at that
critical time the army decided to send a big force from Fort Chadbourne
after the Comanches. A German trader there sent a man to warn Sanaco
and Buffalo Hump that the troops were coming, and that they couldn't
tell friendly Comanches from hostiles. Buffalo Hump and Sanaco and
their people fled at once. Sanaco's father was killed in the Council House
fight in '40, and he doesn't risk getting trapped like his father was."

I'd heard about the Council House fight. A bunch of chiefs and
headmen and their families had gone to San Antonio to make peace.
They were told to bring in all of their white captives, but brought only
one girl, saying the rest were with other bands. Rangers surrounded them
and told them they would be held until they surrendered all of the captives. When they tried to fight their way out, all of the men and some of
the women had been killed. They didn't trust any whites after that.

The Major gave Baylor his instructions and turned the agency over to
him right away, for he'd been gone from his San Antonio headquarters
too long. Jim Shaw and the Major were old friends, and he rode back to
the Brazos reserve with us.

"What do you think of John Baylor?" the Major asked us. "Reckon he'll
make a good agent?"

"Yes, sir," I replied. "I think he'll do just fine." Jim Shaw only grunted
and it sounded like he didn't agree.

"I hope so," the Major continued. "One day soon I want to turn this
job over to someone I have confidence in. He might be the one, especially
if Captain Ross means what he says about not wanting it." Jim Shaw
grunted again. His apparent doubts about Mr. Baylor made me wonder if
I'd judged him right. He did look like he might be pretty mean if anyone
crossed him.

"Baylor has a real challenge with the Comanches," the Major told
Captain Ross when we reached the agency. "They're wild and discon-
tented, and it won't be easy to keep them on the reservation long enough
to take root. Baylor figures it will take a long time to civilize them, but
even if they're never really civilized it's a lot cheaper to feed them than to

fight them, and he's right about that. We can hope that the ones there now and those who are expected soon will keep the treaty and settle down. If they do, it will be Ketumse we'll have to thank." The Major headed for San Antonio the next morning.

Late in September a Comanche raiding party stole a bunch of Caddo and Delaware ponies, so John Connor and eleven other Delawares followed the trail north. They caught up with the raiders and signaled for a parley, John Connor told us after they returned. The two parties camped close together that night, and the overconfident Comanches suggested they do some gambling. Several of the Delawares spoke Comanche but didn't let on. During the play they heard the Comanches talk about killing their party in the morning.

At daybreak the Comanches struck, but the Delawares were ready. They killed four then charged the Comanche camp and killed three more, letting only one warrior escape to tell his people who'd wiped out the raiders. The Delawares also learned from listening to the Comanches that a large war party intended to kill Ketumse and all Comanches who cooperated with the whites. They were angry because when two Clear Fork Comanches accompanied a raiding party to Mexico and returned to the agency with stolen horses, Ketumse turned the animals over to the Major. To the Northern Comanches that was going too far.

Baylor came to the agency to see the Major on one of his visits, and we sat in the office and talked. "The news from Kansas is bad—'Bleeding Kansas,' the papers call it," the Major said. "Sam Houston was right when he predicted that popular sovereignty would disrupt the nation. But his voting against the Kansas-Nebraska Bill means the legislature won't return him to the Senate when his term is over."

"There's talk of the South seceding from the Union," the Captain added. "There's no way it can be done peacefully—it would mean war between North and South."

"I hope we have a war," Baylor exclaimed, "and the sooner the better!" The Major and Captain Ross stared at him in surprise, but neither said anything.

In October the dragoons were transferred to Kansas, leaving few mounted troops anywhere on the Texas frontier. The Major wrote from San Antonio that he'd called on Governor Pease to warn him of the Northern Comanche threat and had urged him to ask federal officials to provide protection. The governor replied that the Secretary of War had already ordered the new Second Cavalry Regiment to march from Jefferson Barracks, Missouri, to garrison the outer line of Texas forts.

About the same time Baylor wrote the Captain that he'd just learned of another Northern Comanche threat to kill Ketumse and his people. "I have no doubt we will have the devil to pay and our frontier is in the greatest danger," he wrote. "I hope the Major's plan for a big Comanche campaign succeeds, as it is our only hope. The Indians here are ready and willing to go against the Northern Comanches and I think they are about the best protection we have if they are managed by some white man. If we kill off a few more raiding parties it will give the Northern Comanches a distaste for these parts anyhow." He added that John Connor had learned that the Northern Comanches planned to set up winter camps near the Red River. "I think there would be no difficulty in finding them if an expedition is gotten up." The Major tried to persuade the army to make a winter campaign, but the army refused because the military department of Texas ended at the Red River. The Comanche camps were in another department.

When the dragoons marched off to Kansas, the only mounted troops left in the state were at the southern posts. "Forts Davis and Lancaster are near the Comanche plunder trails to Mexico," Captain Ross remarked. "Once the troops there start attacking those big raiding parties coming back from Mexico with herds of stolen horses and mules, the Comanches will look elsewhere for loot. That means all of our frontier counties will be fair game now there aren't any mounted troops to protect them. So far it's been fairly quiet around here, but that's not likely to last."

In November the Comanches proved the Captain right. A rider galloped up to the agency one morning on the road from Weatherford. "Comanches coming!" he shouted. Tosche and I headed for the Waco village on the run and called for Ah-ha-dot. When we told him the news he gave some kind of signal and twenty mounted warriors quickly joined him. We loped down the road toward Weatherford, and after about five miles heard shooting and war whoops. At that we loosened our reins and let our ponies run as fast as they could.

Pretty soon we came to a cabin that was surrounded by thirty or forty Comanches, who were making enough noise for a hundred. Two rifles were pointed out through the cabin windows; the Comanches were keeping out of range while one warrior with a flaming stick in his hand was trying to slip up close enough to throw it on the cabin roof.

When they saw us coming the Comanches spread out in a long line and charged, waving their mean-looking lances and shrieking their war cries. The Wacos all hit the ground before their ponies stopped, and aimed their rifles. Tosche and I quickly joined them and saw that they formed two lines. The warriors in the front line fired their rifles and then stepped back to reload while the other line moved forward and fired, so Tosche and I took turns firing and reloading. Those Comanches were a scary sight and their screeching was sure unnerving. Even though they outnumbered us they didn't get close enough to use their bows, for the Wacos were dead shots. When four Comanches had been wounded or killed the others pulled back. Then, riding in pairs, Comanche warriors dashed by those on the ground, leaned down, snatched them up, and carried them off without slowing down. They abandoned a bunch of stolen horses and dashed away. We mounted and followed them until they scattered in all directions. That was my first Indian fight and when it was over I felt pretty shaky—it had happened so fast there wasn't time to feel scared until it was over.

The Comanches and Kiowas made another big sweep around Belknap and Palo Pinto a few weeks later. It was several days before we knew about all the damage they'd done south of us, but it got worse with each report. "If we don't get some mounted troops here soon," Captain Ross said, "this is just a sample of what we can expect."

The rides Tosche and I took to the different villages were longer than before; after we delivered the messages we spent some time keeping the cattle from straying off the reserve. We still practiced roping now and then, taking turns heading and heeling. I figured I must be a pretty good teacher, for it looked like he'd soon be a better roper than I was, and now I didn't even resent it. And I'd wondered if he could ever learn to use a lariat! There was sure a lot I didn't know about Indians, but I didn't mind learning from Tosche.

"I'll teach you to be a tracker like the Tonkawas," he told me one morning. "If you want me to."

"You bet I do." I knew Tonkawas were as good as Apaches when it came to following a trail, and I was amazed at the things he could tell after just glancing at tracks. He pointed to some hoofprints.

"How many ponies were there?" I figured I saw three separate sets of tracks.

"Three?"

"No, four." He showed me four different sets of tracks, one of them nearly blotted out by the others.

"Who were the riders?" I thought that was a silly question to ask anyone, for there was no possible way to know even that the horses had been ridden. Then I remembered that some of the tracks had been made by a shod horse and felt pretty smart. Indians never shod their ponies.

"One white man and three Indians," I said, figuring I should go to the head of the class.

Tosche said nothing but rode on until the tracks spread out and all four sets were visible. "Now look." I looked them over again, trying hard to figure out what he saw that I missed. The tracks of the shod horse were larger than those of Indian ponies or mustangs. One of the unshod horses also made larger tracks, but that didn't help me.

"I give up."

"It was two white men on big horses, one shod, one barefoot, and two Indians on ponies." I felt pretty dumb, but school wasn't over. We rode on until we saw a number of pony tracks away from the trail. "Were the ponies ridden?" Tosche asked.

I looked at the tracks, figuring I'd never be able to learn what he was trying to teach me. The tracks were all heading in the same direction, and that was about all I could tell. "Yes, I guess so," I said.

Tosche dismounted and led his pony a few steps, so I did the same. Then he showed me the tracks our ponies had made when ridden and not ridden. The weight of a man made a slight but barely visible difference to one who had eyes trained to detect such things. After that he showed me the final proof. Near each set of the tracks he pointed to grass stems that had been cropped by grazing ponies. These lessons went on at every opportunity until he was satisfied that I was catching on. I felt pretty proud about that.

Other times he showed me how Tonkawas got around without being seen. We followed gullies or ravines when possible. Before crossing a ridge or a hill we dismounted and crawled to the top, spreading the grass with our hands so we could look over the land beyond without exposing ourselves to the view of anyone who might be there. We took advantage of brush or trees or any other natural cover to shield us from sight.

Tosche also showed me how Tonkawas slipped into enemy camps at night and led the ponies away without arousing the sleeping warriors. They always tied their best war ponies and buffalo runners just outside their tipis, and were used to hearing their stamping and snorting through the night. But if one horse walked steadily away the unnatural sound awakened them immediately. The trick, Tosche said, was to lead them a step or two at a time, then stop. It was much easier with white men, he told me with a smile. Most snored so loud they couldn't hear their own horses walking away. But if they had a man guarding the horses, he added, it wasn't so easy.

"If we could buy a few cows we could start a little herd of our own," I told him one day. "There's plenty of open range around the reserves, and a herd will double every three years." He nodded.

"I'd like that," he replied. "I want to go on looking after the reservation cattle, but that's not the same as tending to your own. There's plenty of grass on the reservation. I hope we can get a start somehow."

"I'm not sure I'd be allowed to run cattle on the reserve," I said. "I doubt if the government would let anyone but a tribal member do that."

"Or someone married to one of the women," Tosche added. I hadn't thought of that, but he was probably right.

At the Tonkawa camp while I was waiting for Tosche one morning, Taka seemed almost friendly, like she'd forgotten I was a cowboy and accepted me as partly human. I hadn't talked to her much, and wasn't sure she knew enough English to carry on a conversation. "Tosche told me your folks were killed by Comanches," I said. "Mine were, too. You and I were probably lucky to escape with our lives." She nodded.

"My father taught me to speak like an American and to read and write a little," she replied. "He planned to put me in a school so I could learn more. He wanted me to learn to live like his people, and he bet that one day I'd marry a white man. Then the Comanches came. Now it looks like I'll never be anything but a reservation Indian. I'll probably soon forget everything he taught me."

I looked at her oval face and light skin, and had that funny feeling again. She was pretty, no doubt about that, and she'd probably fit in better with white people than with Indians. Now that I'd seen another side to her I knew I should forget what I'd been thinking about.

Anyway, she didn't bother me as much as at first. As soon as I'd gotten over feeling scared and embarrassed I'd kept my promise to visit Widder Jones, and saw her at least once a week. That helped me keep my mind off Taka. It didn't even bother me that the Widder had been pulling my leg when she said I looked like her dead husband. She probably figured I was a dumb cowboy who needed some schooling, and she was sure a good teacher. After my first few visits I realized that I was changing. My voice even sounded deeper. The Captain noticed it, too.

"When I came here, Chip, you looked like a lad who'd just turned eighteen. You've sure matured fast. The Major hired a boy and got a man." I thought of who was responsible for the change in me and blushed.

Near as Captain Ross could tell, Baylor was getting along well as Comanche agent, like I figured he would. The Major came up from San
Antonio every month or two and visited both agencies, and he was satisfied with the way things were going. The Comanches were even clearing
patches for planting corn in the spring.

In the meantime Tosche and I kept busy at making him a cowboy and
me a Tonkawa scout. When I thought about that I was surprised. If
anyone had told me six months ago that I'd be learning how to do things
like an Indian and liking it I'd have called him loco. I'd even forgotten
that I could leave at any time.

By December, when the weather was cold and we didn't ride any more
than was necessary, Tosche was a first-rate roper and I could read tracks
and slip around unseen like a real Tonkawa. I didn't know if I'd ever need
those skills, but if I did I'd have them.

One ride I made late in December was the thirty miles to the Clear
Fork Agency with a letter from the Major to Baylor. He wasn't at agency
headquarters. I looked for him awhile then asked John Shirley, Charles
Barnard's assistant sutler, where Mr. Baylor was.

"He left three days ago but didn't tell me or anyone else where he was
going. Seems he told Ketumse our prices are too high and he was goin' to
set up something for DeWitt and Wolfe of San Antonio. He thinks he's
got big influence with the army and that he's popular with everybody. By
gettin' Ketumse and other Comanches stirred up he's vain enough to
think he can swing it. He hasn't even settled his accounts for the beef
and supplies we've furnished the agency. And he lets the Comanches
leave the reserve any time they say they want to go hunting. The Delawares tell me the young men still join raiding parties from north of the
Red River on their way to Mexico. Pretty soon they'll likely hit closer to
home. I smell trouble."

When I returned to the Brazos Agency next day Captain Ross had
gone to Fort Belknap, so I followed him there. I had to let him know as
soon as possible that Baylor had left. I found him talking to the army
sutler, J. T. Ward.

"This is the worst time for him to be away!" the Captain exclaimed
when I told him. "The Second Cavalry left Jefferson Barracks in October
and should have gotten here by now. The Major wrote that Sanaco and
his band are on their way to Clear Fork. They're starving and promise to
keep the peace, but they're mighty skittish. When they see cavalry replace the infantry at Camp Cooper they'll likely stampede. I'd better get
off a letter to the Major and head over there and try to keep the Coman-

ches calm. Chip, keep an eye on things. If a problem comes up you can't handle tell Dr. Stern. If you need to get word to me, send one of the Delawares."

Soon after the Captain left for Clear Fork a cavalryman rode through the gate. "Message for post commander," he told the sergeant on guard. "The regiment will get here late this afternoon." His short blue jacket was trimmed with yellow, and he wore a black slouch hat that had the right brim pinned back with a shiny metal eagle. On the left side a black feather sloped toward the back. He had a carbine in his saddle scabbard, a Colt .36 Navy pistol in a holster on his right side, and a saber on his left. From what the Captain had said, I knew the Second was a new regiment and that Secretary of War Jeff Davis had picked the best cavalry officers in the whole army for it. The commander was a Texan, Colonel Albert Sidney Johnston.

Before returning to the agency I rode to the Tonkawa camp to tell Tosche. "It's a whole regiment, seven hundred and fifty men," I said. "I aim to be there to watch them arrive. Meet me outside the fort."

Word spread fast, and by late afternoon there were several hundred Indians and white settlers gathered near the fort to watch. I saw Tosche coming, with Taka riding behind him, both wrapped in buffalo robes. He tied his pony and the three of us stood together. I wondered why he'd brought her, but didn't ask.

Someone shouted, and the regiment came into view at a slow trot. Colonel Johnston and his staff officers led the way, followed by the separate companies in a column of fours, with their officers in front. Each company's mounts were all the same color—bays, grays, roans, sorrels, and blacks. The regimental band and the company buglers rode white horses.

When they were near the fort the Colonel nodded to a soldier on a white horse a few paces behind him, who turned and blew some call on his bugle. The column halted. He blew another call and each company moved off and set up picket lines for its horses before putting up tents, while the cooks built fires and started preparing the evening meal. Watching the cavalry almost made me want to join up.

By now most of the Indians had drifted away, for the sun was setting. A Tonkawa warrior came from the fort and talked to Tosche. "The army saw a trail that might be Comanche," Tosche told me. "We have to go see. Can Taka ride with you?" He was gone before I could reply.

Might as well get it over with, I thought. Luckily it was almost dark and no one was likely to see us. "Climb on," I told her. "I'll ride behind you." She looked at me, hesitating, then put her foot in the stirrup and swung gracefully into the saddle. I put my foot in the stirrup—she couldn't reach it—and got up behind her. I was trembling like the first time I'd climbed onto a wild mustang. I didn't like that one bit.

Then I remembered what she'd said about cowboys, and that made me feel a bit devilish. Since I was stuck with giving her a ride to the Tonkawa camp I figured I'd tease her a bit by trying some of the things I'd learned from the Widder. If the Widder was right about women liking those things, I'd give Taka something to think about and maybe change her mind about cowboys—not that I cared about that. At least that's what I told myself. Actually I felt a powerful urge to hold her close even though she'd been so unfriendly the first time I saw her.

Whatever my excuse, I slipped my hand inside her buffalo robe and up under the buckskin blouse she wore. The Widder usually wore a layer or two of underthings unless she was expecting me, but under the buckskin there was only Taka. She gasped and pushed my hand away, then turned halfway around to look at me. I held her head and kissed her like I'd learned from the Widder. I'd heard that Indians didn't kiss each other like white folks do, but she didn't object. So I kissed her a few more times and stroked her warm skin in a few places. Each time she was a bit slower in pushing my hand away. The Widder must be right.

When we were close to the Tonkawa camp I slipped off my pony and reached up to lift her down. I held her tight, pressing her against me, not letting her reach the ground. I slid my hand under her blouse again and she pressed it there. Her heart was pounding as madly as mine when she broke away and disappeared in the dark. I managed to climb onto my pony and head up the trail to the agency, but my head was whirling with crazy thoughts. For one thing, I felt guilty for what I'd done just to get even with her. Worse than that, I'd enjoyed it more than I was willing to admit. No matter what Captain Ross said, I'd sure like to teach her a few more tricks.

THREE

I didn't see Taka except at a distance for months; whenever I rode into the Tonkawa camp she disappeared into her tipi the moment she saw me. I told myself I didn't much care whether she talked to me or not. I just wanted her to listen long enough to tell her I was sorry for what I'd done. That's what I'd learned from the Major. "When you're in the wrong," he'd told me, "be man enough to apologize." After that I'd put her out of my mind, but every time she ducked out of sight I had a sinking feeling. Finally I figured the best thing to do was to forget about her. Luckily for me, the Captain kept me pretty busy, but that didn't help me forget her like I intended. I still figured I should tell her I was sorry. After that she needn't talk to me again.

The Major wrote that his first son, Robert Barnard Neighbors, had been born on January 25. The Barnard was for his friend, Indian trader George Barnard, brother of our sutler. This news hit me hard, for now that he had a son of his own there'd be no place in his family for me. He'd never actually adopted me anyway. "There's always a chance that some of your blood relatives will show up and claim you," he said, "and it would complicate things for everybody if I'd adopted you. But I'll be your father as long as you need me." None of my kinfolk ever came.

Now I remembered he'd told me that after Captain Ross had gotten settled at the agency I could leave. I was a bit shocked that I'd forgotten that—it must have been because Tosche and I had gotten to be such good friends. And even though the Captain had said Indian women were off limits for us, I couldn't help thinking about making love to Taka. She was on my mind a lot. I guess what Cornett had said triggered that—I couldn't bear the thought of anyone else making love to her.

But now that the Major had a real son, I thought bitterly, the decent thing for me to do was to clear out. I sure didn't like the idea of not seeing Tosche again, but I knew that wasn't the only reason I wasn't eager to leave. Still, I figured I owed it to the Major, after all he'd done for me. I'd watch for the proper time, then hit the trail for California.

When the Major came to the Brazos Agency in mid-February, Captain Ross had just arrived from Clear Fork, for he still spent most of his time there. He was needed more at the upper reserve, for most of the problems at the Brazos Agency were easily solved or could wait until his next visit. The upper reserve was near the old plunder trail to Mexico, and Northern Comanche raiders often slipped into the camps and kept Ketumse's young warriors stirred up. As the Captain had feared, Sanaco and his band didn't stay long after the cavalry came to Camp Cooper. "Sanaco sent word that he'll stay on the reservation only as long as you supply him with all the whiskey he wants," Captain Ross told the Major.

"It might be worth it," the Major replied. "At least we'd know where the rascal was and what he was doing." I couldn't tell from his expression if he was joking or serious.

"What do you hear from Baylor?" the Captain asked.

"He wrote in January that his wife was pregnant and having difficulty, so he had to rush home. He'll be back shortly with his whole family, and once they're here I think he'll tend to business."

"Let's hope so. The Comanches are the only serious problem we have, but they're a real worry as long as so many of them are on the loose." Remembering what John Shirley had said made the Captain dubious about why Baylor had left, I guess, but Baylor did show up early in March with his wife and six children. He didn't say anything about bringing another trader. Buffalo Hump and about forty of his people had come to the Clear Fork ten days earlier, and Sanaco's band returned a few weeks later. Ironsides of the Tenawish had promised to bring his people, too. There were now more than five hundred Comanches at the upper reserve and it looked like they were ready to settle down and stay, but all the comings and goings kept Ketumse's young men restless.

Lieutenant Colonel Robert E. Lee arrived to take command at Camp Cooper about the same time Baylor returned. Before going to Cooper, Lee called on the Major at the Brazos Agency. Both were Virginians, and they hit it off well from the start. Lee was a couple of inches under six feet and must have weighed about 170 pounds. His shoulders and chest were powerful, and though his hair and beard were turning gray, at fifty he looked absolutely fit. His head was large and well shaped, his eyes dark brown, his lips thin and straight, his expression frank and open. He was an expert horseman, and he seemed to me the perfect cavalry officer.

Like most of the army officers, Lee considered Indian reservations a mistake. I never knew the reasons, but I gathered there was always friction between army officers and Indian agents. Some officers felt they knew a lot more about Indians than agents did, and in some cases that was probably true. They were also convinced they should be in charge of the reservations, since they were the ones who had to fight the Indians. They not only said so, but some openly interfered, telling the Indians they were to do what the army, not the agent, told them. Earlier the officers at Cooper had warned the Comanches not to leave the reservation without permission from the army, but Baylor let them go hunting anytime they asked. The officers didn't actually try to stop them, but their interference had made a difficult job even harder for Mr. Baylor by worrying the Comanches about what might happen to them if they didn't follow the army's orders.

Although I don't think Lee had been around Indians before, he didn't give any of them much credit, and he swore the Northern Comanches weren't worth keeping alive. John Shirley told the Captain that when Ketumse paid him a friendly, get-acquainted call, Lee bluntly said he'd meet him as a friend if possible or an enemy if necessary. Of all the Comanche chiefs, Ketumse was the one trying hardest to get his people to accept reservation life, and he was shocked and puzzled by Lee's attitude. But even Ketumse left the reservation now and then to hunt or to look after the cattle.

Lee at least cooperated with the agents, unlike the infantry and dragoon officers earlier. One time, the Major learned from a settler that whiskey traders were camped near the Clear Fork reserve. "Chip," he said, "ride over to the Clear Fork right away. Tell Baylor there are said to be three men camped near the reserve who are trading whiskey to the Comanches. When I first knew them the Comanches wouldn't touch whiskey, but now they'll trade anything they own for it. That's the work of unscrupulous traders. Tell Baylor to ask Colonel Lee for support and then smash the barrels."

I reached the agency late afternoon, gave Baylor the message, then spent the night. In the morning a corporal and a squad of troopers rode up to the agency office. A Mescalero Apache who served as sort of a constable for Baylor found out where the traders were camped and led the way.

Not far off the reservation we came to a tent and a wagon with four whiskey barrels in it. Three seedy-looking men heard our horses and came out of the tent smiling, like we were their first customers that morning. When they saw the troops and the ax in Baylor's hand their smiles turned to scowls. They grabbed their rifles, but when the troopers cocked and leveled their carbines, the three dropped their guns in a hurry.

Baylor dismounted and handed me his reins. He climbed the wagon, tipped over the barrels, and smashed the heads in with his ax. The rotgut whiskey made a gurgling sound as it poured out and down the slope until it disappeared in the sand. The three whiskey traders looked at the barrels, then at the troopers, their faces black with rage.

I glanced at the eight cavalrymen. One ruddy-faced Irish trooper seemed close to tears, while the others simply stared at the whiskey like they wanted to help it disappear. The Irish trooper licked his dry lips. "It's enough to make a grown man cry. The waste of it! That I should ever see this day. Me father would turn in his grave, rest his soul."

The others chuckled at his unconcealed sorrow, while Baylor mounted his horse. The three men looked like they'd kill him if they could. "You'll pay for this, damn you," one said. "Destroyin' the property of law-abidin' citizens don't go in this state. You'll pay!" Baylor ignored them and we rode back to the agency.

Before leaving I visited John Shirley. "I didn't see Cornett. Has he gone?"

"Yes, and good riddance. Right after Baylor left he tried to drag a Comanche squaw into the office, but she was too strong for him. She ran for her husband, and Cornett left in a hurry—didn't take time to pack his gear."

The owner of the whiskey must have felt as bad as the Irish trooper, for he brought suit against Baylor. The Major got permission to hire a lawyer to defend him, and the suit failed.

There were a few small raids along the frontier south of Belknap and some of the best horses were stolen. "Sanaco's band is probably mixed up in it," Captain Ross said, "along with the Tenawish and Noconas from the High Plains." After much urging by the Major, the army finally ordered a campaign against them. Lee took two companies from Cooper, and two from Fort Mason joined him. The Captain told him where he'd likely find the camps in West Texas and loaned him Jim Shaw and other Delawares as guides and fifteen Caddos and Tonkawas as scouts.

The weather was unusually dry and the grass had been burnt off, so most of the Comanches had gone north of the Red River. The troops rode eight hundred miles over West Texas without finding any big camps. They ran across only one small party, and the Caddos killed two warriors and captured a woman. That was all they had to show for all that riding, but there were no more raids for three months.

White settlers had confidence in the Major's ability to control the reservation Indians, and many families were moving into the country around the Brazos reserve, both farmers and cowmen. The settlement of Belknap was growing up about half a mile east of the fort. These people were all glad that the reservation and fort were near, for both bought corn and beef. Because of the growing populations, the legislature created Erath, Parker, Jack, Palo Pinto, and Young counties. The Brazos reserve was in Young County, and the new town of Belknap became the county seat; a settler named Patrick Murphy was elected sheriff. People had started moving west of Fort Worth as soon as troops manned the outer line of forts, and the towns of Weatherford in Parker County, Golconda in Palo Pinto County, and Mesquiteville in Jack County were taking shape.

One afternoon that spring of '56 a solemn-looking man in a black coat rode up to the agency. "There's a preacher if I ever saw one," the Captain remarked as we watched the man dismount. "If I'm not mistaken, he's Noah Byars. Was blacksmith for the Republic until he was fired for incompetence." The man came to the office, and the Captain invited him to have a seat.

"I'm the Reverend Byars," he said solemnly, waiting for us to look impressed. We told him our names and shook his hand, but the Captain didn't let on he'd recognized him. "I'm a Baptist missionary," Byars continued, "and I want to start a mission for the poor heathen here. Will the government provide the money to support a missionary?"

"Major Neighbors wants a mission and so do I," the Captain replied, "but there are so many different languages spoken here that a mission can't possibly succeed until we have a school. He's already talked to the Methodists about setting up a school and a mission here, and has requested government funds to support them." The Reverend Byars looked pretty glum about that.

"I'm here and ready to go to work. I don't see any Methodists."

"You're too late," the Captain told him. "We don't need two missions and I'm sure the government wouldn't support two. It hasn't agreed to support one yet. But you're welcome to spend the night with us, and tomorrow you can ride to the upper reserve and ask John Baylor if he thinks the Comanches are ready for a mission. There's only one language spoken there."

"Comanches? Are you suggesting I risk my life among them savages?"

"Suit yourself. At least we can put you up for the night."

The Reverend Byars ate a hearty supper, like preachers always do when they're visiting, and afterward he insisted on preaching to us. He ran on so long my mind got to wandering, and I was embarrassed to realize that I was thinking of my first steamy visit to Widder Jones just when he was talking about the wages of sin. I turned red, hoping nobody there could read my mind or notice that I was blushing.

In the morning Byars decided to visit Baylor after all, and he stopped by the agency a few days later on his return. "Mr. Baylor is a real gentleman," he said, rather accusingly, I thought. "He offered to provide rooms, board, and salaries for a teacher and a missionary. I don't see what excuse you have for not doing the same."

"He can't do any of those things unless the Commissioner of Indian Affairs authorizes them," the Captain informed him. "Agents don't have unlimited funds or uncontrolled use of what they do have. We have to follow strict regulations and justify every single expenditure."

The Reverend Byars looked like he didn't believe the Captain and suspected him of trying to prevent a poor, deserving missionary from receiving what was rightfully his. He rode away with his chin in the air and his nose out of joint.

"If what he says is true, Baylor will have a hard time settling his accounts and getting his expenditures approved," the Captain remarked. "The Commissioner's a real stickler about unauthorized payments of any kind—he's got a congressional committee looking over his shoulder in hopes of catching him in some hanky-panky. If Baylor thinks he can get away with things like that he's in for a surprise."

After Ed Cornett had left the upper reserve I hoped we were rid of him for good, but one day at the general store in Belknap I saw him with Sheriff Patrick Murphy. He scowled at me. "Have you diddled that good-lookin' squaw yet?" he asked. "Or won't the Major let you play with his redskin pets?"

I walked away.

Cornett was now Murphy's deputy, and they made a bad combination. Most of the time when they were needed, a man in Belknap told me, either they couldn't be found or they were too drunk to do anything. He said they were waiting for election day so they could choose another sheriff. Murphy's father and brother and sister had a little place near the road to Mesquiteville, or Jacksborough, as most people were calling it. They ran a few cattle and horses on the range, and Cornett bought a few cows and threw in with the Murphys.

A steady stream of visitors came to the agency, among them new ranchers like George Slaughter and his sons, and Kit Carter, whose ranch was not far away on the line between Young and Palo Pinto counties. Carter, who had married the Captain's daughter Ann, was the most frequent visitor. The Slaughters and Jesse Hittson bought range land near the settlement of Golconda before people there changed its name to Palo Pinto.

At the Clear Fork reserve some Comanches were still making an effort to learn farming and cattle raising. The young warriors wanted none of either, however; they continued to slip away and join Comanche-Kiowa raiding parties from north of the Red River, and Baylor seemed unable to stop them. "If we don't control the Comanches and keep them on the reservation so anyone can see they're not away raiding," the Captain said, "people will start accusing them of stealing stock around here. Once that happens, many will turn against our Indians too, though they haven't committed a single offense against anybody."

Tosche got to be such a good hand with cattle that the Captain put him in charge of the reservation herd. It wasn't exactly a herd, for the cows were scattered over miles of country both on and off the reserve. All Tonkawas, women as well as men, were good riders and took to cowboy life like they were made for it. Tosche was nearly as good a roper as a Tejano vaquero, and that's the highest praise. He was also getting to know cattle and could already spot one that needed doctoring. He and a few others circled the reserve each week, pushing strayed cattle back toward it and driving other stock away.

All of the Tonkawas were short of ponies. Tosche had only one, while Taka and many others had none. "Your pony's gettin' worn down," I told Tosche. "You need several so they have a chance to rest. Let's round up a band of mustangs." Tosche agreed.

Captain Ross also approved. "You've run mustangs, Chip, so you take charge. Some of the Tonkawas may know how to do it, but most of the time they preferred stealing horses from enemies to catching wild ones." William Marlin loaned us three of his toughest cow ponies, and three Tonkawas who each owned or borrowed a couple of ponies joined us. I knew where there was a mustang corral that others had used before, so we didn't have to spend a week building one. We set up camp at a spring about half a mile from the corral.

Tosche and I located a mustang band that ranged in the area. Keeping out of sight and downwind, we got close enough to see about thirty mares and colts, mostly bays. The stallion was a powerful animal, also a bay.

From a distance he didn't look all battle-scarred like some of the tough older stallions, so I figured he might be young enough to tame and break to ride if we handled him right. We backtracked the band until we had a pretty good idea of its range so I'd know where to station relay riders to walk the mustangs down. No matter how long or hard they were chased, mustangs always circled back to their own range and refused to leave it. Otherwise we'd never have caught any of them.

Riding a long-winded buckskin cow pony, Tosche set out after the herd early the next morning, and we all rode out to watch the start. When the mustangs saw him they headed south on the run, manes and tails flying. That's about the prettiest sight there is. When they're caught and tamed they're just ordinary cow ponies, but wild and free they look like the greatest animals on earth. An old mare led the way, as usual, with the stallion bringing up the rear to prevent any mare or colt from falling behind.

I told Tosche just to follow them and keep them in sight, but not to push them—walking them down would take from three to five days, and we'd need several fresh ponies at the end. A few hours later I showed one of the other Tonkawas where to wait, for I knew the band might run fifteen or twenty miles before circling back. Tosche rode into camp about noon. "They're good ponies," he said, "especially the stallion." His eyes glowed when he said that. Along the way, he added, a bunch of two- or three-year-old stallions had joined the band. That usually happened, and I was counting on picking up some of the young bachelor stallions, for they were ones that Tonkawas would use for cow ponies. Indian men, like cowboys, never rode mares. We didn't want to gather any other mare bands, for when too many headed into a corral on the run they usually knocked down the fence and escaped. A lot of them were killed or crippled when that happened, and the mustangers came up empty-handed.

At dark the last Tonkawa rider came to camp and hobbled his pony with the others. He described the place he'd left the band, and at the first sign of morning light another rider set out to find it. By the fourth day the mustangs had slowed down so I could get fairly close and turn them in any direction. "Tomorrow we'll pen them," I told Tosche and the others that night.

Late the next morning we drove them into the corral and shut the gate. They raced around it madly until exhausted, then stood with legs apart and sides heaving. Tosche and I shook out loops in our lariats and rode into the corral. One of the Tonkawas had a rifle leveled across a rail with orders to shoot the stallion if he attacked us. Some of those wild stallions would knock a horse down then stomp the rider flatter than a Mexican tortilla.

We were lucky, for he only threatened to charge. Tosche quickly tossed a loop over his head and I caught both hind feet the first throw. We stretched him out on the ground, hog-tied him, and I castrated him. That took care of whatever fight he had left in him. If all went well he'd make a great cow pony for Tosche. Before we let him up I tied a clog to one of his front ankles, a forked limb that stuck out three or four feet behind. If he tried to run, a hind hoof would step on the clog and he'd take a tumble. After a couple of falls the wild ones usually gave up trying to escape.

We spent the rest of the day putting clogs on the mares and young stallions. We'd made a pretty fair catch, for there were fifteen stallions old enough to be broken and ridden right away. The best-looking mare was about four. "Give this one to your cousin," I told Tosche. He knew which cousin I meant.

The next morning we let them out a few at a time and herded them down to the spring, and when they'd drunk their fill we let them graze. After two days of this they'd settled down and we could control them easily. We removed the clogs and herded the mustangs toward the reserve, letting them graze some along the way. By late afternoon we had them penned at the Tonkawa camp. The warriors came out to look them over. Taka watched from a distance, but when I rode toward her she disappeared into her tipi.

We'd been gone a week, so when I got cleaned up I headed for Widder Jones' cabin. She looked a bit solemn when I entered, and I knew something was wrong. "Chip," she said as she put her arms around me, "I'm afraid this is our last time. I'm getting married Sunday."

That set me back on my heels, for I'd gotten so used to seeing her I couldn't imagine what it would be like without her. "Who to?"

"You don't know him. He has a farm over in Parker County. I'll miss seeing you. You can't imagine how much you have meant to me."

"I'll sure miss you," I gulped. "I hope he's good to you."

"He's kind and generous, and I know he'll make a good father. I've always wanted a child, and now . . ."

"You mean?" I'd never dreamed of anything like that happening. She nodded.

"Come," she said, taking my hand. "Let's not make this a sad parting. At least I'll always have something to remember you by."

One or two Tonkawa boys herded the mustangs during the days until they settled down. It didn't take long to tame and gentle them, except for the stallion, only he wasn't a stallion anymore. But by patient and gentle handling Tosche brought it around, and he was one proud-looking cowboy the first time he rode it.

The Major arrived on one of his visits a short time later. "I'm sorry to tell you," he said, "but I just heard that George Hill died." We rode to all the camps and villages, but we didn't say much, thinking about Mr. Hill. Back in the office the Major and Captain Ross talked some about the Comanches.

"I wish Sanaco and Buffalo Hump would bring their people and stay," the Major said. "Buffalo Hump and I used to get on fine. He and some of his people went with me in '49 when Rip Ford and I were marking a wagon road to El Paso. But there was a wild Irishman along, I think his name was Sullivan. Buffalo Hump returned to his camp one day and found Sullivan there, giving a lecture to the women, he told us. I don't know what he was doing, but Buffalo Hump sent all of the women away, so I suspect his lecture was about playing parlor games on a buffalo robe. If they hadn't figured he was crazy they'd have killed him for sure. Buffalo Hump has been a bit cool toward me ever since." The Captain and I smiled, but the Major's face remained impassive as usual.

"As long as Sanaco's and Buffalo Hump's bands don't settle down at Clear Fork the population there will fluctuate," the Major continued. "That will keep Ketumse's young men upset. Sooner or later some of them will be caught raiding around here, or they'll be accused of it, which will have the same result. We'll be in for big trouble."

"We've been lucky so far," the Captain said. "Having Ketumse there is what's made it work, but unless the other bands come in and stay our luck can't last."

"There's only one solution as I see it," the Major added. "That's putting all of the Comanches on a reservation in Indian Territory. The ones at Clear Fork keep asking why the Northern Comanches are free to roam while they're confined to one small piece of land. I've urged the Commissioner to confine all of them, but I'm afraid he'll let things go on this way until a lot of whites and Comanches have been killed, and I hate to see that. The Comanches have a right to go on living even if their old way of life can't last much longer."

The Captain kept the Caddo express rider Fox and me real busy for a while, carrying messages to Indian villages, Clear Fork, and the fort. There seemed to be no letup, for every morning he had something else that would keep us on the go all day or longer. I wondered if Tosche had broken Taka's mare, but had no chance to ask. "It's a good thing the government didn't hire you by the mile," the Captain said, his eyes atwinkle. "They'd have to raise taxes to pay you. I'm glad you've got a tough butt."

"It's about wore out," I admitted.

I knew he was worried about the Comanche-Kiowa raids that had broken out again along the frontier. In May they made a big sweep around Belknap and in Palo Pinto and Parker counties. The Captain heard that some settlers were beginning to claim that the Clear Fork Comanches must be involved. That's what some of my visits to Baylor were about. He swore that his Comanches weren't involved, but since he didn't make head counts except on issue day once a week, and let them leave the reservation at other times, I wondered how he could be so sure. All of these rides kept me from seeing Taka even at a distance for several more months, which made me feel pretty glum.

In July a wagon that Captain Eastman sent from Fort Chadbourne brought four young Comanches to the Clear Fork reserve. They'd come to the fort on foot, armed only with bows and arrows, and had asked to be taken to the reserve. They explained that they'd gone on a mustang hunt with Comanche Sam, but he had died and they lost their ponies. Captain Eastman wanted to know if their story was true.

Baylor had the four put in the guardhouse at Cooper for a week, then turned them over to Ketumse with orders to whip them and shave their heads. They'd gone out looking for trouble, not mustangs, for they'd attacked some white men they saw swimming in a river. Those men got their guns, killed Comanche Sam and two others, then took all their ponies.

Baylor came to the Brazos Agency to see the Major on his next visit. "I can't allow these rascals to stay here and make arrows and fatten themselves, then go out and attack white men," he said. "I aim to stop it, and need your advice. How do I prevent it from happening again?"

"Don't let any leave unless you're absolutely sure you can trust them. If possible, have one of the Delawares accompany them," the Major advised him.

"I've been letting any of them go right along. It got started when the commander at Cooper told them they couldn't leave without his permission. I couldn't let him take over control of the Indians. Now if I stop giving them passes to go hunting they're likely to leave for good."

"You were right not letting the army take over the reserve," the Major assured him. "Somehow, and tactfully, you've got to discourage them from leaving. I know it won't be easy, now that they're used to doing it. They've always been wanderers, and staying in one place isn't to their liking. The Tonkawas were also nomads, yet they're settling down, so it isn't impossible. You've done a good job getting the Comanches to do some planting and to look after their cattle. See what you can do to encourage them to stay put."

"It's their Mexican captives who do the work," Baylor said. "Them and a few of the women."

"Get the captives together and send them back to Mexico. The Comanches must learn to do their own farming."

In September the Major came again, stopping in Dallas on the way to open bids for supplying flour to the agencies. While there he discussed his plans with the editor of the Dallas *Herald.* As usual we spent the day visiting the villages. At the Tonkawa camp I saw Taka; our eyes met, but she lowered her head and neither of us spoke. I hadn't had one chance to talk to her in months. I'd hardly even seen her, badly as I wanted to.

Back at the agency that afternoon we turned our horses into the pen and fed them. "Everything's fine here as far as I can see, Shap," the Major said. "Even the Tonkawas are doing better at farming, and they're taking good care of the cattle. There's only one thing we haven't tended to so far, and it should be next. That's schools for the children." He paused for a moment, then continued. "I'm still worried about the Comanches, although some of them are making an effort and need only time and patience. But not the young men. The only way they can become warriors is by raiding. That's the most important thing in their lives, so we can't really blame them for it or expect them to become saints overnight. When they have a chance to join a raiding party headed for Mexico it's more than they can resist. But it's got to stop. The troops at Forts Davis and Lancaster have cut off raiding parties returning from Mexico recently. That means the Comanches will likely turn their big raids against Texas in the near future. I wish the Commissioner would let me move our Comanches to Indian Territory."

"From all I can determine they aren't mixed up in raids in Texas," the Captain observed, "at least so far. How much longer we can hope that will last I don't know, especially since Baylor still can't keep them on the reserve. But if it's ever proved that any of them are involved in local raids there'll be hell to pay."

"Moving them to Indian Territory won't stop the raiding, but it would make it safer for these Indians here," the Major continued. "If the troops thrashed the Northern Comanches and Kiowas a time or two like I've suggested, and the government offered them a treaty and promised to provide for their needs, the raiding could be controlled. As it is, we'll just have to live with it, but if trouble comes I'm most concerned about what will happen to the Brazos Indians. To most Texans all Indians are alike and fair game even when they're peaceful."

We sat there a while longer, for the Major seemed to be doing some heavy thinking. "As long as you're here, Shap, these people will do fine," he said at last. "I've already told the editor of the *Herald* that in October I'm going to Washington again and try to get approval for schools here and at Clear Fork. Then I'm going to settle my accounts and resign. It's time I looked after my own ranch and spent more time with my family. I don't want my children to grow up wondering who their father is. While I'm away I wish you'd check on the Comanches now and then. Spend a day there whenever you can without getting Baylor's back up."

I sure didn't want to see the Major resign, for he'd go back to his family and I might never see him again. The Dallas *Herald* had a long article on him and the reserves, and the Captain and I read it with delight. "Should this policy succeed, as it now promises to do, too much praise cannot be awarded Major Neighbors—the indefatigable agent, under whose auspices the policy has been inaugurated," it said. It went on to say that he had taken the preliminary steps in 1849, but his removal by President Taylor had frustrated his plans for four years. "On his reappointment, at the commencement of President Pierce's administration, he immediately took steps to test the practicability of the policy. We now see the astonishing results. Major Neighbors, more than any living man, has the confidence and respect of the Indians. His influence with them has doubtless contributed to this result.

"We regret to learn from Major Neighbors that he has determined to resign his agency during the ensuing winter and spring. He has retained it for the last four years at a pecuniary sacrifice. His salary is altogether inadequate to the onerous duties of his appointment. The retirement of Major Neighbors will be a misfortune for the northern frontier. His place cannot be supplied. He originated and carried into successful practice the 'feeding policy' in Texas; he has the entire confidence of the Indians, and exercises an unbounded influence over them. He has faithfully applied the appropriations made by the government to the benefit of the Indians; and by his economical management and disbursement, has saved thousands of dollars for the government. The best evidence of his strict integrity is that he will leave this arduous service, in which thousands of dollars pass through his hands, poorer than when he entered it."

It seems a lot of people around the reserve felt the same way, for when word got out that he'd gone to Washington to quit the Indian service, someone drew up a petition praising his faithful performance of duty and begging him to stay on. A lot of people signed it, and the Captain sent it to him. That changed his mind, at least for the time. I figured maybe I should stay as long as he did, then quit when he resigned.

A couple of weeks after the Major left for Washington, the Captain rode over to the Clear Fork Agency to spend a day with Baylor and talk about the school for Comanche children. This meant he'd be away three days. In the afternoon I rode to the Tonkawa camp and asked where Tosche was. He and some others were out looking for strayed cattle. I'd counted on that.

Taka looked out of her tipi and saw me, then disappeared. I rode over to it and dismounted. I didn't know if her aunt and uncle were in the tipi or if they understood English. I was in a desperate mood. "Taka," I said, "I want to talk to you. Can you hear me?" I knew she could but wanted her to acknowledge it. She didn't. "Please come out, I won't keep you long." I waited a few minutes, but she didn't appear. "You might as well come out and hear what I have to say. I'm going to stay right here until you do. You don't want me to do that, do you?"

I squatted down like I was ready to take root. Finally I heard the tipi flap rustle, and she came out, frowning and looking at her moccasins. "What do you want?" She tried to make her voice sound gruff, but she wasn't very convincing.

"Taka, I'm sorry I tried to make love to you. I couldn't help myself— you're about the prettiest woman I've ever seen. I want you to forgive me so we can be friends. I miss talking to you. Will you forgive me and say we're friends?"

Her frown vanished, and she looked up. I really meant what I said about her being pretty. "I guess so, if that is all you want. You're a friend of Tosche."

"Please don't hide when I come here after this. Talk to me a little. I know you don't like cowboys, but don't forget that Tosche is a cowboy, too." That seemed to thaw her out a bit.

"Did Tosche say I don't like cowboys?" She even smiled at that, proba- bly remembering what else she'd said. "Tosche talks too much. He told me you gave me the pony. Did you?"

"It was the prettiest and the best, so I figured it was just right for you."

"We'll be friends," she said, smiling. That was good enough for me, so I said goodbye and left. I sure hadn't meant to say all those dumb things; I was just going to say, "I'm sorry," and "Goodbye, sister." Those words had just blurted out and I couldn't stop them. I must be losing my marbles.

The Captain returned a few days later. "How is it at Clear Fork?" I asked him. "Things have been quiet here."

"Baylor swears everything's dandy, but if he believes that it's only because he thinks that as long as he's in charge nothing can happen without his permission. I couldn't ask him much or he'd have thought I was spyin' on him." He smiled and his pale blue eyes twinkled, then he was serious again. "He's sittin' on a hornet's nest and doesn't even seem to know it." He shook his head.

There was some excitement at Clear Fork, the Captain said. Someone dressed like an Indian shot at Lieutenant Herman Biggs but missed. Baylor, with a few Indians and soldiers, tried to follow the man's trail through the Comanche camp. When the women saw them coming, they and the children ran for the hills and hid out until dark. The soldiers at Cooper had accused the Comanches of trying to kill them, and kept them constantly alarmed by threats that they'd all be massacred. During all this Ketumse was away looking after the stock, he said. Baylor told the Captain he was sure it would take troops to get Ketumse back on the reserve, but he did return.

"Baylor is losing control," the Captain told me. "The Comanches won't plant crops until he gives them presents. I told him that was a bad idea. He said he'd done it only to get them started the first time, but now he can't stop it. He seemed to have things under control at first, but now it looks like they've got him buffaloed, and it's getting worse rather than better. Ketumse won't even talk to him."

The next morning he had a message for the Tawakoni chief, whose village was about four miles away. On the way I stopped at the Tonkawa camp. Taka seemed to sense that I was there and came out of her tipi, smiling. Of course I was all smiles, too. "Why don't you come with me for a little while? I'll wait for you down the trail."

"I'll come," she said.

I waited for her under a Spanish oak, then led the way to a spring surrounded by oaks and willows. "Let me tell you something," I said. "I had convinced myself that I just wanted to tell you I was sorry, and then not talk to you anymore. I knew all along that wasn't true, that I was trying to fool myself. I still think of our ride from the fort that night."

She smiled a little. "I liked that too." She leaned over and kissed me.
"What do you call that?"

"Kissing."

"I like kissing," she whispered. We sat there awhile, and I gently caressed her. I didn't want to scare her away or make her sorry she accompanied me, so I didn't try much of what I'd learned from the Widder. But I sure thought about it and barely resisted the temptation.

"Taka, I want to see you anytime I can. When you see me lift my hat it means I'm comin' here and want you to meet me. Will you?"

She didn't answer right away, but looked at me as if trying to figure out something. "If we come here many times, maybe Taka will love you too much. Then one day you'll ride away and not come back. What will happen to Taka then?"

That left me fumbling for an answer. I'd promised myself I'd leave when the Major resigned so he could think only of his real family and forget he'd raised me. Now he'd decided to stay on a while longer. I hadn't given much thought to the future. All I had in mind was teaching Taka all I'd learned about making love, not looking beyond that. But that might complicate things.

"I'm not planning to leave anytime soon," I finally told her, a bit lamely. "If you want, we can meet once in a while and just talk." She nodded. I kissed her and lifted her onto her mare, then headed down the trail. My mind was as clear as a buffalo wallow. I couldn't see us just sitting and talking unless she had more power to resist temptation than I did.

The Major returned from Washington to his San Antonio headquarters in March '57, and in April came to the agency just in time for a little excitement at Clear Fork. A soldier from Camp Cooper had been shot, and others claimed it was by a Comanche. I accompanied the Major there as soon as we heard the news.

"It wasn't one of my Indians," Baylor said. "The soldier was drunk and probably shot himself."

The Comanches were alarmed, for the soldiers had told them many times they'd all be wiped out soon. They were ready to run, for they'd brought in their ponies and kept them handy. If other troops had suddenly appeared, in five minutes there wouldn't have been a single Comanche anywhere on the reserve.

"I have bad news for you, John," the Major told Baylor. "Commissioner Manypenny is sending Colonel Matthew Leeper to replace you. I asked him why, but he wouldn't give me much of an answer, just mumbled something about you being absent without leave and your accounts not being in order. That was what he emphasized, the accounts. His mind was made up and he didn't care to discuss it with me. It may be that the army or some congressman on the appropriations committee put pressure on him to hire Leeper. That happened to me in '50 when the Whigs took over. I was called to Washington, but when I got there I was out of a job and John Rollin had replaced me because a Whig senator wanted some patronage. I'm sorry, but there was nothing I could do about it."

Baylor's naturally swarthy face turned almost black and his dark blue eyes burned like live coals. Remembering Jim Shaw's doubts about him, I was glad it wasn't the Major who'd fired him, for he sure looked like he was in a killing mood. I guess maybe he deserved to be replaced, for he'd bungled and lost control of the Comanches. I didn't know about his accounts, though I recalled his extravagant promises to the Reverend Byars, and what the Captain said. But it was obvious that he considered this an enormous insult. I shivered a little as I wondered what he'd do about it.

FOUR

Colonel Matthew Leeper, a large, black-haired man in his thirties, arrived at the Brazos Agency with his wife and son in mid-May '57. Without telling anyone he was leaving, Baylor had already moved his family to his ranch near Hubbard Creek. One of the Delawares got word to Captain Ross, so he stayed with the Comanches for three weeks before Leeper came to take over.

Sanaco and Buffalo Hump had come in again, for their people were starving, but about the time Baylor left, Sanaco and his band disappeared. "I couldn't find out for sure," the Captain told the Major later, "but I gather that something Baylor said scared him off. My hunch is he told Sanaco the troops would seize him if he stayed. Ketumse gave me the idea. He said Sanaco was afraid he'd be arrested for stealing horses."

The Major was silent for a few minutes, and his usually expressionless face seemed sad. "That sounds likely," he said at last. "Baylor probably hopes all the reserve Comanches will leave since he's no longer their agent. How many are there at Clear Fork now?"

"At last count there were about three hundred and eighty, but only seventy are men. All the rest are women and children." The Major frowned.

The Brazos Indians' farms were, as Mr. Hill had predicted, as good as any in the state the past year. They had raised enough corn and wheat to meet their needs. The government had sent them some Chinese sugar cane, or sorghum, and it was growing well.

The Comanches were also doing much better at farming, Leeper reported later. "I tried something different," he explained. "I divided the cornfields and melon patches into separate family plots. Now they're looking after them much better than before. The only problem is their impatience. They won't wait until their crops are ripe—so they eat half-grown ears and melons the size of apples. But they're catching on, so there's hope for the future."

A few days after the Major returned to San Antonio an excited young Caddo rode up to the agency on the dead run and tried to tell us something in a mixture of Caddo and English. About all we could tell was that there was some calamity in their cornfields. We mounted and followed him to his village at a fast lope. When we neared it we saw all of the Caddos in the fields flailing about with shovels, clubs, or anything handy. At first it looked like a free-for-all—what Captain Ross would call an Irish picnic—but we saw they were hitting the ground, not one another. When we got closer, we could see the ground was covered with huge grasshoppers flowing northward like a flash flood in a dry streambed and devouring every green thing in their path. It was a scary sight, like watching the world coming to an end.

"It's no use," the Captain told the Caddos. "There's nothing you can do. They'll eat everything, then move on. When they're gone you can plant another crop." The despondent Caddos trooped in from their fields, looking back to watch their corn vanish, as if they couldn't believe what they saw.

Several days later, after every cornfield on the whole reserve had been stripped bare, the hoppers flew north, all at once. I was riding toward the agency when the sky suddenly grew dark. My pony jumped, then stopped and stood there, trembling, for as the hoppers flew over us they blotted out the sun. It's hard to describe the sound they made, a sort of metallic clicking and whirring that reminded me of a twister that went over us once without touching down. When that wave of hoppers passed over them, the birds and animals went wild for a few minutes. It was sure enough scary.

I wondered if they'd been sent to tell the Indians they were doomed, that they'd all starve to death. Their coming reminded me of a camp meeting preacher I heard once who worked up a big sweat ranting about hellfire and brimstone, the work of the Devil, and a lot of stuff I didn't understand. If it was the Devil's work, I figured he'd done a pretty thorough job. I asked Tosche what he made of it. "Bad medicine," he said. Whether the hoppers were sent from above or below, the Indians didn't need a setback like that.

The Indians planted another crop and it survived. Before they would plant again the Comanche men demanded presents, as usual, but somehow Colonel Leeper jollied them into doing it. Anyway, it was the women, not the men, who did the planting and looked after the crops.

The Comanches loved roasting ears so much that some families ate all of their own in a hurry and then helped themselves to ears belonging to others. That caused the men to guard their gardens like they were their best war ponies. Colonel Leeper told us that if he needed to see any of them he had to go to the fields. They wouldn't leave them unguarded.

I didn't go to the Tonkawa village for a month after Taka and I had met at the spring. Too many things had happened, and I needed to do a lot of thinking before I talked to her again. Every day I'd think about seeing her, and I even started toward the Tonkawa village a couple of times before turning back. I wanted badly to see her alone, but I still wasn't sure about anything. I even thought about asking her to marry me, but pushed that crazy notion out of my mind. Marry an Indian! I could never do that.

Finally I figured I'd better see her and talk some more—that should help me decide what to do. At least that's what I told myself. The fact was I missed seeing her. The next chance I had I stopped at the Tonkawa village, gave her the signal, and rode toward the spring. She caught up with me on the way and we rode to it together. We sat on her robe and I kissed her. "Taka, I hate it when I don't get to see you," I admitted.

"I watch for you ever' day," she said. We lay back on her robe and I fondled her like I had that night on the way back from the fort. She sighed and closed her eyes. I was sure tempted to teach her everything I'd learned, but resisted. We were both on fire and my willpower was getting weaker by the minute when she arose, looking a bit frightened.

"I must go," she said.

One of these days, fool, I thought, it's going to happen. And what will you do then? She'd expect me to marry her—maybe by their customs we'd already be married, and I'd have to skip out in a hurry. Then what would the Major think of me? He'd likely feel he'd failed me as a father, and for sure that I'd failed him as a son. I couldn't let that happen just because I . . . I should head for California right now before I ruin everything, I thought, but I didn't start packing.

Captain Ross had to attend court in McLennon County for a month, so the Major came and took his place as agent. Right after he arrived the Northern Comanches and Kiowas made a raid through the ranch country around the reserves, scaring the settlers and stealing about sixty of their best horses. They also drove off about twenty from the Brazos reserve, mostly Caddo and Waco ponies.

Local ranchers sent word to the Major that they were rounding up a party to follow the raiders and asked for some Indian scouts and trackers. I headed for the Anadarko village to tell José María. He sent riders to other villages, and about thirty warriors were waiting at the agency when the ranchers and cowboys got there. I had already gotten my rifle, blankets, and some grub, and was ready to mount up.

Tosche also joined us, along with five Tonkawa scouts. We took the lead, following the raiders' tracks—so many horses were easy to follow. We rode all day, trotting or loping, and I figured we must have gained on them. At night the ranchers stopped, for it was too dark to see the tracks.

Tosche spoke to some of the other Tonkawas, then came to me. "Tell them we'll follow trail some more. We know where they're going and can find the trail in the morning."

I told the ranchers. They looked like they could use some sleep, but they wanted badly to recover their horses, so we pushed on until midnight. We tied our ponies where they could graze, then rolled up in our blankets and slept. At the first sign of light the Tonkawas mounted their ponies and rode ahead, me with them. They soon found the Comanches' trail.

We followed it at a fast clip until midday. By then the raiders must have seen our dust and figured they were being followed, for they split up into a dozen small parties and scattered. Maybe that was what they always did, just to be safe. We waited for the ranchers to catch up.

"They do this to throw off pursuers," Tosche told me. "They come back together later. We'll follow some of the tracks and find all of them."

I explained this to the ranchers. "We just keep going," I told John Dayton, a slender young cowman with a black beard. "They'll lose some time trying to hide their tracks, so we've got a better chance of catching 'em."

"Let's go," he said. We rode on.

Late afternoon, sure enough, the trails all merged. The Tonkawas slid off their ponies and examined the tracks carefully. Tosche talked to them, then came to me.

"The Comanches aren't far ahead," he told me. "The Tonkawas and Caddos will go on, and get past their camp in the dark. You come on at daylight. We'll chase the Comanches this way. Shoot a heap of them."

I explained this to Dayton and the others. "How do we know they'll do what they say?" one asked.

"At least twenty of their ponies are in that bunch," I told him. "They'll kill all the Comanches they can and try to recover every animal." He looked like he doubted me.

"When they strike the raiders' camp on the north side they'll drive them toward us," I told them. "We'd better be ready or we'll miss a chance to shoot some Comanches."

We were up and on our way as the eastern sky turned pink. Just as the sun appeared we heard whoops and gunshots, then the sound of running horses. We spread out and leveled our rifles. Pretty quick a dozen Comanches dashed toward us, whipping their ponies. They were almost on us before they realized we were there. All of us cut loose at them, but they made poor targets, flattened on their ponies' backs and moving so fast. They quickly scattered. If we hit any of them they didn't fall.

Right behind them came most of the Caddos and Tonkawas, but by then the Comanches had disappeared. The rest of the Caddos soon appeared, driving a herd of ponies and waving six gory scalps. The ranchers smiled.

When we got back to the agency, tired and hungry, John Dayton stopped at the office to see the Major. "They split up and tried to hide their trails," he said, "but we just followed one trail. When they got back together they must have thought they were safe, but the Tonkawas could track a bumblebee in a blue norther. And those Caddos and Anadarkos are real scrappers. They killed six and maybe wounded others. But for the Indians I doubt if we'd have recovered a single horse or killed one Comanche. They're good folks to have around and I'm glad they're here." Everyone we talked to after that had nothing but praise for the Major and the Brazos Indians.

One morning Tonkawa chief Plácido came by the agency to see the Major, and greeted him like an old friend. I didn't hear what they talked about, but it was clear they'd known each other before. "How well do you know Plácido?" I asked after the chief had left. "I remember you mentioning him once."

"He's one noble old chief. Before the Whigs took over in '50 and replaced me, I visited the Comanche camps to try to talk them out of raiding in Mexico. In the Treaty of Guadalupe-Hidalgo the U.S. promised to end the raids from our side of the border, and as Indian agent it was my duty to try to stop them. Ketumse was willing, but Buffalo Hump and Santana were outraged at the idea. Some Kiowas were camped near the Comanches at the Double Mountain Fork of the Brazos, and they were pretty ugly when they heard what I was asking them to do. They sent word they were coming to kill me. There were only four of us—Captain Ross and two others—and we didn't have a chance against so many. Plácido and seven of his warriors were trading with the Comanches, and they joined us. 'Before they kill you they'll have to kill us,' he said, and they got ready to fight. That stirred the Comanche chief into action. He told the Kiowas we were on a peaceful visit, but that didn't stop them. Then he told them they'd have to fight his warriors, too. The Kiowas left, but just to be sure we were safe, thirty Comanches and the Tonkawas escorted us clear back to the settlements. But if it hadn't been for Plácido, no telling what might have happened to us."

"Now that I know some Indians pretty well, I've got to admit you were right when you told me to keep an open mind," I said. "Tosche and I couldn't be closer if we were kinfolk." The Major flashed one of his rare smiles.

"I'm glad to hear you say that. It's easy to hate people you don't know, not so easy when you know them. These Indians need all the friends they can get."

"Have you known any white men who married Indian women?" I asked him another time. "I'm not planning to," I added hastily, "but I'm curious to know what it would be like, that is, what other people would say." He looked at me sort of thoughtfully, and I wondered what he was thinking.

"I've known several. Some adopted Indian ways and stayed with the tribe. A few were ranchers, and you couldn't tell their wives from other ranch women except by their appearance. But folks call them squawmen and their children breeds, and not as a compliment. If you're around them long enough you just might decide to marry one. If you do, best think about it some so you're sure you know what you're doing. That way you won't change your mind about it and regret it later."

"If I ever do I'll remember that, but it ain't likely." I sounded a lot more sure than I really was. I figured he must have guessed that I'd already thought about it, and I was grateful he didn't ask me who I had in mind. But because of Taka I'd wondered what it would be like to be a rancher with an Indian wife. How would our neighbors treat her? She was, after all, half white. Or if we lived with her people, how would they treat me? The Major didn't make it sound real bad, and he didn't say don't even consider it. That meant I could think about it, even though I'd never thought I'd ever consider it.

When Captain Ross returned the Major left for San Antonio. A few days later Jim Shaw galloped up to the agency. "Seventy Comanches are headin' for the Anadarko village," he shouted. "Looks like they mean trouble." We saddled up and the three of us started for the village on the run.

The Comanches were already in sight when we got there, and it was clear they weren't paying a social call. José María and about thirty of his men stood facing them with rifles ready, and others were coming on the run. The Comanches, their feathers fluttering in the wind, were in a long crescent, and they stopped their ponies about a hundred yards from the Anadarkos. Ketumse and Buffalo Hump were a few yards in front of the warriors, and the latter was talking in sign language. We pulled up near José María, who was making signals in reply.

"What is he saying?" the Captain asked José María.

"He wants men who killed Comanches," he told us. "If not, he says they kill all of us."

"What did you tell them?" the Captain asked.

"I say come on. We're ready."

By now a good-sized crowd of Anadarkos and Caddos had gathered, all of them warriors who feared no Comanche. The Captain and Shaw turned their horses toward the Comanches. Not sure what I was getting into, I trotted my pony until it was even with them. The Captain and I hadn't taken time to get our rifles, which was probably just as well, for the Comanches were less likely to kill us than if we were armed. At least I hoped that was true. Jim Shaw had a rifle, but he left it in the scabbard.

As we rode toward that long line of grim-faced Comanches I hoped the Captain knew what he was doing. Some of the warriors wore feather warbonnets, while others had a feather or two in their hair. Their faces were painted red and blue, and some had white stripes from eyes to chin or white dots on their foreheads. I'd never laid eyes on a meaner, scarier-looking bunch. Each held a lance in his right hand, and those murderous-looking lance heads of polished steel reflected the sun in every direction. Most of the warriors had bows, but a few held rifles. They must have gone to a lot of trouble getting all painted up, and I figured they'd be mighty disappointed if there wasn't any party. All they were waiting for was a signal from the chiefs.

I glanced back at José María and his men; even without war paint and feathers they looked every bit as grim and determined as the Comanches. If anyone on either side fired a shot, even accidentally, blood would surely flow, and since we were in the line of fire between them, some of it would be ours. We'd stop arrows on one side and bullets on the other. I set my jaw and tried to look calm like the Captain and Jim Shaw, but my heart was sure pounding.

Ketumse and Buffalo Hump rode forward to talk, while the warriors scowled at us. Both chiefs were short and heavyset, like most Comanches I'd seen, and both wore eagle-feather warbonnets and had strings of elks' teeth around their necks. Their faces were painted like the others. Their buckskin jackets and leggings were beaded and fringed with hair. Seeing them so close was enough to make my skin tingle at the thought of one of them scalping me. Compared to Buffalo Hump, Ketumse, even in his war paint, looked almost peaceful. Buffalo Hump, with polished brass bands on his arms, was grim-faced and mean-looking.

"Why are you here?" the Captain asked through Jim Shaw.

"They killed Comanches," Buffalo Hump replied. "It's our duty to avenge them."

"They killed Comanches who stole their horses. When you came to Clear Fork you also promised to fight raiders. That's your duty, not starting a war between the reservations." The Captain let that sink in.

I glanced back at José María. By now at least a hundred warriors had gathered around him. The Captain nodded his head in their direction.

"If you attack those warriors they'll kill many of you. Then other Comanches will come to avenge you, and more will be killed. Is that what you want? Are the Comanches all tired of living?"

Buffalo Hump thought about that some, looking madder than ever. "Are the Caddos going to accompany white men after Comanches again?" he asked. "If they do we will kill."

"Anytime Comanches steal their ponies or those of the settlers, they will."

Ketumse and Buffalo Hump wheeled their ponies and rode back to the others, who gathered around them. Ketumse talked fast, while they sullenly listened. When he stopped, others spoke. Ketumse talked some more, swinging one arm toward the Brazos warriors, who had spread out in a long line, each of them holding a rifle pointed toward the Comanches. Then Ketumse rode through the warriors toward Clear Fork, with Buffalo Hump following. The others shouted threats or insults at José María, then sullenly rode after the chiefs. I felt like a big boulder had rolled off my chest and I could breathe freely again.

"That was a close call," the Captain said. "Ketumse was forced into this, no doubt about that. Lucky for us he's a reasonable man." I sure thought so, and Jim Shaw grunted his agreement.

In July Lieutenant Colonel Lee was transferred and Captain Stoneman replaced him as commander at Camp Cooper. Lee had little use for Indians and considered the reservations a mistake, but at least he didn't interfere with the agent. Stoneman made trouble from the start by counteracting Leeper's orders. He nearly stampeded all of the Comanches by trying to make a head count without first informing the agent.

Head counts were the agent's responsibility anyway, but Stoneman told the Comanches they were now under army control and that he'd send troops to kill any who left the reserve without his permission. He also claimed that the Clear Fork Comanches were showing raiders where the ranches and settlers were and helping them steal their stock. The Delaware scouts, who knew what went on, said this wasn't true. The raiders, they said, were mostly Northern Comanches and Kiowas, but some were Kickapoos. None of them needed any help in finding ranches or isolated cabins.

Leeper wrote the Major, warning him that Stoneman's threats were making the Comanches so nervous they were likely to leave. The Major requested General Twiggs to replace Stoneman with an officer who wouldn't interfere with the agents or spread false reports. Captain Plummer soon arrived and Stoneman left. Plummer cooperated with Leeper, but some of the officers still claimed that the Clear Fork Comanches were involved in the raids.

There wasn't any question about the damage the growing number of raiding parties was doing, for they stole horses all along the frontier. The cavalry had been sent to protect the settlers, but they couldn't stop the raids without attacking the Comanches in their main camps on the High Plains and north of the Red River. As long as they waited for raiders to strike and then tried to punish them, they weren't much more useful than infantry. They did send out a lot of patrols, and once in a while they stumbled onto a raiding or hunting party.

Thirty or forty Northern Comanches and Kiowas sought refuge at Clear Fork after tangling with a cavalry patrol. Ketumse didn't like them being there, but some of his people did. The Indian agent at Fort Arbuckle sent them word that their annuity presents had arrived. They made a fast trip to Arbuckle, collected their loot, then returned to Clear Fork, boasting of the gifts they'd received from the government because they refused to settle down and live like women. They even traded guns to the Wacos. Leeper and Ketumse finally got them to leave by threatening to bring cavalry onto the reserve to drive them away.

"It's hard to understand what the government is doing," the Captain said, shaking his head. "We're at peace with a fraction of the Comanches and at war with all the rest. The agent at Arbuckle supplies them with guns and ammunition, giving them the means to continue their war against Texas."

The Major wrote that he had again urged General Twiggs to send a large force to attack Comanche and Kiowa camps on the High Plains and in Indian Territory, for that was where the raiders had to be stopped. He offered to furnish scouts and guides, but Twiggs still hadn't requested permission to send troops into another military department. A few settlers moved their families to safer places or left the area, while many wrote the government demanding protection. Because the Indians on the two reserves were the only ones they could see, many frustrated men turned their anger on them.

After one raid John Dayton and two other ranchers came to the agency when the Major was there. Dayton, who'd praised the Brazos Indians for helping recover his horses earlier, did the talking. "Baylor tells us the raiders are from both reserves," he said, "and that you know it but won't do anything to stop it. Instead you feed and protect them while they're robbing white people. We're here to find out when you're going to do something about them."

The Major looked each man in the eye before replying. "I assure you that what Baylor told you is not true. No raiding party has come from either reserve. When one is trailed to either agency I'll do something about it, not before. As you know, the Brazos Indians have also lost many horses to the Northern Comanches. Have you forgotten they helped you recover yours? You had to follow the thieves nearly to the Red River, so you know where they come from."

The men shifted uneasily in their saddles. "We remember that," Dayton said, "but it's different now. Baylor was at Clear Fork and swears he knows what goes on here as well. He says it's your responsibility to protect us from Indians, yet you refuse to do it."

"I have no troops to protect anyone," the Major told them. "You can see that. The cavalry was sent here to protect the settlers. Why don't you talk to the army?"

"We did," Dayton admitted. "Most of the officers say the Clear Fork Comanches show the raiders where the ranches are. Give them control of the agencies, they say, and they'll put a stop to all the thieving and killing. Why won't you let them do it?"

The Major drew a deep breath, for all of this palaver was leading nowhere. "I assure you the reserve Indians are not involved in the raids in any way. They suffer from them same as you. I'm a federal officer and my sworn duty is to manage and protect these Indians. As long as they're innocent of wrongdoing I'll protect them as best I can. They are, after all, the same ones you said were good people to have around. They haven't changed, and you'd be in a lot worse trouble if they weren't here."

The ranchers pulled down their hats, wheeled their horses, and rode away while we stared after them. I felt sick, hearing them talk like that, for they'd been friends of the Indians before. Now they weren't satisfied with what the Major had told them. "They've swallowed Baylor's lies," the Captain said, "and they don't want to admit the truth. But I can understand their frustration over the raids and thefts."

When the ranchers were out of sight the Major, Captain Ross, and I went into the agency office and sat there for a while in silence. "I'm afraid this is just the beginning," the Major remarked at last. "Looks like Baylor's on a crusade to destroy the agencies and the Indians, and he's already won some converts."

"What he wants most are scalps—mine, Leeper's, and especially yours," the Captain added. "If he gets them it may slake his thirst for the Indians' blood. If not, it looks like he'll try to destroy anything and everything to get at us."

"I see only two things I can do that might prevent him from inciting the settlers into attacking the reserves," the Major said. "One is to keep after Twiggs until I convince him that only a strike at the main Comanche camps will do any good. The other is to persuade the Commissioner to move our Comanches to a reserve in Indian Territory. So far I haven't been able to manage either, but I've got to keep trying. If I fail we may have to move all Indians out of Texas just to save their lives."

In August Colonel Johnston and most of the Second Cavalry were transferred to Utah because of some Mormon trouble there. Once more the frontier had few mounted troops, and the Comanches and Kiowas were quick to take advantage of their absence, striking dozens of places along the frontier.

We didn't hear any more about Baylor for a while. The Major sent Captain Ross word that the schools had been approved for both reserves. Workmen got busy putting up one-room buildings, and the schools opened in November. About thirty-five youngsters started attending the Brazos Agency school even though some of them had to come four miles or more. A young man named Zacharias Coombes was hired to teach them, and we took our meals with him and his wife. The Comanches weren't eager to have their children learn anything from a white man, but Ketumse sent his young sons to school. As long as a few attended there was hope that others would follow.

In the November election Hardin R. Runnels defeated Sam Houston for governor. "All I know about Runnels," Captain Ross said, "is that his only policy is to find out what's likely to be popular with the voters, and do it. Protecting Indians has never been popular. It would have been different if Sam had won. He'd support us all the way."

In mid-December Captain Gabriel Paul of the Seventh Infantry at Fort Belknap learned that a large Kickapoo camp had been seen on the West Fork of the Trinity. Everyone knew that the Kickapoos were better armed than any other tribe, and there were no better fighters. Captain Paul ordered the commander at Cooper to send all available troops and asked for fifty or sixty Tonkawas and others to accompany them. The Kickapoos must have learned they were coming or had business elsewhere, for when the troops and Indians found their camp it had been abandoned. At least now the army couldn't claim there were no Kickapoos in the area.

Because of the destructive raids along the whole cattle frontier, in December the legislature authorized the governor to raise a company of mounted volunteers to defend the settlers. We learned that a couple of Baylor's friends, Allison Nelson and Thomas Frost, had joined it as lieutenants. Frost was ordered to raise the company in Coryell and Comanche counties for three months' service. He announced a brilliant idea for fighting Comanches—when citizens killed any raiders, he'd have his men watch the bodies and shoot any Indians who came to bury them. When the Captain heard that he snorted in disgust.

As soon as he got to the Belknap region Frost wrote the governor that it was well known the Indians on both reservations were involved in the raids. "Major Neighbors has been petitioned time and again by our citizens to give some attention to the affairs yet they have received nothing but curses, insults, threats, and renewed outrages," Frost wrote. The letter wasn't published, but we soon knew its contents.

FIVE

The Major left for San Antonio late in December, and wrote the Captain several letters in January '58. "If you didn't see the governor's message to the legislature," he wrote, "he called attention to affairs in Kansas, where the pro-slavery men seem to be losing. Then he made it clear that he favors secession. Fortunately, most of the legislators don't agree with him." The legislature did agree to send delegates to a meeting of men from all Southern states if one should be called, and there was a lot of loose talk about Texas resuming its independence, the Major said. "This talk is madness. It would be the greatest folly for Texas to leave the Union."

Later he wrote that he'd called on General Twiggs, who showed him Frost's letter, which the governor had sent him. The Major told Runnels that he was surprised the governor would circulate a letter that was absolutely false in every particular. He was responsible to the Commissioner of Indian Affairs for protecting the Indians, he said. The army's duty was to protect the settlers. "It appears from the frequent censures I receive from some of the extreme frontier citizens, that they think the General Government employs me as Indian agent to herd the horses of the citizens, generally, when the fact is that I have not a single soldier under my control, and I am not charged with the defense of the frontier against Indian depredations. My duties are specific and I can only act as a civil magistrate to execute the Indian Laws and Treaties."

He'd heard that the legislature was excited about the false reports, he told the Captain, so he was going to Austin to assure the legislators that Indians didn't leave the reserves without permission. He would also warn them that if the state took no action to prevent it, war between settlers and reservation Indians was likely.

The legislature responded by authorizing the governor to enlist one hundred and ninety rangers for six months, and Runnels named Rip Ford to command them. That was good news—Ford was able and honest, and not one to be buffaloed by Baylor and his cronies. But about the same time Captain Newton Givens was made commander at Camp Cooper, and that was bad, for he was a friend of Baylor.

The officers had always denied that Kickapoos were involved in the raids even though the Delawares knew they were. Givens told anyone who'd listen that he'd never seen any sign of Kickapoos. Everybody on the frontier knew, he claimed, that the raiders were from the Clear Fork reserve. He swore he'd seen twenty-five or thirty Comanches leave the agency when Leeper had given passes to only six. He said a lot of other things that were also lies, like whenever the reserve Indians went on raids the agents blamed the Kickapoos.

In mid-January Captain Ross sent out a scouting party under Waco chief Ah-ha-dot because of frequent thefts of Indian horses. Across the Red River they attacked a Comanche camp, captured four men, and recovered eighty horses. Many of them bore the brands of local ranchers, and they were sure glad to get them back. The captives told Jim Shaw that the raiders were Comanches, Kiowas, and Kickapoos led by Sanaco's son. A council of Brazos chiefs decided that the four Comanches should be shot. When I saw ten grim-looking Brazos warriors and four glum Comanches heading off the reservation, I felt sorry for the prisoners. The ten Brazos men were all from different bands; that way no one band could be held responsible for executing the Comanches.

When Ah-ha-dot had returned to the agency, José María and Campo remained on a scout for Comanche raiding parties. Worried that a big war party might find them, the Captain sent a number of Caddo and Anadarko warriors to join them. They didn't see any more Comanches, but they ran across the last of the Tonkawas and brought them to the agency. There were eighty-three of them, mostly women and children, starving and nearly naked.

In January we got word that Baylor had called a meeting of settlers on the Clear Fork below the Comanche reserve. The meeting, to be held on February 1, was said to be for the purpose of organizing volunteer companies to defend the settlers of the area. When he heard about the meeting, the Captain sent me with a note to his son-in-law Kit Carter, asking him to attend it and see what Baylor was up to. Carter said he'd go and then stop by the agency afterward to report.

He came to the agency a couple of days after the meeting. "Baylor's a real demagogue," he told us. "That meeting wasn't for organizing companies to protect people. He ranted and raved about how the reservation

Indians are the ones who'd burned their cabins and stolen their horses. He kept repeating that, trying to turn them against the reservations and the men who run them. 'Major Neighbors knows what's going on,' he said, 'but he cares more for his redskin pets than for white people. Is a man like that fit to be agent?' He claimed he'd been dismissed because he defended the settlers, and he wants them to demand that the Major resign or be fired. He was vicious and long-winded."

"How many you figure were there?" the Captain asked.

"I'd say between eighty and a hundred. Baylor's friend Allison Nelson was there, and every time Baylor damned agents or Indians he hoorahed and tried to get them worked up."

"Reckon Baylor convinced them?"

"Some, at least temporarily, like when a camp meeting preacher gets everyone excited enough to swear off sin. After a while they get over being excited and wonder what they were doing. I talked to some of the ranchers and farmers and others who live near the reserves, and except for Patrick Murphy and Ed Cornett, they swear by the Indians to a man. They know the raiders don't come from around here, and that they steal horses from the reservation as well as ranches. Some figure there's a ring of white horse thieves who get Kickapoos or other Indians to do the dirty work and make it look like Comanches and Kiowas did it. I reckon that's true, and I wouldn't be surprised if that boozing braggart Cornett is mixed up with them."

After he left Clear Fork I'd run into Ed Cornett on the range a few times in places I didn't expect to meet anyone. Each time I met him he acted nervous and asked if I'd seen any stock with his brand. I'd figured he was out doing some mavericking, trying to pick up a few unbranded calves the ranchers or Indians had missed at branding time. It hadn't occurred to me that he might have been meeting someone in secret.

In February the Major wrote he'd asked that the Commissioner request the Secretary of War instruct the troops at Belknap and Cooper to protect the Indians against bands of armed whites. He pointed out that Major Paul at Belknap and Captains Stoneman and Givens at Cooper had consistently kept the Indians stirred up, hoping they'd have an excuse to attack them. If the Secretary of War issued special instructions we didn't hear anything about them, and the officers didn't change their ways.

While he was recruiting rangers Rip Ford sent Lieutenant Edward Burleson ahead to set up a base camp where Hubbard's Creek enters the Clear Fork, between the two reserves. They called it Camp Runnels. In

March Ford authorized William Marlin to raise a company in Young County, then came to the Brazos Agency to see the Major. He was a tall, eagle-eyed, gray-haired man who had been doctor, lawyer, surveyor, newspaperman, and Indian fighter. His name was John, but during the war with Mexico he had to write so many letters to families of men who'd died he finally shortened "Rest in Peace" to R.I.P. Pretty soon "Rip" was his nickname, and it stuck. He and the Major had surveyed a wagon road to El Paso in '49 and both were in the state legislature in '51. It was their joint resolution that got the governor to negotiate with federal officials over setting up the two reservations for Texas Indians. Whenever there were emergencies in the state Ford's was one of the first names governors usually remembered.

When Ford came to the agency the Major sent Fox and me to the different villages to ask the chiefs to meet him for a council, and they didn't waste any time getting there. As soon as all had arrived the Major asked them if they'd be willing to accompany Captain Ford on a Comanche campaign. They grunted their approval. They were already at war with the Comanches, Ah-ha-dot explained, but even if they weren't, and the Major wanted them to fight Comanches, he had only to ask them. At least a hundred warriors were ready to go whenever he called on them.

Ford smiled. "They'll be valuable, no . . . indispensable auxiliaries," he told the Major.

José María didn't volunteer to accompany Ford's rangers. He had made a treaty with the Creeks and Comanches, he explained. They had agreed that no one of them should make war on another without first informing the third tribe. If one of them did that, the other two would join in a war against it. He sent a messenger to the Creeks. When the man returned, José María came to see the Captain. "I am ready," he said, "whenever you need me."

Soon after Baylor's meeting on the Clear Fork a letter addressed to Captain Givens and bearing twenty-five names was published in several papers. They had put up with the state of affairs on the frontier as long as they would, they stated. Henceforth any Indians found off the Comanche reserve without a white man or a Delaware with them would be killed. If any settler in the area was killed by an Indian they would raise a force and break up the reservation. The letter also charged the Major with incompetence and demanded his removal. Many of the men whose names were on the letter swore they'd never seen it until it was published. James Swindell, surveyor for the Young County District, came to the agency to see the Major, but he was in San Antonio.

"Prior to the meeting at which the document referred to was hatched, or rather born," he told us, "I was but slightly acquainted with Captain Baylor. I and a good many others supposed from the positions he'd held both as an officer of the government and as a citizen of the state, that he was entitled to credence, particularly upon so serious a matter as making charges against Major Neighbors and the statements of alleged depredations by the reserve Indians. I couldn't believe that he would tell a deliberate falsehood upon so grave a subject, and to a meeting that looked to him to verify or deny rumors about the Indians. I as well as others supposed him to be a gentleman, scorning to do little things."

He went on to say that Baylor had lied about being authorized to sign his and other men's names to the letter. He also lied when he said that Ketumse had admitted some of the raiders were from Clear Fork, for at the time Ketumse wouldn't even talk to him.

"Had I known what I know now of Baylor's character for veracity, I should have given the lie direct to all his statements. Since the people have been enlightened as to his real character, they are sorry for what they have done."

William G. Preston, who had helped organize the meeting and whose name was also on the letter, was outraged, calling it a "base forgery." Givens had written a statement on the bottom of the letter attesting to Preston's reliability.

Publication of Baylor's letter and the others stirred up some support for the reservation Indians and raised our hopes. John von Hagen wrote that he was the outside man on the Clear Fork frontier and he'd never had any trouble with the Comanches. There might be, he admitted, individuals at the agency who communicated with the Northern Comanches, but most were contented and doing well. If the government planned to break up the reservation he wanted to know, for in that case he would no longer feel safe.

Thomas Lambshead and J. N. Gibbons wrote from their Clear Fork ranch: "We the undersigned are in favor of the Comanches and the Caddos and the other small tribes for still to remain on the present reservations in Texas. We the undersigned are in favor of our present Agent Major Neighbors for still to remain in office."

The attack on the Major included identical letters to the Secretary of the Interior from Williamson and Lampasas counties demanding his removal as supervising agent. They claimed he hadn't protected the frontier like he should have. And although he had been told repeatedly that reservation Indians had committed depredations ever since they had been settled there, he denied it in the face of positive proof, such as finding stolen horses on the reserves. The Secretary of the Interior sent copies to the Major. The four men whose names were on the letters declared their signatures had been forged. "This is more of Baylor's work," the Major told us later.

One morning just after the Captain left for a few days to confer with Rip Ford about the expedition, white-haired Isaac Lynn walked up to the agency office while I was there alone. He farmed on Keechi Creek but had only oxen, not even one saddle horse. He looked worried.

"My daughter promised to visit me yesterday," he said, "but she didn't come or send word like she always has before. I've got a feeling that something's bad wrong, but I'm not up to walkin' that far. Can you or someone else check on her for me?"

His daughter had married Tom Mason and they'd settled at Lost Valley in Jack County, where they and their children shared a double log cabin with James Cameron and his family. I'd stopped there a few times and knew them.

"I bet they're all right, Mr. Lynn," I told him, "but I'll be glad to make sure for you. Let me tell Dr. Stern and then I'll head over there right away and be back by late afternoon."

Dr. Stern, the agency doctor, doubled as acting agent when the Captain was away. He was short and slender, with wispy, colorless hair and spectacles perched on his nose, giving him a sort of owlish expression. He was solemn and unsmiling, like he figured doctors should be, I guess. He was nodding over one of his medical books when I told him about my errand for Mr. Lynn. He yawned and waved his hand, then went on with his reading.

A few hours later I could see the cabin in the distance, and stared at it. There was no smoke rising from either chimney, nor any other sign of life. Fear rising, I urged my pony to a fast lope. Maybe they just got mixed up on dates and had all gone to see Mr. Lynn today, I thought, but that didn't seem likely.

When I was a few hundred yards from the cabin I saw bodies lying in the yard with arrows sticking in them. As I got nearer I recognized the Camerons and two of their children, dead and mutilated. Sickened, I rode past them looking for the Masons. I soon found the bodies of Tom Mason and one of his children, but saw no sign of Mrs. Mason. Maybe she'd escaped somehow, I hoped, but I soon discovered her body in the cow lot, still clutching her baby in her rigid hands.

With trembling hands I took the baby from her arms, for it was still alive, and carried it into the cabin. There I found a two-year-old Cameron boy hiding. I gave each child a drink of water, then somehow managed to mount my pony with one arm wrapped around them. I'd passed a cabin about five miles down the trail and had seen children in the yard. I hurried there, told the startled woman what had happened, and left the little ones in her care while I rode hard to Fort Belknap to report the murders. A troop of cavalry trotted off to bury the bodies while I headed for the agency.

I couldn't get the sight of the Masons and Camerons out of my mind, for it brought back a vague memory of a similar sight in my early years. I still remembered my mother hiding me and ordering me to remain quiet when my father shouted that Indians were coming. That memory revived my nearly forgotten hatred of Indians, and it swept over me like a sheet of icy rain in a blue norther. I wanted to get far away from the Brazos reserve, so far I'd never see another Indian to remind me of this day. I could hardly bear the thought of seeing Tosche and Taka again.

I sure hated to tell Mr. Lynn what I'd found, but I had no choice. It seemed he'd expected bad news, for he knew from my expression that his worst fears had been realized. When I told him about the two little ones he exclaimed, "Thank God for that!" I told him I figured that one of the Cameron boys was missing, for I hadn't seen any sign of him.

That same afternoon we learned what happened to the boy, for some white men stopped at the agency with him asking the way to Fort Belknap. Mr. Lynn recognized him at once. He was a bright little fellow, about five or six, and he told us the story.

After the Indians had killed the Camerons and Masons they caught an unbroken mule and tied the boy to its back, driving it in the herd of horses they'd stolen. At night they took him off, and in the morning put him on a horse behind a white man who had red hair. There were, he said, two other white men with the Indians.

As they headed north, they came in sight of an emigrant train bound for California. About twenty of the emigrants started after the Indians, the boy said. The redheaded man had pushed him off to lighten the load on his horse. "Stay here till I get back," he ordered. The tired boy lay down in the tall grass and fell asleep.

Unable to overtake the Indians, the emigrants returned to the wagon train. The boy heard their horses and thought the white man had come back for him. "I'm here yet," he said. He told the emigrants who he was and that Indians had killed his parents. They were taking him to Fort Belknap when they stopped at the agency.

The fact that white men were in charge of the Indians changed the whole picture for me. I remembered Skinny and Jake saying that a man called Red was going to get Indians to help them steal horses. I remembered, too, who had saved my life when I was in their clutches. The Delawares had often claimed that some of the raids blamed on Comanches were the work of white men and Kickapoos, and these killings proved they were right, at least about white men being involved. Some folks in Lost Valley suspected that a white rancher had arranged the murders, for he'd been trying to get the two families off their land so he could add it to his own. Baylor wrote the Dallas *Herald,* blaming the killings on reservation Indians.

The Mason-Cameron murders were the first in the area, and many families were naturally terrified. Most settlers had come from states where Indian troubles were unknown, and they were shocked by the brutality. A lot of them talked about leaving for safer country.

Tosche came by the agency that same afternoon. "Let's follow the trail," he said. I told Dr. Stern we intended to find where the Indians and the white men had gone.

"Good! Then the army can destroy those murderers. They don't deserve to live another day."

The trail was nearly three days old by the time we set out, but they were driving a bunch of stolen horses and mules, so it was easy to follow. Having to watch constantly for Comanche war parties slowed us some, but we made pretty good time. After we crossed the Red River the trail was fresher, so we had to be even more cautious.

The next morning Tosche slipped to the top of a ridge, peered over it, then trotted back down. "Many ponies," he said. "Their camp is near."

We hid our ponies in a bushy ravine, then climbed the highest point around and watched. When some of the horses grazed fairly near where we were hiding, I saw that many were branded, which meant they were stolen ranch horses, not Indian ponies. In the afternoon some riders came from the east to drive the grazing animals back the way they'd come. Most of the riders were Indians, but they didn't look like any I'd ever seen.

"Kickapoos," Tosche whispered.

With them was a red-haired man on a big bay horse with a blaze face. "That's Cameron's horse," I told Tosche.

We waited until they were out of sight, then got our ponies and headed south, traveling as fast as we dared. Dr. Stern was in the office when we reached the agency, so I knew the Captain was away again. He bent his head, peering at me over his spectacles. "Well?" he said.

"We found the camp," I told him. "Kickapoos. With them was a red-headed man riding Cameron's horse." Dr. Stern leaped to his feet.

"I'm off to the fort!" he said. "I'll get the army to send an expedition after those murderers and kill every last one of them. You and Tosche can show them the way."

He was gone about three hours, while Tosche and I rested, figuring we'd better be ready to ride. Finally I saw Dr. Stern riding toward the agency at a walk, his shoulders slumping. He looked pretty glum and seemed to be talking to himself. It was obvious he was upset.

"Damn the army! Damn their idiotic regulations!" he exclaimed. "They can't cross the Red River—they'd be in another military district, and they can't do that without permission from the Secretary of War. Here's an opportunity to rid the world of a bunch of murderers, and all they can say is, 'Sorry, it's against regulations.' I argued with them for an hour, but I was just wasting my breath." He went off mumbling to himself, and I recognized a few words I'd never heard the Major use.

He was still in a bad mood the next morning and cussed out a mixed-blood Shawnee who helped Dykes, the agency blacksmith. The doctor had wanted his horse shod, but Dykes had some government wagons to repair and needed help, so the horse hadn't gotten shod. I walked with Dr. Stern to his cabin, while he grumbled about Indians in general and halfbreeds in particular.

"What would you think of a man who'd marry a squaw?" he asked, but didn't wait for my answer. "The only squawman I've seen was as lazy and good-for-nothing as an Indian. Had a flock of halfbreed brats who didn't want to do anything but ride and hunt. None of 'em had any ambition, yet they were as happy as if they owned a farm and had a barn full of hay."

"I've known white men like that," I ventured. He snorted.

"That's different. If you ever get the stupid idea of marryin' a squaw get a friend to knock you on the head. The Lord didn't intend for the races to mix like animals."

I didn't argue with him, for his mind was made up, but he sure gave me a different picture than I got from the Major. Most folks probably looked at such things like the doctor did. The Major didn't even call Indian women squaws, like everyone else. "It's a word that once meant 'woman,' " he told me, "but it has come to be a term of contempt."

What the doctor said really set me back and made me do some heavy thinking. The more I thought about it, the more I realized it would be a mistake to marry Taka. To hear my wife called a squaw and my sons referred to as halfbreed brats was more than I could face. Now I wished I hadn't asked Taka to be friends, and I used any excuse to avoid stopping at the Tonkawa village.

The Comanches made one of their biggest raids around Fort Belknap, running off so many horses that ranchers and reservation Indians were left shorthanded. Everyone hoped that the rangers and Brazos Indians would kill a flock of Comanches and recover the stolen stock.

Ford was ready to march in late April, and the night before we set out the Indians put on a big war dance. The warriors were all painted, and they whooped and hollered and went through the motions of killing Comanches. The women cheered them on, and if all that didn't put them in a fighting mood I don't know what would. It was enough to make the hair stand up on the back of my neck.

Before we left, the Captain asked the Reverend Tackitt, an old frontiersman turned preacher, to give the Indians a send-off prayer. While Jim Shaw interpreted, Tackitt prayed for the success of the expedition and safe return of the Indians.

Ford, with his rangers, was in overall command, but the Captain was in charge of the Indians and I was his lieutenant. Among the Indians were famous war leaders like José María, Jim Pockmark of the Caddos, Plácido of the Tonkawas, the Waco Shot Arm, and Shawnee Jim Linney. I counted one hundred and thirteen Indians, among them a dozen Tonkawas on foot—Comanches had stolen their ponies.

"Can they keep up with the riders?" I asked Tosche.

He smiled. "They'll keep up," he said, "and come back on Comanche ponies. You'll see."

We took two light wagons to carry grub, blankets, and ammunition, and it was hard going for them. Soon after we crossed the Red, Ford set up our supply camp and left ten rangers to guard it. The Captain sent Tonkawa scouts out to look for Comanches, while the rest of us traveled slowly, waiting for them to return with news.

When they rejoined us, it was clear the scouts were excited. "They saw Comanches hunting buffalo," Plácido told Ford and the Captain. Judging from the direction their pack ponies traveled, the scouts knew the Comanche camp was in Antelope Hills, five miles to our west.

Everyone got busy checking guns, tightening cinches, and generally getting ready for battle. I knew there were hundreds of Comanches north of the Red River, and the prospect of facing five times our number made my mouth dry. There were two hundred and ten of us, not counting the men at the supply camp, and everyone, rangers and Indians, seemed eager for a scrap. The Captain and his Indians led the way, with the Tonkawa scouts well in advance.

From just below a ridge the Tonkawas signaled to the rest of the Indians. "Small camp ahead, not main camp," Plácido told us.

The rest of the Brazos Indians split up and headed off to the right and left in order to surround the camp, while the Captain and I followed and the rangers waited. As we crossed a hill I saw our Indians charging the camp—half a dozen tipis—while the Comanches dashed for safety. The Brazos Indians shot a few warriors and captured the pony herd. In a few minutes the Tonkawas who had been on foot the whole way were mounted.

We followed the fleeing Comanches toward their main camp in Antelope Hills and soon saw several hundred warriors coming toward us, to delay us while their women and children escaped. We were on the right of Ford's rangers when the Comanches, led by chief Iron Jacket, charged. They were armed mostly with bows and lances, but the Brazos Indians all had good rifles. Iron Jacket wore a coat of mail one of his ancestors had taken off a Spanish soldier. He was a famous war chief who had come through many a battle unscathed, for his coat of mail stopped arrows. But it wasn't proof against bullets, for Jim Pockmark felled him with one well-placed shot, while the deadly fire of other Brazos Indians killed many of his warriors. Then Ford's rangers hit the big camp and all of the Comanches fled. In all that excitement I noticed that the Tawakoni George Washington stayed close to his adopted brother, the Captain, like he was his guardian angel. I'd gotten off a few shots before the Comanches turned and fled, but in all the smoke and dust I wasn't sure I'd hit anyone.

There must have been another big camp a few miles away, for several hundred more warriors appeared in a long line on the crest of a hill overlooking the captured camp. They advanced slowly toward us, whooping and shouting threats. The Brazos Indians rode out to meet them, telling them by sign language to come on and fight, but the Comanches wisely stayed out of rifle range. They circled around as if to cut us off, but Ford sent half of his rangers to join us, and the Comanches pulled back.

Ford signaled the Captain to hold the camp and captives while he and his rangers took off after the Comanches. They chased the fleeing warriors a mile or two, then returned. From a captive woman a Delaware learned that Buffalo Hump was about ten miles away with a large number of warriors. The Captain relayed this news to Ford.

"They're liable to discover our camp and wipe out the men there," Ford said. "We best pull back before that happens." He made a quick count of the dead Comanches. "Counting those at the little camp, I figure we killed seventy-six," he told the Captain. "How many captives?"

"Sixty," the Captain replied, "all women and children."

We'd lost one ranger and one Waco warrior killed, and a few rangers and Indians had been wounded.

Back at the supply camp Ford and the Captain told José María that the Indians could divide the Comanche ponies; we'd return the branded stock to the owners.

"Our horses are run down," Ford said, "and there must be five hundred Comanche warriors within ten or fifteen miles. I say let's head back before they surround us."

"Suits me," the Captain replied, so we headed for home.

Our return march was made without any more fighting, although the scouts said a big bunch of Comanches was following us at a safe distance. It was clear they wouldn't attack us unless they could take us by surprise, but Ford and the Captain didn't let that happen. The Comanches did try to stampede our horse herd one night, but we kept a heavy guard around it, and the attempt failed.

When we were only a few hours' ride from the Brazos reserve we made a camp for the night while Fox rode on to inform the Indians that we'd been successful. That way everybody could be on hand when we arrived in the morning, for the return of a successful war party was a time for celebrating. The women wore their finest buckskins and loudly praised their husbands, brothers, or sons. When the Indians drove in the big herd of captured horses and waved fresh Comanche scalps, everyone went wild. I had to admit I was as excited as anyone.

Tawakoni George Washington remembered the Reverend Tackitt's send-off prayer and praised his medicine. "It must have been mighty strong," he exclaimed. "We killed seventy-six men—some weren't counted. We took sixty prisoners, three hundred ponies, many fine buffalo robes, and other things. We lost two men killed and only a few wounded. He is a wonderful medicine man!"

In his report to the governor, which we soon read in several papers, Ford praised the conduct of the rangers. "In justice to our Indian allies," he added, "I beg leave to say that they behaved excellently on the field of battle. They deserve the gratitude of the state and all our frontier people."

The governor wrote a letter praising Captain Ross and the Brazos Indians for their help in protecting the frontier settlers, and it was also published. "That ought to convince everyone that what Baylor says isn't true," I remarked to the Captain.

"It should, but I bet he'll keep trying," he replied.

I met John Dayton not long after this when he was delivering steers to sutler Charles Barnard. "Tell the Major for me we were dead wrong to believe Baylor," he said. "He's damn convincing and he fooled a lot of folks. No more of that for me. I admit I was taken in and I'm sorry for it. My friends feel the same way. I say again what I said before—the Brazos Indians are good people and I'm glad they're here. We'd be a lot worse off without 'em." That was the best news I'd heard in a while.

All of the praise for the rangers and Indians didn't sit well with the army officers. They grumbled that Captain Ross favored volunteers over regulars and wouldn't provide them with guides and scouts. When he heard that the Captain was furious, for both he and the Major had repeatedly offered them scouts anytime they wanted them. When he cooled off he went to the commander at the fort and assured him that scouts and guides and fighting men were available whenever the army requested them. The army knew that—they were just feeling guilty because civilians and Indians had done what they were supposed to do.

Ford wrote the governor another letter about the Brazos Indians, and it was also published. It should have ended our troubles.

"They have cut loose from the wild Indians for good," he wrote, "and have, so far as they can, identified themselves with whites in every way. They say they wish to become Americans. The strides they are making in the way of becoming civilized are great and, I might even say, astonishing. They are trying to imitate the whites in manners, in dress, in agriculture, and in all essential particulars. They have large fields of wheat and corn, which they have planted themselves and are now cultivating. Wagons drawn by oxen are driven by Indians; women and children dropping corn; all give the scenes at the different villages quite an American appearance. There is no disorder, no discontent, and no disposition to give trouble to the Agent or the Government. They are endeavoring to fulfill the treaty stipulations and to give satisfaction to the Americans. I speak of what I have seen and heard, and believe it is true. I should view any combination of circumstances that tended toward the breaking up of this reserve as a serious misfortune to the State of Texas and a calamity over which the philanthropist might mourn."

It wasn't long before Baylor wrote more letters to the papers and held meetings in Jacksborough and Weatherford, still claiming the reserve Indians were the ones who stole horses and who had murdered the Masons and Camerons. None of the settlers living near either reservation believed him, but he convinced some of those in other counties who hated all Indians.

Congressman John Reagan wrote from Washington that Ford's rangers and Indian allies, two hundred and twenty in all, had done more damage to the Comanches in one expedition than three thousand troops had in five years. This really stung the army, and some officers began talking about carrying the war to Indian Territory.

While Baylor was accusing the Major of incompetence and of protecting guilty Indians, Senator Sam Houston praised him. "The only improper thing Major Neighbors had done," he stated, "was that $80,000 had been appropriated for the agencies, and there is still an unexpended balance of $60,000." This, too, was published.

A few weeks after we returned, an old Comanche named Bear Paw headed for the Brazos reserve with his family and some ponies to trade. On the way they fell in with a party of white men from Lampasas, who were going in the same direction. All of them camped for the night at J. R. King's place. That evening King heard one of the whites say, "Let's kill that old redskin in the morning and take his ponies."

"For God's sake don't do that," King begged them. "That would put all of our lives in danger, and innocent folks would be killed. Don't do it."

That didn't stop them, for on the way the next morning they killed the old man, but his wife and daughters escaped into the woods while the men shot at them. They hid awhile before returning to the reservation. Leeper called on Captain Nathan Evans at Camp Cooper for an escort to accompany the burial party, but Evans refused. Leeper and a bunch of angry Comanches buried the old man. Fortunately they didn't run across any white men, for they'd surely have killed them, Leeper said. The Comanches were outraged over the murder of a harmless old man, and many settlers feared retaliation. Baylor or one of his cronies wrote the papers that Bear Paw was a notorious horse thief and the white men had recovered animals he'd stolen from them. Bear Paw, they said, had scalped many whites; his killers deserved medals.

After Captain Givens' charges against the agents and reserve Indians had appeared in the papers the Major had written the Commissioner demanding an investigation. The Commissioner agreed, but by May hadn't ordered one, so the Major went to Washington. He was there when he heard about the killing of Bear Paw. That news helped him convince the Commissioner that the situation was getting serious.

Soon after returning to Camp Runnels, Ford held a council with his officers, but we didn't learn about it until a few weeks later. He was still convinced that some of the raiders were Clear Fork Comanches, and he said that if he caught them in the act he'd break up the reserve. His men were to patrol all around the Comanche reservation and watch for signs of raiding parties leaving or returning. He made them swear to keep all of this secret. If the Comanches were guilty, as he suspected, he wanted absolute proof.

One of the officers remarked that a trail leading to the reserve from the scene of an attack on whites would be all the proof Ford needed.

"That can be managed," Allison Nelson said. "The trail can be made."

Ford exploded at that, we heard. "No, sir, that won't do. I am responsible to the state and to public opinion, and I will take no step in the matter unless I am backed by facts of such a character as to justify me before the public. I am willing to punish the Comanches if they are found guilty, but I am not disposed to do so unjustly and improperly." Nelson shrugged and walked away.

For days Nelson and others rode around the Comanche reserve looking for plunder trails. Finally he had to admit that they'd seen no sign of trails implicating the Comanches. He was also surprised to discover that all of the people living near the reserve were opposed to breaking it up. That set him back a bit but didn't stop him. It was pretty clear that Nelson wanted the Major's job as supervising agent. Ford told the Captain he'd heard Nelson remark that the Major had escaped removal only because his accusers hadn't used the right methods. "The men are after him now who will hurt him—he will be removed," Nelson said.

"I'm sure he was referring to himself and Baylor," Ford said. "I told him to keep out of Baylor's feud with agents and Indians, but he said he'd do what he damn well pleased. I also heard that Baylor promised Buck Barry he'll do all in his power to get Nelson in the Major's job."

About this time Captain Givens moved the Camp Cooper troops off the Clear Fork reserve to his ranch, which was twelve miles by road from the agency. This was another attempt to embolden the Comanches so they would cause trouble and the cavalry could attack them. Givens was, of course, a friend of Baylor and willing to do anything to help destroy the Indians and their agents. When Leeper wrote the Major about it, he protested to General Twiggs.

"If the agent is worried about his safety," Twiggs replied, "let him move the agency closer to Camp Cooper." The Major didn't leave until Twiggs agreed to station an officer and twenty men at old Camp Cooper.

Because reserve Comanches also suffered from Northern Comanche raiders, Ketumse was willing to help the army attack their camps. I was at the fort one afternoon when he and Jim Shaw rode in. Through Jim Shaw, Ketumse told the commander that he and his warriors would lead the troops to the Comanche camps near the Wichita Mountains in Indian Territory. That's where they'd find a heap of stolen ponies, he said.

The officer thanked him. They'd have to talk about it, get permission to enter another military district, figure out the logistics, and things like that, he said. He'd write the general about it.

It was clear to Ketumse that the army wouldn't do anything at the moment, at least, so he told the commander to forget it. "All white soldiers want to do is sit and drink coffee and talk," the old warrior said, "and talk and talk and write and write but never fight." Because he feared an attack by the Northern Comanches, he took his sons out of school so he'd be able to protect them. He didn't care, he said, if the troops killed all of the Northern Comanches, but he didn't expect them to kill even one.

In June the rangers' six-months enlistments expired and most were mustered out. Only William Marlin's company remained on duty near Fort Belknap. All along the frontier there was a rising protest against the army for its failure to protect settlers, but Twiggs still had taken no action except to allow the troops to pursue raiders after the damage had been done.

I'd thought a lot about what Dr. Stern had said, and finally figured I had to tell Taka she should go ahead and marry a Tonkawa, because there was no future for us. I guess it was mainly because I didn't have the guts to face Stern and others like him. When the Captain sent me with a message for one of the chiefs, I stopped at the Tonkawa village for the first time in a month or more. I saw Taka with some of the women and gave her the signal, but she acted like she didn't see me. Then she slowly went for her pony, so I rode on down the trail and waited for her. She hardly looked at me, but followed as I led the way to the spring. She spread her robe on the grass and we sat on it. She was still looking down.

"Taka, something bad has happened. What is it?"

She raised her face toward me, and she looked so sad I instinctively wanted to comfort her. Her answer made me feel like I'd fallen out of a tree.

"Uncle says I must marry White Buffalo."

"Marry White Buffalo?" I couldn't believe it. "Why him? He's got a wife."

"He's a friend of Uncle. His wife needs a younger woman to help."

I knew White Buffalo was a famous warrior, but he had married daughters as old as Taka. It didn't make sense, marrying one half his age just so she could wait on his wife.

She looked so sad I held her face in my hands and kissed her. She threw her arms around me like she'd been waiting for that and held me so fiercely I could hardly breathe. I kissed her again, and she sort of went limp. I hadn't planned on anything like this, but in a moment we were making love.

"Be careful," she said. "Hurts."

We lay there awhile after that, but neither of us spoke. I'd almost forgotten I was supposed to be delivering a message. I hated to leave her looking so sad, but had no choice. We clung to each other for a moment, then I climbed on my pony and rode down the trail. I had been about to tell her to marry some Tonkawa, so I should have felt greatly relieved, but for some reason I didn't. I guess I was mostly sorry for her having to marry an older man who already had a wife. I didn't really know White Buffalo very well, but I found it easy to hate him. As I thought about it, I had to admit I'd have hated any man who took her away from me. I tried to think of some way to stop it, but I couldn't think of any solution but killing White Buffalo. That was out of the question.

SIX

A few weeks after all of the rangers—except William Marlin's company —were disbanded, someone in eastern Palo Pinto County thought he saw Comanche sign. Everyone was still jumpy over the Mason-Cameron killings, so women and children forted up together in the strongest cabins while the men went Comanche hunting. A rancher from over Palo Pinto way stopped at the agency a few days later and told us the story.

Anne Lasater, who lived with her husband and children near Black Spring in the northeastern part of the county, was looking after her own sons and a neighbor's boys while her husband was with other men scouting for Comanches. With Mrs. Lasater was a black woman, Aunt Liz, and her son Hez. She told the boys to stay near the cabin.

Late in the afternoon of the second day Mrs. Lasater discovered that three of her sons, Hez, and some of the other boys were missing, and suspected they had gone to the spring for a swim. Black clouds indicated an approaching thunderstorm, so Mrs. Lasater and Aunt Liz headed for the spring. They had nearly reached it when the rain started. Just then they heard war whoops and screams, and the buck-naked boys dashed by on their way home. "The woods are full of Indians!" they shouted.

Terrified, Mrs. Lasater told Aunt Liz to hide while she went to a ranch north of Black Spring for help. In the storm and darkness the poor woman lost her way, wandering about the whole night in the wrong direction. At dawn she found herself on the road to Weatherford, where she met a teamster. They hurried on to Weatherford to warn the people there. It was Sunday, and Parson Keenan was holding a camp meeting. He ran to the square and rang the bell. "Indians coming! Indians coming!" he shouted.

That really panicked the whole town as well as the camp meeting, for everyone remembered the Mason-Cameron murders. Some people headed for Fort Worth. Some left for the country, on the way meeting others racing to town. But no Indians appeared.

It was a false alarm, the rancher told us. Some cowboys from Erath County had stopped at Black Spring to water their cow ponies and saw the boys swimming in it. Not knowing about the Indian scare in the area, they decided to have a little fun by pretending to be Indians. After that, there was some talk in Palo Pinto County of declaring war on Erath cowboys.

When Northern Comanches ran off a bunch of ponies from the Clear Fork reserve, Ketumse sent a war party after them. They trailed the raiders to their home camp near the Wichita, killed several, and captured most of their pony herd.

Among the captured horses were many bearing brands of local ranchers, and eight of them had Buck Barry's triangle on their left hips. Barry, whose ranch was at Flag Pond in Bosque County, had reported the loss of nearly sixty horses in a big raid in December '57, and the Major had helped him make out a claim for them. In it Barry had blamed Northern Comanches, Kickapoos, and renegades from the reservations, which covered most possibilities. He was surprised to learn that Clear Fork Comanches had recovered some of his horses, but he came to pick them up. Even this didn't stop him from accusing the Indians on both reserves of stealing horses, for he was a friend of Allison Nelson. Baylor quickly claimed that the Clear Fork Comanches had stolen Barry's horses and then returned the ones that were worn out and useless.

After Rip Ford and his rangers could find no evidence that the Clear Fork Comanches were implicated in the raids he was finally satisfied that Ketumse and his people were innocent. Baylor and his friends claimed again and again that they were horse thieves and murderers, and that Major Neighbors knew it and sheltered them just so he could collect his salary. I guess they thought that if they repeated the lies often enough some people would believe they were true no matter what Ford and the Major said. Unfortunately they were right about that, for Indian haters in other counties were glad to believe anything bad about Indians and their keepers.

Earlier, Ford had sent out word that anyone who accused the reservation Indians of thefts or killings should submit the charges to him in writing and under oath. Not one man complied. "I have never been able to detect the reserve Indians in the commission of a single depredation," Ford announced, "or to trace one to their doors." Because he was widely known and respected, people with open minds believed what he said, but there were too few of them on the frontier. By this time some of the army officers, but not Baylor's friends, admitted they were convinced the reserve Indians had nothing to do with the raiding.

Ford went on to say that horse stealing was so widespread in the state many had long been convinced that a ring of white men were using Kickapoos and other Indians to steal horses for them. The Mason-Cameron murders were proof of that. The editor of the Dallas *Herald* agreed. "The present opinion is that horse stealing and other depredations on the frontier cannot be attributed to the reservation Indians," he wrote. "The existence of a band of robbers in the state, extending across it and into Mexico on the one side and the United States Indian Territory on the other, is doubted by few—these scoundrels are in league with the Indians. They find where the horses are and the Indians, under their guidance, steal them."

The Major had requested the army to provide him with copies of the officers' reports about the depredations, for it was clear that Baylor had seen them. But Colonel Wilson of Twiggs' staff had merely forwarded the request to the War Department. The Major asked for copies so the agents could defend themselves and the Indians against the accusations, but he never received them.

After leaving the Clear Fork Agency, Baylor had moved his family to his ranch, but they didn't stay there long. He knew who the real raiders were, so he settled his family in Weatherford for safety. In the third week of June he held another of his meetings there, and from what we heard he ranted about the Mason-Cameron killings and warned the people to break up the reservations and destroy everyone on them. Yet everybody knew the killers of the Masons and Camerons had been Kickapoos led by white men.

A man named H. A. Hamner started publishing a paper called *The White Man* in Jack County, but when his plant there was burned he moved to Weatherford. Someone left a copy of his paper at the agency, and after the Captain and I read it about all we could do was sit and shake our heads. It was so vicious it was hard to believe that anyone could tell such a pack of lies. He called Ketumse and José María horse thieves and murderers, and accused the agents of "protecting redskins whose hands were gory with the blood of white women and children."

Even with all this commotion, Ketumse's people were still doing well. They'd planted larger fields and their crops were better than ever, the Clear Fork Agency farmer reported. Leeper was also pleased with the school, even though attendance was irregular. Most of the reservation

Comanches now wanted their children to learn English, he said, and that was a hopeful sign. At the time there were sixty boys and girls in the Brazos school.

When the Major returned from Washington to San Antonio in June he again called on General Twiggs to send an expedition against the Northern Comanches and Kiowas. As usual, he offered to furnish guides and scouts. For the first time Twiggs liked the idea and agreed to it, since it was clear that remaining on the defensive had accomplished nothing. Most of the Second Cavalry was still in Utah or Wyoming. Twiggs said he'd recommend that the regiment be sent to Indian Territory and ordered to follow the Comanches summer and winter. Maybe then they'd leave Texas alone, he said. In the meantime he'd request permission to send an expedition into Indian Territory in the fall and to allow it to remain there.

I hadn't seen Taka since she married White Buffalo, and I figured I probably wouldn't ever see her again, but I still couldn't put her out of my mind. The idea of being called a squawman didn't bother me anymore and now it was too late. I knew I had to forget her, but I kept seeing her sad little face when she told me the bad news, and I ached to hold her and comfort her. Then I'd remember that she was White Buffalo's wife and I'd better put her out of my mind. I tried.

Every time I went to the Tonkawa village for any reason I looked for her, but in vain. Once someone was watching me from the doorway of White Buffalo's thatch house but disappeared as I turned my head in that direction. It had to be Taka! I had that funny feeling like the first time I saw her. After that trying to forget her was a losing battle.

Another morning I rode to the village with a message for Plácido and Campo, then stopped to talk to Tosche about the cattle. The herd had grown to more than a thousand head, and he and his Tonkawa cowboys were kept busy. As I was leaving I saw Taka with several other young women. She looked solemn but gave me a quick smile.

Without thinking about what I was doing I gave her the signal. She smiled again, said something to the others, and walked toward the corral. I couldn't believe it, but she caught her mare, threw her robe over its back, and hopped on. I trotted my pony down the trail and waited, my mind whirling with the thought of holding her again. I was trembling when she caught up with me and we headed for the spring.

She spread her robe on the grass. I crushed her and kissed her, feeling her grow limp in my arms. I'd often thought of my last visit with the Widder Jones, sure that nothing could ever surpass it. I was wrong.

"I'm your woman," Taka whispered. "I can never belong to anyone else."

I thought a lot about that over the next few weeks. I wanted her more than ever, now that she belonged to White Buffalo. Unless he got himself killed there was nothing I could do about it except try to see Taka at every opportunity. But if White Buffalo ever got suspicious . . . I wished there was someone I could talk to. How could I tell the Major or Captain Ross "I'm mixed up with another man's wife and need your advice, like how do I keep from getting caught at it, or how can I run off with her without getting myself killed?" Neither of them would have much use for me after that.

When I first came to the Brazos reserve, agency farmer J. J. Sturm spent a lot of time with the Tonkawas, teaching them to farm. He was a pleasant, good-natured man about thirty, and we hit it off well. Lately every time I went to the main Caddo village I saw him there. That surprised me, for the Caddos were already good farmers.

"You used to spend more time with the Tonkawas," I said one day. "Aren't these people already pretty good at farming?"

He shuffled his feet and looked a bit sheepish. "Yup. They're the best. That's not why I'm here. I'm tryin' to persuade Deer Woman she oughta marry up with me."

"Good luck," I said, and rode back to the agency, my thoughts on Taka.

The next time I saw him he was all smiles. "Deer Woman said yes, and the Reverend Tackitt is goin' to hitch us."

The wedding took place under a big oak at the agency. A number of Caddos, friends or relatives of Deer Woman, stood solemnly at one side in their best beads and buckskins. Most of us whites who worked on the reserve were also there, but I didn't see Dr. Stern. Remembering what he'd said, I knew he was showing his contempt for such marriages by staying away, but at the last minute he appeared. He wasn't even frowning.

After the ceremony I walked with him to the office. "I reckon you don't approve, do you?" I asked.

"On the contrary," he said to my surprise. "I've gotten acquainted with Deer Woman and I find her a most gracious young lady. I think Sturm did well to marry her and I expect them to be happy. As you can see I've had a change of heart. I'm afraid working with the Major and Captain Ross has corrupted me." He smiled, but I didn't.

I was happy for Sturm but at the same time envious, cursing myself for not marrying Taka when I had the chance. Dr. Stern was partly responsible for that, but I couldn't blame him for my chickenhearted mistake. I'd let my chance slip away only because I was afraid of what others would say about us. I felt real sorry for myself and even more for what I'd done to Taka. Now that I knew for sure I wanted to marry her it was too late.

During the summer Baylor started attacking Leeper in letters to the Dallas *Herald,* accusing him of allowing Comanches to leave the reservation even though he knew it was to rape white women and murder their husbands. Leeper accepted the challenge, answering each wild accusation with the facts. He also pointed out that Baylor had asked for a detail of rangers to protect his ranch. After gaining the confidence of two young rangers, Baylor had showed them a Comanche bow and some arrows. If they would go with him at night to the farm of a neighbor named Shaw, he told them, they could destroy his crops and shoot arrows into his hogs and cattle. Then they could make a trail to the Clear Fork Agency and drop arrows along the way. Rip Ford would blame the Comanches for the attack and break up their reserve.

The two young men had refused and told Lieutenant Burleson, who informed Leeper. Baylor claimed that everyone knew he was joking, but few men believed that. He changed the subject, again accusing Ketumse's people of stealing Buck Barry's horses.

In one letter Baylor declared that if Major Neighbors died prematurely he'd set up a tombstone with "Viva la Humbug" on it. I couldn't believe a man could be so full of poison. He claimed again that he'd been fired as agent because he stood up for white settlers against Neighbors' redskin pets. When the editor of the *Herald* refused to print any more of his rubbish, Baylor shifted to the Waco *Democrat.*

In August, the Major wrote us, he'd received a letter from the governor asking him to help get the federal government to provide relief for frontier families. It was clear, the governor said, that Northern Comanches had begun a campaign to break up the reservations. "He doesn't believe that," the Major said. "The frontier families need protection, no doubt about that, but he still believes the reports blaming the reservation Indians. He knows what I think, so he mentioned the Northern Comanches just to butter me up. I intend to ask the Commissioner again to request that the Secretary of War station enough troops here to protect both peaceful Indians and citizens."

In his next letter he told us that four companies of cavalry and one of infantry had been ordered to march from Fort Belknap to Otter Creek west of the Wichita Mountains in September. They were to set up a supply depot and then comb the country for Comanches. At the same time two companies of cavalry had been ordered from Kansas to Fort Arbuckle, where they would locate sites for new military posts to restrain the Comanches. "At last!" the Major concluded. "If they pursue this policy aggressively we may yet see peace on the frontier. But I wonder if it will come in time to save the Texas reservations."

One afternoon a few days later a Delaware brought a message from Leeper that renegade Comanche chief Santana and a few of his warriors had come to the Clear Fork reserve and he was trying to wrest control from Ketumse. "Get over there right away and tell Leeper to call on the army for help," the Captain told me. "If Santana gets away with that it could mean the end of the Comanche reservation."

I headed for Clear Fork at a pretty fast clip and got there in mid-afternoon. I told Leeper what the Captain had said.

"I've been hopin' the Comanches could handle it by themselves," he said. "Right now Santana's holed up in Ketumse's cabin. Not many support him, but if troops interfere no tellin' how the others will react. But I guess we'll have to find out." He sent me to Lieutenant Cornelius Van Camp to ask him to bring his infantry company and eject Santana and his warriors.

On the way Leeper, Ketumse, and a Delaware interpreter joined us. When the reservation Comanches saw us heading toward Ketumse's cabin, they knew what was afoot. By the time we got there, more than fifty sullen-looking Comanches had made a circle around us, with bows strung and arrows on the bowstrings. Behind them was a big crowd of women and boys, all armed with clubs. It didn't take a prophet to see that if the troops made a move against Santana the Comanches would cut loose on us.

Just then Van Camp's sergeant spoke softly to him, and his words made my legs feel like they'd turned to water. "Sir," he said, "we just had target practice and ain't drawn a fresh supply. Not a man in the whole company has more than one round."

Van Camp and Leeper both turned pale, and I'm sure I was even whiter. Leeper quietly explained the problem to the Delaware, who told Ketumse. Then the three of them walked toward the Comanches who surrounded us. My ears were ringing and I couldn't make out what they said; I just froze there, knowing if I had to run for it my legs would fail me. Finally they returned.

"They agreed to escort Santana and the others off the reservation," Leeper said, his voice a bit husky. "That was one close call. Some of these people still have strong ties with other bands."

Leeper had to report the incident to the governor and the Major, and I guess Van Camp or another officer also reported it to General Twiggs. At least he soon knew about it.

"General Twiggs is greatly annoyed to think that a company of his troops would go into a possible fight with only one round of ammunition," the Major wrote Captain Ross. "He's ordered a full investigation and there's talk of a court-martial for Van Camp. Because of that I asked the governor not to publish Leeper's report of the affair, for it could only harm Van Camp."

That's the way the Major was. Some of the army officers had never missed an opportunity to embarrass him or give him trouble, but when he was in a position to repay them in kind he refused to do it.

Major Earl Van Dorn assembled the cavalry and an infantry company at Fort Belknap for the Comanche campaign Twiggs had ordered. He was a sandy-haired, egotistical Mississippian, but from all accounts he was a good cavalry officer. He came by the agency to ask Captain Ross to bring his Indians to the fort on the morning of September 15, when the troops would march.

Sul Ross, the Captain's nineteen-year-old son, had arrived from college in Alabama a few days earlier, and had ridden to the villages to see Indian friends. He was about six feet tall and slender, with black hair and blue eyes. I'd gotten to know him earlier, and we got on well. Right after Van Dorn's visit, Plácido and other chiefs solemnly called on the Captain. Plácido was spokesman.

"You are sick," he said. "You must not accompany us on any more campaigns. You might be killed and white people would say we did it or that we betrayed you to the enemy. They would like to believe that. You are as likely to be hit as any of us. Think what your death would cost us. We depend on you like children depend on their father. We would mourn your loss as if we were your children. We have a leader now." He pointed to Sul.

It was true the Captain was ailing, and he wondered if he'd be able to stay in the saddle day after day.

"You have chosen this boy as your leader," he said. "I want you to promise to obey his orders as he will obey the orders of Major Van Dorn. Will you?"

"We will obey him," Plácido promised, and the other chiefs quickly agreed.

"Why don't you and Tosche come along?" Sul asked, and that suited us. We and the Indians rode on ahead of the troops—four companies of cavalry and the infantry under Lieutenant Van Camp. A doctor in an army ambulance, sutler J. T. Ward and his supply wagons, and the infantry brought up the rear, but we didn't wait for them. We crossed the Red River with no difficulty and set up camp on the south bank of Otter Creek. We had to wait five days for the troops to get there, so we had a good supply of buffalo meat ready for them.

Van Dorn put the infantry to work building a stockade around Camp Radziminski, which he named after a lieutenant who had died a few months earlier. In the meantime the scouts cautiously combed the country for miles in every direction. Two Wacos discovered a big Comanche camp near the Wichita village at Rush Spring. After dark the two slipped into the village to visit friends or relatives, for they spoke the same language. The Wichitas told them the Comanches knew we were on Otter Creek but didn't think we were after them. We didn't learn about it until later, but the Comanches had just made a treaty with federal Indian agents at Fort Arbuckle. All we knew was what the Wacos told us— Buffalo Hump was there with his band and others who had just returned from raids in Texas. That was all we needed to know.

The two scouts reported to Sul; he quickly told Van Dorn the news, but he was suspicious. "How do I know it isn't a trap?" Sul and I both did some talking and finally convinced him all of the scouts could be trusted —they had their own reasons for wanting to fight the Comanches. The Wacos said the camp was about forty miles away.

"If we ride all night we should be able to hit them at daybreak," Sul suggested. Van Dorn agreed. He'd take the cavalry and leave the infantry guarding the camp.

Indians don't have a very good idea how long a mile is. We rode all night, but when the sun rose we weren't halfway to Rush Spring—it was close to one hundred miles from Camp Radziminski. We rode all day, stopping to rest a few times so horses and men didn't give out. I sure felt sorry for Sul—he'd been at college all year and hadn't done much riding. His rear end was pretty tender. At dark we stopped to rest and eat.

Then we pushed on all night without stopping to rest, and by early morning the scouts said we were getting close. The ground was covered with a heavy frost and the fog was so thick we could have ridden right through the Comanche camp without seeing a tipi. Van Dorn ordered a halt and called his officers together to give them battle orders.

"When the bugler sounds charge," he told Sul and me, "you and the Indians drive off their pony herd. After the fighting starts, you stay on the right so none of your Indians will be mistaken for Comanches." Then he assigned one company to hit the lower end of the camp while the other three struck the upper end.

The fog was gradually thinning, and the Comanche tipis slowly appeared, rising ghost-like out of the mist. It was spooky, and I felt the hair on my arms sort of writhing. We rode quietly around the camp to where the pony herd was grazing. Then the early morning stillness was shattered by the shrill notes of the bugle—hearing it really made me feel like throwing myself into battle. From the camp came the shrieks of women and children, the whoops of warriors, and the chatter of cavalry carbines.

We raced around the pony herd and drove it off. A dozen Caddos stayed with it while the rest of us headed for the camp. The smoke and fog were so thick it was hard to tell friend from foe, so all was confusion. Women and children were fleeing while the warriors fought furiously to give them time to escape. Even though we'd surprised them, they didn't panic. Tosche and I, along with a dozen Tonkawas, attacked some Comanches who were trying to cut us off. The air was thick with their arrows, but we picked off several of them and the rest pulled back, then came at us again.

I heard Sul shouting for men to follow a bunch of Comanches, but we were pinned down and fighting for our lives. I saw a soldier and Lieutenant Van Camp, along with an Indian or two, rushing to join Sul, then lost sight of them. He told me later what had happened.

"I saw a bunch of them escaping," he said. "That's when I yelled for help in cutting them off. Only Van Camp, poor fellow, a private named Alexander, and the big Tawakoni George Washington heard me, I guess. I discovered we were after women and children and was ready to let them go when I saw a young white girl. I yelled to the Tawakoni to grab her, and he did. Big as he is, he had his hands full, for she was so terrified she gave him a whale of a battle while he carried her away."

I knew that George Washington had been sticking close to Sul like he did to the Captain, ready to sacrifice his own life for his adopted brother or his son. I'd gotten to know him well after he'd called on the Captain that day. Grim-looking though he was, he liked to joke and play tricks. If I didn't already have Tosche as sort of an adopted brother, I'd gladly join his family. I wasn't sure I could have run a mesquite thorn through my flesh like he did, but having him for a brother or uncle would have been worth it. It really tickled me to see him hovering around the Captain or Sul, determined not to let any harm come their way. It was bad luck for Sul that he had him capture the white girl.

Sul and the other two now found themselves cut off by about twenty warriors, and he said it looked like the end of the trail. Arrows were coming thick and fast; both Van Camp and Alexander fell. The percussion cap in Sul's carbine failed, and before he could draw his pistol, an arrow struck him in the shoulder. A Comanche jumped from his pony, picked up Alexander's carbine, and shot Sul point-blank, knocking him from his horse. Stunned, he lay there, his pistol under him.

"I tried to roll over and draw my pistol, for the Comanche was coming at me with his knife in hand. I sure thought my time had come, and just a few days after I turned twenty. Luckily for me, the cavalry got there on the run and one of the officers dropped the Comanche not ten feet from me."

Caddo John saw Sul and pulled the arrow from his shoulder. He put something on both wounds to stop the bleeding, bandaged them, then helped Sul onto his horse and took him to the doctor at the upper end of the camp. Van Dorn had been badly wounded, and the doctor was tending to him and some soldiers who'd stopped arrows.

The fighting went on for over an hour before all of the Comanches scattered. We counted fifty-six dead, including several women, and we knew many more had been wounded. Buffalo Hump and most of his warriors had escaped. Lieutenant Van Camp and three soldiers had been killed and twelve were wounded.

I heard the doctor praising Caddo John for his medical skill. "What in the world did you put on the wounds to stop the bleeding?" he asked. "I'd sure like to know." Caddo John smiled and shrugged. He wouldn't tell.

We'd captured close to three hundred ponies. The soldiers wandered through the tipis, collecting trophies and dried meat. Then they set fire to them, 120 in all. Fox and a few other Caddos set out for the agency to tell Captain Ross about the victory and Sul's wounds.

All of the wounded except Sul and Van Dorn were taken to Fort Arbuckle, but those two lay under a tree for five days, too weak to be moved. On the sixth day the soldiers made litters for them between two pairs of mules, and we set out slowly for Camp Radziminski. Both men were in great pain, so we didn't hurry. When we had to cross steep inclines or ravines, two of the Indians carried Sul while soldiers looked after Van Dorn.

One of Sul's wounds got infected, and he was delirious part of the time and sure he was dying. He begged George Washington to kill him, but the big Tawakoni just patted him on the head. "You get well," he said.

I did some scouting with Tosche and other Tonkawas in the next two weeks while waiting for Sul to be able to travel. "Van Dorn said he'll write the Secretary of War recommending me for a commission as captain in the regular army," Sul told me one afternoon. "I haven't done anything to deserve that, but it makes me feel pretty good. Right now I'm not sure that's what I want. I don't think a twenty-year-old captain would be welcome among regular army captains who are in their mid or late thirties."

When he was well enough to travel, we put him in the army ambulance and, with a dozen Indians for an escort, started for the agency. Sul looked thin and puny, but claimed he felt pretty good and was as chipper as usual. When we reached the agency Captain Ross wasn't there. Fox had brought him news of the battle but he thought all of the wounded would be taken to Arbuckle, so the Captain and a dozen Indians had gone there. They returned a few days later, and the Captain was sure glad to see Sul. After a week he put Sul on a horse and sent him to Waco, so he could recuperate at home.

On the way Sul stopped at the Dallas *Herald* to tell the editor about the scrap, and the paper reported it. "The result will probably be a cessation of depredations upon the border settlements for a time, at least, and an end to the war should the blow be followed by active, energetic operations," the editor concluded. But since the fight raiders had already stolen a hundred horses in North Texas. One campaign against the Comanches wasn't enough—there were too many different bands.

Everyone praised Van Dorn and Sul Ross, and the Brazos Indians came in for their share of credit. From Waco, Sul wrote that he'd received a letter from Commanding General Winfield Scott offering him a commission in the army and promising to help if he wanted to make a career in the cavalry. "I thanked him," Sul wrote, "but told him I've had no military training and felt I wasn't prepared for it. Anyway, I want to finish college, then Lizzie and I plan to marry." He'd told me about Elizabeth Tinsley, the daughter of a planter near Waco. I didn't have any prospect like that and sure envied him.

Sul hadn't been gone two weeks before Comanches ran off one hundred and sixty ponies from the Brazos reserve. Tosche had kept his bay mustang close to his tipi and saved him, but other Tonkawas weren't so lucky.

It was obvious that one defeat only made the Comanches eager for revenge. They would have to take some real lickings before they learned to leave the frontier settlers and reservation Indians alone. I was glad that Van Dorn had remained at Camp Radziminski to continue after the Comanches, and that most of the Brazos scouts had stayed with him. He

sent Captain Ross word that he'd rescued a Mexican boy from the Comanches. The boy said that they and other tribes were preparing for
revenge. First they'd kill Van Dorn and the Indians on the reserves; then
they'd attack the nearest white settlers and kill as many as they could
find.

Before the Van Dorn expedition had marched north we'd learned that
Thomas T. Hawkins had been appointed to investigate the charges
against the agents and Indians. The Major had requested an investigation
earlier in the year, but nothing was done until he went to Washington in
May. Hawkins announced the hearings in the main papers of North and
Central Texas, and wrote letters to those who had made accusations,
inviting each to testify. He also asked the Major to be present to cross-
examine witnesses and to advise the Captain and Leeper. The reports
and petitions circulated by Captain Givens had been the main reason the
Major had requested the investigation. Givens was now stationed at the
military department headquarters in San Antonio. "I notified him that
Hawkins would be at Camp Cooper and Fort Belknap from October 1 on
to look into his accusations against us," the Major wrote Captain Ross. "I
told him I was giving him notice so he could make arrangements to
appear. I also said I would be pleased to know what he intended to do so
that I could make my own plans accordingly. General Twiggs gave him
permission to attend the hearings. I am anxious to confront him."

When Sul and I returned from Camp Radziminski we learned that
Hawkins had reached Camp Cooper on September 30, and Captain
Palmer provided quarters for him and his assistant, J. T. Pickett. Haw-
kins found no one but Leeper interested in the hearings, he told the
Major later.

The Major had arrived from San Antonio on October 4 in a carriage
drawn by four government mules and driven by his slave Cipio. "I hope
all of our enemies show up," he told the Captain. "This is our first
opportunity to face them and to give the lie to their baseless charges."
After resting a day he'd gone on to Camp Cooper. As soon as I got back
to the agency with Sul I rode over to the Clear Fork to be with the Major.

Hawkins was a pleasant-mannered but firm man who was determined
to give everyone an opportunity to have his say, so none would have an
excuse to complain afterward. Just as he was ready to open the hearings
at old Camp Cooper, the army again abandoned the post in favor of
Givens' ranch. It looked like the army was trying to break up the investigation or place obstacles in Hawkins' way, but with difficulty he per-

suaded Twiggs to leave a detail of troops with him until the hearings were concluded.

He and the Major waited and watched for witnesses to arrive, for no one could have been unaware that the hearings had begun. By October 16 only three men had come forward, and none of them was a Baylorite. The first one said that everyone knew Indians were trained from birth to steal horses, and if they were hungry and no buffalo were available they'd kill cattle. The idea was, I guess, that if all Indians were taught to steal horses and killed cattle when they were hungry, that must prove that the Clear Fork Comanches were guilty of such misdeeds. The other two had nothing to add.

Givens simply declined to attend, and the others made excuses. Allison Nelson wrote Hawkins that he didn't even know Major Neighbors. He'd received Hawkins' letter so late that the hearings would be over before he could gather evidence to present. We knew, of course, that in July he'd talked about the investigation and bragged he was gathering damaging testimony against the Major. Now he said he would gather evidence to support his charges as soon as possible and furnish the Major a copy so he could prepare a rebuttal. But that was as far as it went; Hawkins heard no more from him.

At the Major's suggestion, Hawkins had written Buck Barry and invited him to testify. Barry also claimed he hadn't learned about the hearings in time to prepare for attending them. "Although my testimony might not be worth much for or against him," he wrote Hawkins, "permit me to say in behalf of Major Neighbors that he treated me fairly and gentlemanly in the information of some of my horses that was stolen notwithstanding I am satisfied from many circumstances that the Indians on the upper reserve was knowing to the stealing of my horses and some of them directly concerned in it though I was not thus satisfied when I made affidavits in presenting a claim to the government for damages done therefore those upper reserve Indians were not included in my affidavit." Barry, T. C. Alexander, and several others in Bosque County had signed a petition asking that their neighbor Allison Nelson be appointed in place of the Major. They gave no evidence of misconduct by the Major to support the petition except to say that he took the side of Indians against white men.

Baylor also claimed that he hadn't known about the investigation in time to gather evidence. Yet in late July or early August he'd boasted that he had evidence against the agents and redskins that would destroy them. The government had sent a commissioner all the way to Texas so Givens,

Baylor, Nelson, and Barry could make their charges under oath, but not one of them came to testify.

Although none of the accusers of the agents and Indians had any real evidence to present, the Major, Ross, and Leeper had a mass of affidavits and sworn statements from citizens living near the reserves. These concerned the behavior of the reserve Indians, the false statements of the Baylor crowd, and the forging of signatures.

One evening a man from Belknap warned the Major that Sheriff King of Young County was coming the next day with a big posse to arrest a young Comanche accused of attacking Allen Johnson's son several months earlier. Hawkins was sick in bed at the time. "This must not be allowed to happen," he told the Major. "Civil officers have no authority over federal property. Call on the army for support."

The Major and I rode to Givens' ranch to see Captain Palmer. "I'll meet you at the agency with a troop of cavalry first thing in the morning," Palmer promised. Although still ailing and too weak to mount a horse, Hawkins came out when we met the troops a little after sunrise.

"You must prevent this outrage from happening," he told Captain Palmer, and he was a high federal official. He sent his assistant Pickett to accompany us as we rode toward Belknap. We started none too soon, for we'd gone only about five miles when we met the sheriff and a posse of fifty. The two bodies lined up facing each other, while we rode forward to talk to the sheriff.

"I have a writ from the district court of Wise County for the arrest of a Comanche Injun," the sheriff said, holding out a paper. "I aim to arrest him no matter what."

The Major pulled an envelope from his coat pocket and removed a sheet of paper. "This is the act of the legislature of the State of Texas granting the reserves to the United States and giving the federal government exclusive jurisdiction over them," he said. He read it aloud, then added, "What you are trying to do is illegal and will get you in trouble with the federal government. You'd better think about that, all of you. Being prosecuted in a federal court isn't the same as facing a cowboy jury out here."

After some argument and discussion among themselves the posse turned around and headed back to Belknap. Cursing them, the sheriff followed.

"It was your presence, you and your troops, that persuaded them," the Major told Captain Palmer. "I don't think that legal scruples had much to do with it other than give them an excuse to back off."

When we reported to Hawkins he commended the agents and Captain Palmer on the moderate and judicious manner in which they'd handled a dangerous and unpleasant situation. Since there was little for me to do and the hearings would soon end, the Major sent me back to the Brazos reserve, but I waited until the posse had a good head start. I didn't want to run into them.

A man named Barclay came to the agency about the time I arrived; with him were four Alabama-Coushatta Indians from East Texas seeking a new home on the reserve. A few days later the Major arrived from the Clear Fork, accompanied by Ketumse and one of his wives.

The next day I rounded up the chiefs for a council with the Alabama-Coushatta visitors. All of the Brazos Agency chiefs welcomed them and invited them to make their home on the reservation. Ketumse also greeted them, then spoke to the Tonkawas in Spanish and to the Caddos in their own language. I didn't understand all that he said, but it was clear he was friendly. Nothing came of this visit, however, for the legislature decided against moving the Alabama-Coushattas to the Brazos reserve; instead it assigned them their own agency at the Big Thicket in East Texas.

On the previous night Comanches had stolen twenty-eight Tonkawa ponies and five from Charles Barnard. Tosche and I went to see if other villages were missing stock, but when we made our first stop at the Tawakoni village there was no one in sight. Puzzled, unable to imagine what could have happened to them, we searched among the native houses. We saw an old Tawakoni man peering out of a doorway and asked him where the others were.

"Man have dream of dead friend long time," he told us, struggling for words. "Dead friend say, 'Run for life—Comanches come!' Everybody hide in woods."

Tosche and I checked on other villages and found them all empty, so we went back to the agency to tell the Captain.

"Let Sturm and Dykes know," he said. "Then all of us will spread out through the woods and search. Tell them the Comanches are gone and it's safe now to return to their villages."

We spent the rest of the day tracking down the frightened men, women, and children and persuading them to return. They'd run because so many of their men were still with Van Dorn and they knew there weren't enough to fight off a big Comanche war party.

Near the end of October several mean-looking men from Jack County came to the agency. "We trailed stolen horses to this reserve," one said.

"They were headin' for the Caddo village. What are you goin' to do about it?"

"Which direction did they come from?" the Captain asked.

"The north."

"Those were the tracks made by a party returning from Fort Arbuckle a week ago," the Captain said. "No doubt about that." The men rode away, muttering something about damned Injun lovers.

When his health improved Hawkins ended the hearings at Camp Cooper and reopened them at Fort Belknap. It was a waste of time, for not one man came to testify. Hawkins visited the Brazos Agency for a council with the chiefs ten days later. Plácido told him about Tosche and me trailing the Mason-Cameron killers and learning that they were Kickapoos led by white men. Other chiefs also spoke, praising the Major and Captain Ross.

The Major had written Rip Ford, asking him to send a statement to Hawkins, and Ford was happy to comply. He stated that he had kept the reserve Indians under surveillance but had never detected them in wrongdoing. He had invited all who had complaints about the Indians to give him written statements under oath, but not one had come forward. At first he had suspected the Comanches of raiding and Leeper of incompetence, and had been prepared to break up the reservation. After a visit to the Clear Fork he saw that Leeper was able and that the Comanches were making remarkable progress. He had high praise for Captain Ross and for the Brazos Indians, who were rapidly adopting the ways of white men. And finally: "The ordeal through which Major Neighbors has passed endorses him. He needs no recommendation from any quarter."

Hawkins concluded that the charges of Baylor, Nelson, and Givens were false and malicious. The agency system, he observed, was sound and effective, but it would be wise, as the Major had recommended, to move the Clear Fork Comanches to a new reservation in Indian Territory. He had high praise for the Indians of both reserves.

Hawkins' investigation had completely vindicated the agents and the Indians. In mid-November he ordered the hearings closed, and with Pickett departed for Washington while the Major returned to San Antonio. We shook hands with the Major when he was ready to leave. "I'm under no delusion that our troubles are over," he said. "We've got to move the Indians away from here before anything else happens. In the meantime I intend to ask the Commissioner to publish Hawkins' report. Let's hope that will quiet the agitators and give us time to arrange the move."

The editor of the Dallas *Herald* as usual supported the Major and his policies. "Some anonymous writers continue to snap and snarl at Major Neighbors through the columns of the Waco *Democrat,*" he wrote. "We tell all such that they 'gnaw a file' and had as well betake themselves to the mountains."

While the Major was in San Antonio he wrote the Captain that the Southern Indian Superintendent had protested Van Dorn's attack on the Comanches while they were visiting the Wichitas. The Comanches concluded that the Wichitas had betrayed them and attacked the band and destroyed its village. The destitute survivors had fled to Fort Arbuckle. But Major William Emory of the First Cavalry, who was also at Arbuckle, pointed out that some of the Comanches had just returned from pillaging in Texas. They would never settle down until they had been soundly defeated, he added. "They have received nothing more than they deserve."

SEVEN

We had some excitement of a different kind that September, for the Butterfield Overland Mail stage route between St. Louis and San Francisco opened, and Belknap was one of the way stations. Twice a week the stages stopped there to change teams while the passengers ate lunch. The stage brought newspapers and the passengers swapped news of the outside world for local gossip. What they learned about Indian troubles in Texas they passed along to editors in St. Louis and San Francisco. It was sure strange to read about Fort Belknap in papers from other states.

A lot of people gathered around Murphy's stage station when the stage was due. About half a mile from the station, the conductor blew a blast on a bugle so fresh teams would be harnessed and a meal would be ready for the passengers. Horses were used east of Belknap; westbound stages used mule teams. Harnessing those half-broken mules was an exhibition of kicking and biting on their part and an artistic display of agility and profanity on the part of the handlers. It was even better to watch the stagecoach approach, with the horses or little mules at a gallop, wondering if they had decided to stop this time. Getting to talk to passengers on the way to far-off places made me feel like somehow we'd suddenly become attached to the real world. The Butterfield company had "swing" stations every fifteen or twenty miles where the drivers changed teams, and "home" stations like Belknap, where the passengers could get meals. The Comanches and Kiowas were as pleased about the opening of the stage line as we were, for here was a new supply of good horses and mules to steal. They didn't attack the stagecoaches, but many a driver who stopped at a swing station for a change of teams discovered that every animal had been stolen.

In November Ketumse's brother and other Comanches came to Clear Fork, followed a few days later by eighty more of his band. He told Leeper that he'd sent his son to bring the remainder to the agency from their camp on the Arkansas River. About a month later the Kotsotekas—Buffalo Eaters—also came to the Clear Fork. These were survivors of the Ford-Ross attack on the Comanche camp in Antelope Hills. Carrying the war to the Northern Comanches at last seemed to be bringing them around.

In November, too, the governor authorized Rip Ford to enlist another ranger company for six months. Knowing that one company couldn't protect the long frontier, Ford suggested that a whole regiment of rangers be raised. Everyone agreed, but the legislature demanded that Washington pay for it; controlling the Indians was, after all, a federal responsibility. Congressman Reagan introduced a bill to that effect in the House of Representatives, but it was defeated. That convinced a lot of people that the government intentionally neglected Texans, and there was a lot of angry talk about seceding from the Union.

Late in November Captain Ross went to Waco to tend to some business and to spend Christmas with his family, leaving Dr. Stern in charge. People were still praising Van Dorn, Sul Ross, and the Brazos Indians for their victory over the Comanches. Nothing much had been heard of Baylor since the campaign, so it seemed a good time for the Captain to be away.

In mid-December a dozen scouts who'd been with Van Dorn returned to the agency to let their lean ponies rest and recover their strength in time for Van Dorn's spring campaign. The best grass available was below the reserve boundary along a bend in the Brazos near where Keechi Creek entered it. Dr. Stern gave them passes to camp there.

Choctaw Tom, one of the most reliable men on the reservation, also asked for passes for his family and others to hunt in the same area. He was a longtime friend of the whites who'd served as interpreter for Sam Houston when he was negotiating the treaty of Birdville back in '43. He'd married an Anadarko woman, and they had a flock of children and grandchildren.

About mid-morning a couple of days after Christmas, Dr. Stern, reservation farmer J. J. Sturm, and I were in the agency office trying to keep warm when a young Caddo rode up on the dead run and pulled his lathered pony to a halt. "White men shoot Choctaw Tom's people!" he shouted. "Many die!"

That can't be true, I thought as Sturm and I quickly saddled our horses and followed the Caddo toward Keechi Creek on the run. There was no possible reason for attacking them. We got to the camp just as a big party of Caddo and Anadarko warriors galloped up, grim-faced and painted for war. Young C. C. Slaughter was with them, talking fast to any who'd listen. I looked for Choctaw Tom but didn't see him.

Seven Indians, four men and three women, lay dead, among them Choctaw Tom's wife and one of his daughters. Most had been shot in their sleep and were still wrapped in blood-soaked blankets. Two women, one man, and a young boy were badly wounded but still alive. For a moment I could only stare at them, unable to move or to believe what I saw.

One warrior wasn't in his blankets. Apparently his wife had been killed and he sprang up and shot the man who'd done it before falling himself. The white man also lay where he'd fallen, not far away. He was Samuel Stephens, and he'd been shot in the back of the head at the same time the Caddo shot him in the chest. Someone in his own party had given him the head wound.

When I looked at those shattered bodies of people I'd known and respected I nearly exploded. I saw myself an avenging angel, tracking down those murderers one by one, to the last man. I'd let them beg for their lives while I slowly cocked my pistol and blew their brains out. I'd never even shot at a white man and had never wanted to before, but I'd enjoy seeing those men crawl before I killed them.

C. C. Slaughter woke me and brought me back to earth. "Chip," he said, "will you ride over to the ranch and get a shovel while I talk to them. I've got to keep trying to convince them no one around here had a hand in this." The Slaughter ranch was about a mile away, so I rode over and brought back the shovel.

The Caddos and Anadarkos were ready to set out on a revenge raid. If they couldn't find the killers they'd attack any whites they saw, for that was the custom of most tribes. C.C. kept explaining to them that the people of Palo Pinto County were innocent—the killers were from another county. José María was also telling them they must not take vengeance on white people in general.

We took turns with the shovel, and in an hour had dug seven graves. Sturm, C.C., and I took off our hats as the bodies, still wrapped in gory blankets, were lowered into the earth and covered with soil and a layer of stones to prevent coyotes from digging them up. I was still in a daze, unable to comprehend the tragedy. The Indians were grim-faced, but they gently picked up the wounded and carried them to their village. I figured the longer they could be kept off the warpath the less likely they would be to go on a killing rampage.

"Ride over to Palo Pinto and see what you can learn about who did this," Sturm told me. "I'm going to stay with these people the rest of the day and try to calm them. Lord, how I wish the Major or Captain Ross was here."

C.C. and I rode to the Slaughter ranch together. He was about my age but a bit shorter and stockier, with black hair and beard. I'd seen him frequently since his family moved their cattle out here early in '56. His father had become a circuit-riding preacher, leaving the cow work to C.C. and his younger brothers, and they were all good cowhands.

"The gunshots woke me up," C.C. told me. "I saddled a horse and rode here as fast as I could. It was the most awful thing I've ever seen. I figured those who'd gone to the villages would raise a revenge party, and every family in the county would be in real danger. I figured they might even kill me, but I had to take that chance and try to talk to them, so I headed for the reserve. About halfway there I met them. Man, they were a scary sight, and I know some of them were ready to kill me without thinking about it. Luckily for me, my friends surrounded me and saved my life. I did some fast talking to convince them nobody around here had anything to do with it. If they could find the killers I wouldn't try to stop them, but if they got their revenge on innocent people it would bring on an Indian war for sure and they wouldn't have a chance."

In the little town of Palo Pinto a big, silent crowd of men stood in front of the general store and stared at me as I rode up. Off to one side women and children huddled together by themselves, all of them pale and plenty worried. I saw the storekeeper, with his grimy apron around his waist, and rode to his side. He was also ashen-faced.

"What do you know about the attack on the Indians?" I asked him.

"Yesterday some men here asked the Indians to hunt bears with them. Choctaw Tom had just bought a wagon and was going to return to his village, but he said the others could stay if they wanted to. He went on home or he might have been killed." He drew a deep breath.

"Last night Peter Garland and twenty men from Erath County rode into town. He said they were out to kill any Indians they found off the reserve, bucks, squaws, or papooses, they didn't care which. He said they just wanted to have some target practice before they joined Baylor and Nelson in wiping out all of the Indians and their Indian-loving agents. Fonderberg told them he could show them where some Indians were camped off the reservation.

"All of us told them to leave those Indians alone. They're friends of ours and we're going hunting with them tomorrow, we said. We don't want the reserves broken up and we don't want an Indian war. All our families would be in danger. Leave those Indians alone. Garland said in that case they'd camp the night and go home in the morning. We offered to put them up in our cabins, but he said they didn't mind camping out." He drew another deep breath and continued.

"They came through here this morning, crowing about what they'd done. 'We've opened the ball,' Garland bragged. 'Now others can dance to the music.'" He paused again. "Tell the Indians for us that we regret very much what those men have done and we share their grief." He turned and looked at the solemn faces around him.

"What do you think the Indians will do?" he asked, nervously rubbing his palms together. "A lot of folks are scared and talking about leaving. They're afraid the Indians will think we condone it or had something to do with it, and that they'll kill any whites they see. Some families are packing their belongings just in case. We don't want any of them to leave —we need every man, every family."

"I can't speak for the Indians," I replied, "but if the men who did it are brought to justice I think they'll be satisfied. I heard José María warning them they mustn't take revenge on people who haven't wronged them."

At the back of the crowd a bearded man in greasy buckskins squirted a stream of tobacco juice on the ground and wiped his mouth on his sleeve. "I don't go fer tryin' no white men for killin' no damn Injuns," he said. "Let 'em stay on the reserve or get outa Texas. Whose country is this, anyway?" Several others loudly agreed, while most frowned at him. I didn't see any point in arguing with his kind, so said nothing.

It was almost dark when I got to the agency, just as Sturm was entering the office. A worried Dr. Stern was waiting. "A more terrible sight I never expect to see," Sturm said. "There, in their beds lay seven of the most unoffensive Indians on the reserve, their bodies pierced by buckshot and rifle balls. I can't believe anyone could be so depraved as to commit such an atrocity."

In the next few days many people around the reserve came and expressed their indignation about the killings and damned Garland, but others were silent. "It was a dirty piece of business," young rancher Charlie Goodnight said. "They just wanted to kill some Indians. Jack Bailey told me that all the time they were shooting at them Caddo Jake was giving the Masons' hailing sign. Bailey just laughed about that."

A man named McNeil, who had been with Garland, claimed that they were on the trail of horse thieves and it led to the Indian camp. Even though the Indians had been killed in their sleep, he swore they had shot first. I suppose he figured people in other counties would be glad to believe that. He added that a man named Barnes had died of his wounds a few days after the attack. From what we heard it seemed that he had also been shot by his own party. Garland sent the paper a similar account, adding that they intended to kill all the Indians and agents on both reservations. "We have no apology for what we have done," he concluded.

In January '59, about a week after the killings, a man from Palo Pinto came to the agency. Dr. Stern was busy tending the wounded, so Sturm was in charge. The man said that Allison Nelson was in Palo Pinto with a hundred and fifty men, on their way to attack the reserve Indians.

"Get over to the fort right away," Sturm told me. "Tell Major Thomas we're in imminent danger of attack and ask him to send troops. In the meantime I'll send Fox to tell the Indians to come here. God, I hope Captain Ross and the Major get here soon."

I headed for the fort at a fast lope and told Major George Thomas what was happening. He was in his fifties and his hair was turning gray, but he looked fit for a hard campaign. He stood about six feet tall and must have weighed close to two hundred pounds. He always looked like he was about to stand inspection or go on parade, for he was dressed as neatly as anyone could be in a frontier outpost. Thoughtful and deliberate, he seemed a man who didn't make up his mind in a hurry, but once he decided what needed doing, nothing could stop him. He sent for Captain Palmer.

"March your company to the Brazos Agency on the double," he ordered Palmer. "Don't take time for your gear or provisions. Tell the sutler to send them in wagons." He paused while Captain Palmer waited. "If armed civilians attack the agency or the Indians," he said in a steely voice, "repulse them with every weapon you have."

Palmer saluted and left. I rode to William Marlin's ranger camp and told him about it, and he said he'd be along as soon as he could round up his patrols. By the time I got back to the agency most of the Indians were already there. I saw Taka and Tosche but didn't have a chance to talk to them.

When I told Sturm an infantry company and Marlin's rangers were coming his tense face relaxed. "Thank God," he said. "I wasn't trained to handle things like this. All I really know is pushing a plow and making things grow."

Captain Palmer soon marched up with thirty-six men and posted sentries. When the sutler's wagons arrived, the soldiers set up their tents.

José María and other chiefs kept scouts out watching for the enemy, but they saw no one for several days. On the seventh a man rode up to the agency and stayed on his horse while looking around at the soldiers and Indians. Sturm and Palmer and I went out to hear what he had to say. "Mr. Nelson is sending a delegation with his peace proposal tomorrow," the man said. "Will you receive them?"

Unsure what to do, Sturm looked at Captain Palmer, who nodded. "We'll receive them," Sturm told the rider, who turned his horse and left. Late the next morning George Erath, J. N. Norris, and Dixon Walker rode up, followed by a twelve-man escort. I'd met Erath, an Austrian with a thick German accent and a dislike for violence. I wasn't acquainted with the other two.

"We're representing the citizens," Erath told Sturm and Captain Palmer. "They asked us to settle this difficulty between whites and Indians. Can we talk to the chiefs?"

José María and the other chiefs joined them. Nelson's peace proposal, Erath said, was that the Indians stay on the reserve at all times and not leave it for any reason. They must ignore the killing of Choctaw Tom's people and any others that might occur. I didn't see any of the Indians answering Erath, but Sturm said later they had promised only that they wouldn't take revenge against all whites for the Garland killings.

Erath and the others stayed overnight, then returned to Nelson's camp in the morning. Word quickly spread that Nelson had made a peace settlement with the agency Indians. The chiefs, he announced, had agreed to keep their people on the reserve at all times, and that none should leave it for any reason. Both Captain Palmer and José María swore that no chief had made any such promise, so it looked like another of Nelson's tricks to win support for killing Indians found off the reservation. As far as we knew they still intended to attack both reserves and kill everyone on them.

Captain Palmer and his company returned to the fort and the Indians went back to their villages. On January 15 Captain Ross and his oldest son, Peter, arrived; Sturm and I were sure relieved to see them. If anything happened now the Captain would know how to handle it.

Kit Carter stopped at the agency next day to see the Captain. "How's Sul doing?" he asked.

"Recovering nicely, thanks. He's about as good as ever."

"What do you think will happen next? Will this madness ever end?"

The Captain looked solemn and his eyes weren't twinkling. "Baylor and his crowd still swear they're goin' to kill us and the Indians. If Garland and that bunch are arrested and get half what they deserve,

Baylor and the others will likely go wild. I don't think this state has ever punished even one white man for murdering a friendly Indian. With everyone already up in arms, it would give Baylor all the leverage he needs to raise enough men to kill every last one of us. Our only hope is to move the Indians out of Texas before that happens. The Major has been working on that for over a year. Maybe these murders will wake up the Commissioner to the fact that all of us are in the gravest danger."

"Why don't you quit right now and go back to your farm?"

The Captain looked thoughtful. "That's a temptation," he admitted, "but it's not for me. I've never run from trouble before and I don't intend to now. I couldn't let either the Major or these Indians down. I'll stay."

"I figured as much."

The Major arrived a week later. "I had to stop in Austin to see the governor and demand that the murderers be punished for their crimes," he told us. "He promised to order state troops to assist sheriffs in making arrests, and Rip Ford agreed to help. The governor also said he'll issue a proclamation ordering armed bands to disperse, but I'm not sure what good it will do. I reminded him that Twiggs has no more troops to spare, so it's his responsibility to protect the reserves. But if he does anything at all it will be because he's afraid Congress will cut off funds for the state if he makes no effort to protect the Indians and punish those killers, and for no other reason."

The Captain had said that with an election coming up, Runnels wouldn't do anything except what he figured would win him votes. A letter from a J. G. Thomas to the governor published in the Birdville *Union* made it clear his judgment was correct.

"To His Excellency, Dick Runnels—

"You wished me to ascertain the *'facts* in the case' and if the Indians under Ross and Neighbors *should show* out to be *guilty* (of which you entertained no doubt) to report the same to your Excellency by the first mail, that you might take *popular steps* by the sitting of Houston Convention. You wished me also to ascertain the *feelings* of the people along the frontier, as to the *popularity* of our *mutual friends* Maj. Neighbors, Capt. Ross, Charley Barnard, Jo. Walker, and others of like reputation— whether they are considered *real actors* behind the scene or *merely accomplices* in the Indian depredations along the frontier! Whether Neighbors and Ross are *longer* able to keep the public in the *dark,* as to the guilt of *their Indians*—(which we both held they could not do.) And to ascertain if the frontier would instruct their delegates at the Houston Convention to favor the renomination of Your Excellency for Gov. &c, &c! All of

which I have been *intensely* anxious to ascertain—I have spared neither
time nor expense (as you requested) to get the facts in the case. I *now*
with an *amalgam* of feeling of sorrow and joy, give your Excellency the
result of my labors. In the first place, in regard to the guilt of the Reserve
Indians, the *facts like cactus prickles jut out all around!* The Reserve Indians (or as Col. A. G. Walker would say, the 'Red roguish rascals'!) have
committed ALL the depredation in the counties of Erath, Jack, Palo
Pinto, Comanche, and other counties adjoining the Reservation, to the
citizens of which you addressed your late Circular (or Bull, as these
people out here call it!) of the 12th March. There has been a meeting of
delegates, just come off at Col. Loving's in Palo Pinto County, the object
of which is to ascertain the facts in the case—that is, to get the *proof,*
showing that the *pet* Indians are the aggressors.

"At the convention, I am informed, is a letter from a friend, that the
testimony, riveting guilt on the red roguish rascals was as *numerous* as
grasshoppers or as pigeons at roosting time."

Someone from Palo Pinto told the Major that Fonderberg had left for
Waco. Knowing that he was the scoundrel who led Garland's party to
Choctaw Tom's camp, the Major sent agency blacksmith A. J. Dykes and
a man named Callaher to Waco to arrest him so he could be tried along
with the Garland bunch. Fonderberg may have been warned that men
were after him; at any rate Dykes and Callaher couldn't find him.

The Major next had me round up the chiefs for a council. Their faces
were more solemn than usual, but their affection for the Major was still
obvious. "I'm determined to see those murderers brought to justice," he
assured them. "The governor has promised that it shall be done."

"We're no longer safe here," José María said. "Our families are in
danger every day. We're determined to leave this place."

"I shall inform the Commissioner in the strongest terms that we must
move as soon as possible. I hope to receive permission shortly."

"A man doesn't need permission from anyone to move his family away
from danger," Ah-ha-dot said.

"You're right, of course. But we must be assigned land and the army
must be ordered to protect us on the way and after we get there."

"We can't wait much longer," José María added, "even if we don't have
permission."

Judge N. W. Battle of Waco issued writs for the arrest of Garland's
party and ordered Rip Ford to bring them to Waco for trial. Governor
Runnels published a proclamation calling on all commanders of state

troops to assist civil officials in making the arrests. He also published an order to all armed bands of citizens to disperse.

On the last day of January the Major, Dr. Stern, and two others took several of Choctaw Tom's people to Waco for the examining court and to be present to testify at the trial of Garland's party. We waited eagerly for word that the Garland bunch had been arrested.

There were a lot of comings and goings at the agency, for both Indians and whites were nervous and apprehensive. Ketumse came to ask what could be done about the bands of armed men who constantly prowled around the Clear Fork reserve. His people couldn't round up their strayed ponies or cattle without being shot at. The Captain could promise only that he'd request Major Thomas to send out cavalry patrols. "Urge your people to avoid clashes with them," he advised Ketumse.

William Marlin came to ask the Captain what he wanted his ranger company to do in case of trouble. "I hear that Baylor, Nelson, Garland, and several others are trying to raise a thousand men," he said. "It's not likely that so many will be willing to join them, but they seem to be having some success."

We expected daily to hear that Garland and the others had been arrested, but what we learned blasted any hope of that. All of the commanders of state troops, including Rip Ford, refused to make the arrests. No civil official had authority to give him orders, Ford said. He would assist only if a sheriff certified that he had exhausted all other possibilities. "I shall use force only to repel force," Ford added. If he wouldn't help make the arrests they wouldn't be made. We all felt pretty sick when we heard this, for it meant that nothing would ever be done to those butchers.

When Ford appeared unexpectedly at the agency, the Captain's reception was cool. "I'm making another drive on the Comanches toward the end of the month," Ford said. "I've got forty-five men and will need as many Indians as are willing to go with us. Will you ask them for me?"

Captain Ross took his time replying. "If you had arrested that bunch of killers they'd all want to go with you. As it is, I'm not sure any will."

"You know I'd make the arrests if there was any possible way to do it," Ford said. "They're in the heart of Baylor country, and even those who don't support him would fight anyone who tried to arrest white men for killing Indians. It would take a whole regiment to do it, and plenty of blood would flow. Then they'd all head for the reserves and kill the agents and every Indian. Believe me, there's no way it can be done."

Captain Ross thought about that some. "I reckon you're right, Rip," he said at last. "It's a sad state of affairs when good people, men and women, are murdered in their beds and this state does nothing about it. I'll see what I can do about getting some Indians to go with you. But the smartest thing for us would be keeping all of our warriors right here to defend their families."

On the night of February 22 Comanches ran off about fifty Caddo ponies, so when Ford and his ranger company arrived the next morning, seventy-five angry Caddos, Anadarkos, and others were ready to accompany him. They headed north together, following the trail of the Comanche raiders.

Right after they left Fox rode up to the agency with a message from Van Dorn. He was preparing for his spring campaign, he said, and he needed more scouts and guides. The Captain sent two of the best scouts still available with a note informing him about Ford's rangers and Indians. He also sent a rider to tell Ford about Van Dorn's plans.

A few days after Ford left we learned that Baylor had held a big meeting at Jimmison's Peak. He warned the government that unless the Indians had been removed by March 20 he'd raise a thousand men to destroy the reserves and kill the agents and Indians.

When Ford received the Captain's message he headed straight for Camp Radziminski, he told us later. A severe blizzard hit them about the time they got there, and Van Dorn's welcome wasn't much warmer. He didn't want any undisciplined volunteers, he said, just Indian scouts. Ford left the Indians with him and returned to the Brazos Agency. After he arrived he paid off William Marlin's rangers and sent them home.

The frontier families he'd seen were frightened and forted up, Ford said, expecting either Comanches or reservation Indians to attack them. "I'm writing the governor that the threatened combination of frontier settlers against the reserves has not passed," he added. "Indeed, there are many causes to render the apprehension of coming difficulties, dangers, and troubles not only reasonable but alarming. If he takes no action to protect the reservations from attack he must bear the full responsibility for whatever happens."

The Palo Pinto grand jury met to consider the evidence against the Garland killers but refused to indict them. Garland and his men, they said, "had performed a public service." The only action they took was to indict José María and Ketumse for horse stealing because Baylor had accused both of being horse thieves. They were two of the most dependable chiefs on the reserves. José María had taken part in campaigns against the Northern Comanches and Ketumse had offered to help the army against them. But all along the frontier Indian haters were calling for a war to the death against the reservation.

"I can't understand it," the Captain remarked. "The Indians are the aggrieved party, yet they're willing to forgive and forget. The settlers fear retaliation for crimes against the Indians, so they want to destroy them."

When Ford and his rangers returned to their camp in Leon County, they passed through Palo Pinto on the way. Everyone thought they had come to arrest Garland's party, and a huge crowd of armed men followed them clear out of the county, ready to attack them if they attempted to seize anyone. There was no way the Garland men could be arrested short of calling on the army.

Dr. Stern and the Indians who'd gone to Waco to testify against Garland returned to the agency, for it was clear there'd be no trial. The Major had gone on to San Antonio to inform the Commissioner that a blowup was imminent and to plead again for permission to move the Indians out of Texas.

It was soon known that Baylor didn't intend to wait for the government to remove the Indians. Reports came in from Jack, Palo Pinto, Erath, and Comanche counties that he and his cronies were trying to raise an army. Dykes learned in Belknap that a man named Dillingham had gone to Jacksborough to tell the Baylor people there weren't any troops at the Brazos Agency. Dykes also heard that rancher Oliver Loving had raised a force to prevent the arrest of the Garland bunch.

"What do you make of that?" I asked the Captain. "He sells steers to the agencies and knows the Indians. I thought he was on our side."

"He is, in a way. He doesn't approve of what those men did, I'm sure of that. It's just that killing Indians has never been a crime in this state, and arresting white men for it is something that Loving and others like him can't accept. I'm writing the Major that we need him here. Baylor is likely to show up with a large force at any time, and it will take all the influence we can muster to reconcile the Indians."

He sent me to ask Major Thomas for a cavalry company to protect the agency Indians. "There's not one troop available," Thomas replied. "But tell Captain Ross I'll send Captain King and his infantry company with a piece of artillery." Captain King and his company soon arrived, but at night they returned to the fort.

Someone called on Young County citizens to meet at Belknap on March 12, to discuss the Indian problem. "You'd better get over there and hear what they decide," the Captain told me.

On the morning of the twelfth I rode into the little county seat and tied my pony to a hitching rack, then walked around while the crowd gathered. I saw Ed Cornett, Patrick Murphy, and a lot of others, some I didn't recognize. At ten o'clock everyone crowded around Henry Vollentine, a local merchant.

"There are men raising an army to destroy the reserves," he said. "We must . . ."

"Let's do it!" Cornett interrupted. Murphy and a few others shouted agreement. Most of them yelled "No!"

They argued back and forth for a while, when one man came forward holding a piece of paper. He held up his hand and the crowd became quiet while he read. "Resolved, that breaking up the reserves and forcibly expelling the Indians would expose us to immediate danger and threaten the lives of our families. We shall, therefore, petition the secretaries of War and Interior to remove them. Only if our petition is ignored will we join others in expelling the Indians."

There was a lot of shouting and milling around before they voted. Most of them opposed violence and what Baylor was trying to do, so the resolution passed by a big majority. Ed Cornett spat in disgust.

"You and the Major and his redskins will get what's comin' to you yet," he said. "First I'd like to get me a piece of that little squaw." I turned my back and left.

"Most are for peace," I told the Captain, "but there are a few like Cornett and Murphy who are with Baylor." O. H. Fitts, a man who lived in Belknap and who opposed breaking up the reserves, came to the agency one morning. "I rode over to Jacksborough to see what was goin' on there," he told us. "Someone recognized me and they grabbed me. Luckily, I did have some legal business there and they finally let me go. Baylor had been in town, and all they talked about is killing every Indian and anyone who tries to protect them. For a while I was afraid they'd force me to go with them. They've beaten up men who refused."

A few nights later a fellow named McLewan showed up at the agency, having walked the twelve miles from his cabin. "The Jacksborough men are camped at Rock Creek," he told us. "I couldn't tell how many, but must be at least two hundred and more are coming. It's likely they're fixin' to start some mischief. They're holding several men who refused to join them."

The Captain sent a note to the fort, and Captain King and his infantry company came back to the agency the next morning. About noon the Major arrived from San Antonio and found us and the Indians preparing for battle. Everyone was excited as the Indians flocked to the agency for safety, fearing for their families. If the infantry and its cannon hadn't been there the Indians would have abandoned everything and fled. The women and children huddled around the buildings, watching fearfully for enemies.

An old Caddo man approached Captain Ross. "I don't see Narchicox or his wife and son," he said. "I've looked everywhere. They're not here. Maybe those bad men found them."

"You know his cabin?" the Captain asked me. I nodded. Narchicox was one of those who'd built a regular log cabin instead of a native house. "See if you can find them," the Captain continued. "We'd better keep all our people close by."

I knew Narchicox, for he was one of the friendliest men on the reservation. He'd been worried about all the threats, and I suspected he had decided to take his family to a hideout.

At the cabin I checked my pony and called for Narchicox. No answer. I looked through the open door. Narchicox, his wife, and son were sprawled grotesquely on the dirt floor, circles of blood beside them. The rifle he'd used lay near Narchicox. He'd been so upset by the dangers to the Indians that he'd killed them and then taken his own life. This was something else Baylor and his friends could claim credit for.

We waited all day but the enemy never came. "I wonder if they really planned to attack us," Captain Ross said. "This may have been just a diversion to screen Garland and his killers from being arrested. They must know that writs have been issued for all of them and delivered to the Palo Pinto sheriff."

After a few days Captain King and his troops returned to Fort Belknap. I watched them march away, wondering if they could return in time if we really needed them.

A few days later George Erath came to see the Major. "When we heard that Baylor was raising an army to attack the reserves," he said, "Colonel Johnson and I decided to try to talk some sense into the people and get them to wait for the government to act. He went to some settlements while I went to others. We urged the people to remain calm and not let themselves be talked into brutal acts they'd regret later. We reminded them that even now seventy-five Brazos Indians are helping the army against the Northern Comanches. In some places we were able to restore a degree of sanity, at least for the moment. But we learned that as soon as we rode on some of Baylor's men came and tried to undo whatever we'd accomplished. Colonel Johnson finally had to give up, for one crowd threatened his life.

"All of these people are a long way from the reserves and know little about Indians except what Baylor and others have told them. But to all frontier people, Indians are like buffalo—they're crazed at the sight of either and have to kill. They don't need a reason." He cleared his throat and continued.

"I hate to tell you this, but you need to know. Baylor, Nelson, Garland, and Motherell are determined to murder you and Captain Ross. They've even offered rewards for your scalps." The Major and Captain Ross looked at each other silently. I figured their eyes must have had a message, for neither spoke.

No attack came during March, for the Baylor people found that too few men were willing to join them. Early in April Rip Ford published another letter of warning.

"The frontier is in a bad way," it began. "The feeling of insecurity and hostility toward the Reserve Indians, and many imaginary and dreadful evils they persuade themselves are near, render the frontier people violent and, in many respects unreasonable. It has been a difficult matter in the last seven years to sustain the frontier settlements, but we have had the assistance and cooperation of the Reserve Indians. Place them on the opposite side, throw in 400 of the best warriors in the United States, imbued with a belief that we have been unfaithful to our pledges and thirsting for revenge, then tell me where you think the line on the settlements will be within five years, and when the war will end. Let an infuriated mass of men attack the Reserves, break them up, interfere with the United States Government's settled Indian policy, and we may apprehend danger, trouble, and bloodshed from the Red River to the Rio Grande."

He went on to say that federal authorities would view it as a war between frontier people and Indians with whom we were at peace. "We should then have worse than a Florida war saddled upon us. I don't take it upon myself to sit in judgement upon the border settlers—they may be right—but I have never been able to detect the Reserve Indians in the commission of a single depredation or to trace one to their doors, and I do think the measures instituted by the people have been impolitic and precipitate."

About the same time that Ford's letter was published the Major heard from the Commissioner that he was taking steps to lease land from the Choctaws to provide reservations for Texas Indians. Because of the Comanche-Kiowa hostility toward the Texas tribes, a fort would have to be built nearby to protect them, and that would take time. The Major left for San Antonio to await instructions concerning what action to take if the reserves were attacked in the meantime. He was there on April 19 when the Commissioner authorized him to abandon the reserves in the fall or winter and relocate the tribes in Indian Territory. The Major wrote the Captain that he had immediately notified the governor and the leading newspapers.

"Thank God, at last," he concluded. "This should have the effect of calming the agitation. Those who want the Indians removed shall have their wish. In six months all Indians will be gone from Texas. There is no longer a shadow of an excuse for making war on them."

EIGHT

Knowing that the Indians would soon be out of Texas satisfied most frontier settlers but not Baylor and Nelson. We soon heard they were still demanding the destruction of the Indians and their agents. The Reverend Tackitt heard Baylor speak to a big crowd in Palo Pinto.

"He wants scalps—yours, Leeper's, and the Major's," he told the Captain. "His language was as threatening as any I've ever heard. He's downright bloodthirsty. His men are undoubtedly prowling around the reserves right now, watching for an opportunity to kill Indians, and he made it clear they don't care if they are women and children. I've never seen a man so filled with hatred."

The Captain sent word to the fort asking for troops to protect the Indians, and Lieutenant William Burnet brought his infantry company from Cooper. Unlike many of the officers, he was a Texan; his father, David Burnet, had been president during the Texas Revolution. Although he was Texan, he made it clear that he would carry out orders to defend the Indians. In the meantime we'd gotten word to the chiefs to bring their people to the agency, and all were there when Burnet's company arrived.

"Baylor's men attacked some Comanches on the Clear Fork reserve yesterday," Burnet told the Captain. "They were trying to steal Comanche horses. They got away with some, but the Comanches killed one and lost one warrior. A cavalry troop was sent after them, but they got a pretty good head start."

"I hope they catch them and make them pay," the Captain said. "I thought that now everyone knows the government will remove the Indians soon they'd be willing to wait. But what they're after now is ponies, not protection, and they're doing pretty well at the pony game."

The Major sent word that he'd warned the Commissioner it was unsafe to wait until winter and he'd urged immediate removal. He enclosed a letter to Agent Blain at Fort Arbuckle, asking him to make arrangements to receive and feed the Indians. Fox, with an escort of six Caddos, took the Major's letter to Arbuckle.

A week later we were waiting for Fox to return with Blain's reply when his escort galloped up to the agency office without him. As they rode past Murphy's stage station, they said a bunch of white men shot at them and pursued them. They headed for the timber, but Fox's pony was worn down and they captured him and took him to the stage station. He was carrying official dispatches and had a pass from the Captain.

Thirty-seven Indians, including a brother and a cousin of Fox, ran for their ponies. Sturm and I mounted and joined them, along with Burnet and two soldiers, all three of them mounted. As we loped to the stage station, ten miles from the agency, Burnet took command. One of the hands at the station told him that fifteen men calling themselves Jacksborough Rangers had taken Fox. We strung out along the road to Jacksborough, with several Indians about half a mile ahead of us. After about ten miles they stopped and started wailing. When we caught up with them Fox was dead and scalped alongside the road. The mail pouch was missing.

We were all shocked and furious at the sight, but Burnet was livid. While the Indians buried Fox, Sturm and I talked to Burnet.

"I'm determined to capture or kill those murderers," he said, "even if we have to follow them to Jacksborough."

Sturm looked worried. "If we even go near Jacksborough with Indians no telling what will happen. I figure it's bound to make things worse."

I agreed with Sturm. "We'll be playing into Baylor's hands if we go there. We'll only make it easier for him to raise a big crowd of Indian killers."

Burnet's jaw was set and the knuckles on his clenched fists were white. "Those men are criminals of the worst sort. I've got to try and catch them. It's my duty."

Sturm and I looked at each other, both of us feeling helpless. I glanced at the Indians. They wanted revenge and I figured they might take it out on any white man we happened to meet. They weren't ready to turn back, so there was nothing we could do but stay with them and do our best to keep them out of trouble. We rode on toward Jacksborough; it reminded me of the time the Captain, Jim Shaw, and I rode out to meet the Comanche war party. Luckily, we didn't see anyone the whole way.

We waited while Burnet and the two soldiers rode into town to see what they could learn. It was dark when they returned, so there was nothing to do but camp for the night without blankets or food.

"No one would tell me anything except that the men aren't in Jacksborough," Burnet told us. "None of them was very friendly or cooperative, even though we were after mail robbers and murderers. In the morning we'll see if we can pick up their trail."

I knew we should head for the agency, but we tried to sleep on the bare ground with empty bellies. Before dawn it rained hard, which added to our misery. "After all this rain there'll be no trail to follow," I told Burnet. "We'd better get back to the agency quick before those people come after us." He glumly agreed.

There'd been little time to think about Fox, but on the long ride back I thought about him plenty. He'd wanted to be like a white man in every way, and lots of times he'd asked me how we did some things or what the word was for this or that. He'd served the army and the agents as loyally as any man could. And now he was dead, murdered by a bunch of frontier riffraff for no reason at all, just for being born an Indian.

We were all famished when we reached the agency that afternoon, but Lieutenant Burnet was still fuming. I wanted to see them get what they deserved as bad as he did, but he didn't know those frontier people. He thought they'd support us in catching murderers, but to them killing an Indian was an act of public service. The Palo Pinto grand jury had said that about the killers of Choctaw Tom's people. If he'd found the men who'd killed Fox and tried to arrest them it's unlikely that even one of us could have escaped.

"What took you so long?" the Captain asked.

"Jacksborough Rangers killed Fox and took his dispatches," Sturm replied. "Against our advice the lieutenant insisted that we follow them clear to Jacksborough. We waited while he went into town, but fortunately he couldn't find them. God knows what would have happened if he had." The Captain looked shocked.

"That was madness! If any act was calculated to give Baylor an excuse for a war on the reserves, that was it. We must prepare for the worst."

Lieutenant Burnet came to report to Captain Ross. "While they were burying Fox," he said, "I was thinking about what it was my duty to do. I decided it was to follow those mail robbers and murderers as long as possible, and if I overtook them, to arrest or shoot them."

"I understand your feelings," the Captain replied, "and I might do the same if I have the opportunity. But given the explosive conditions here, nothing could have been more imprudent. Following those men to Jacksborough with a party of Indians has given Baylor and Nelson all the fuel they need to inflame the settlers into destroying the reserves. They were having trouble raising men before, but now it will be easy. We can expect trouble."

I felt sorry for Lieutenant Burnet, for he certainly had no intention of making things worse and putting us and the Indians under the gun. But that's what he'd done. He saw that now, but it was too late for regrets.

Men who still refused to join the Baylor crowd stopped at the agency from time to time to tell us the latest news from Jacksborough. The whole town had gone wild because a party of "murderous Indians" had tried to avenge the killing of a "noted horse thief and murderer" by "public-spirited citizens." A man named Boyd started raising a force of volunteers; Baylor and Garland heard the good news and hurried there to take charge. They were aiming to raise five hundred men, saying the Indians must be driven out or destroyed before they committed any more atrocities against white women and children; it was useless to wait for Washington officials to make up their minds.

Another man reported that the women of Jacksborough had made a banner for their men. On it were the words "Necessity Knows No Law!" The Reverend Noah Byars, who'd been angry at the Captain for not letting him start a mission on the Brazos reserve, piously blessed the lawless crowd as "righteous crusaders."

We also learned that traitors among the troops at Camp Cooper got word to Baylor that there were only about thirty soldiers there. He made plans to send Garland with two hundred and fifty men to seize the field artillery, carbines, and ammunition. I headed for the fort to warn Major Thomas, who was now the post commander.

"We have barely enough troops to defend both reserves," he told me. "I'll send what reinforcements I can spare to Cooper. I can't allow those outlaws to seize government property or attack the agencies. Tell Captain Ross that I'll request General Twiggs to recall Major Van Dorn and his force. And thank him for keeping me informed. We're all in this mess together."

All of the Indians were camped around the agency, and the men put up a stockade to protect the women and children. During the next week a lot of them came down with cholera, and Dr. Stern was busy night and day tending them. I've got to admit that even though he may not have admired Indians, he treated one and all and was gentle and considerate. But even though he did the best he could, a few of the sick ones died each day.

"I've got to have more medicine before this gets completely out of hand," he told the Captain, handing him a list.

"I'll send word to Dallas on the next stage," the Captain promised. "I'll ask them to send what they can by stage and have the rest come by wagon with the supplies I've ordered. No tellin' how long we'll be cooped up like this, and Barnard says he's getting low on provisions."

Some of the medicines arrived on the next stage from Dallas. "Just in time," Dr. Stern said. "I was getting desperately low."

A few days later three men walked up to the agency from the east. "We're the teamsters who contracted to haul your supplies from Dallas," one said. "A crowd of armed men forced us off our wagons down the road a piece. I thought they figured on killing us, and maybe they did. They looked mean enough. Finally one said, 'You tell Ross and Neighbors we aim to starve them and their damned Injuns out.' Then they let us go. We didn't argue with them."

After that Baylor's men stopped the stage several times and took the mail bags. They'd gotten as lawless as possible, but still nothing was done to stop them. It looked like Baylor could do anything he wanted to by pretending he was defending the settlers from the reservation Indians.

The chiefs kept scouts out, watching for Baylor's "Army of Defense," as he called his bunch of outlaws. The scouts said Baylor still had a big camp at Rock Creek, and figured he must have about three hundred men there. It was clear that Baylor was getting ready to strike.

His attack on the Brazos reserve was timed to take advantage of the absence of seventy-five of the best warriors, who were still serving with Van Dorn in Comanche country. Early on the morning of May 23 excited scouts reported that Baylor and two hundred and fifty to three hundred men had left camp and were riding toward the agency. The Captain sent Dykes to the fort. Captain Bradfute's cavalry troop arrived about two hours after, followed by Captain Plummer and Lieutenant Burnet with an infantry company.

In the meantime, all of us checked our rifles and pistols, for it looked like we'd soon be using them to save our lives. Then for hours we watched nervously. In mid-afternoon we saw them approaching, spread out in a long line and coming toward us with their horses at a walk. I watched them, rubbing my moist hand on the butt of my carbine.

The infantry company and Captain Bradfute's cavalry troop were all under arms and calmly watching the enemy. When they were about half a mile from the agency Captain Plummer called Lieutenant Burnet:

"Take your company and tell them I demand to know for what purpose a body of armed men has come onto this reservation."

Burnet saluted and marched toward the invaders at the head of the infantry. We watched while he and Baylor talked. Soon the troops returned.

"Baylor says he has come for the purpose of attacking certain bands of Indians," Burnet reported. "He says he will not attack whites, but if they or the soldiers fire on his men, he will destroy them. He requests that the troops leave the reservation at once."

"Inform him that my orders are to protect the Indians on this reservation from attacks by bands of armed citizens, and that I will do so to the best of my ability with the weapons at my disposal," Captain Plummer told Burnet. "Order him in the name of the government of the United States to leave this reserve."

We waited again while this message was delivered and Burnet returned. "He says that doesn't change his determination to destroy the Indians on this and the upper reserve, and he will leave when he's ready. He swore he'll carry out his purpose if it costs the life of every man in his command. He also said that we'll likely be hanged if we kill a single citizen. I told him I don't know about civil law but would take that chance. He went on and on about the law. I finally cut him off by telling him I'd said what I came to say and had his answer."

"That's about what I expected," Captain Plummer remarked. The troops spread out in a battle line with the field artillery in front of them, while a dozen or more warriors rode out on the flanks. The Baylor men rode off toward the Waco village, where the oldest Indian on the reserve was squatting in the shade while his wife worked in her garden. Some of Baylor's men made friendly gestures to him, and although he was deaf and nearly blind, he approached them. One threw a loop over his head and dragged him away while another shot his wife. Then they shot the old man and scalped him.

Between fifty and sixty enraged warriors galloped toward them, shrieking their war cries. Others would have followed, but the Captain begged them to stay and protect the women and children. When the Baylor men saw the Indians coming they fired wildly, then spurred their horses and fled.

Captain Bradfute with his cavalry troop and Lieutenant Burnet and his infantry company followed, so I went with them. It was a running fight for about eight miles, until the Baylor crowd reached William Marlin's ranch. They shot at Marlin and forced him to head for the timber—he'd always supported the Indians, and when he was a ranger Baylor had threatened to hang him.

Baylor and others dashed into the house, where Mrs. Marlin and their children were. The rest hid in the outbuildings or corrals, with the Indians shooting at them. I saw Tosche, and rode up to him, out of rifle range. If Mrs. Marlin and the children weren't in the house, he said, they'd set fire to it and burn Baylor out.

The battle went on the rest of the afternoon, with the Indians shooting whenever they had a target. Jim Pockmark rode toward the house, with bullets whistling around him. "Baylor," he shouted, "come out and fight me, just the two of us." He circled around and waited. We watched for Baylor to appear, but he apparently declined the invitation.

I rode back to the agency to tell the Captain what was going on, that Baylor and his army were holed up at Marlin's ranch, pinned down by at most sixty warriors.

"They're finding out it's not the same as shooting Indians in their beds asleep," the Captain remarked.

At dark the Indians returned to the agency, carrying the body of Caddo John, or Hatterbox. Several were wounded.

"We killed maybe six or seven," José María told the Captain. "I don't know how many were wounded. The way they ran it looked like they didn't expect us to fight."

I didn't sleep much that night, wishing morning would come. When the sun finally rose, José María and a party of warriors headed for Marlin's ranch. The Captain and I accompanied them. When we were nearly there, scouts rode up.

"They're gone, all of them," they told the Captain. At Marlin's ranch we saw Mrs. Marlin staring at seven freshly filled graves in the yard. "I never saw such a frightened bunch of men," she said. "I told Mr. Baylor what I thought of him—he's worse than any Comanche. The cemetery is right over yonder, but they were afraid to go that far to bury these men. What cowardly scoundrels they are."

About that time William Marlin rode up. "Are you and the children all right?" he called. "I tried to get the soldiers to come from the fort, but they said it was the sheriff's responsibility as long as those men were off the reservation."

"We're all right. Some of the men were so scared they pulled up boards and hid under the floor. I haven't heard so much prayin' since the last camp meeting."

Marlin looked around. "Where are the horses?"

"They stole every last one they could find."

"Which way did they go?" the Captain asked Mrs. Marlin.

"They took the wounded to Belknap. I guess the others went to their camp, wherever it is."

The Captain turned to me. "Chip, ride into town and see what you can learn. Some may have stayed with the wounded, or maybe you can talk to them. Try to find out what Baylor aims to do now."

I headed for Belknap, and saw quite a few folks standing outside the general store. "We let 'em leave the wounded but told the rest of 'em to git," Vollentine told me.

"I'd like to talk to them. Where are they?"

"At Doc Robinson's, yonder." He pointed to the doctor's house.

I knocked on the door and Mrs. Robinson opened it. "Captain Ross asked me to see what I can learn from these men," I told her. "Are there any I can talk to now?"

"Most of them are just boys," she said, leading me to an alcove where a pale-faced young man lay on a cot. I told him my name and he told me his. "How come you got mixed up in this?" I asked him. "You look like you got better sense than that. You might have got yourself killed, and for no good reason."

"I know." He looked like he was fighting back tears. "They lied to us, said there wouldn't be any fighting. They bullied us into coming. When we heard him say he'd destroy the Indians if it cost the life of every one of us we knew we didn't belong there." He drew a deep breath. "Baylor told us they'd be too scared to fight. Most of us don't know anything about Indians and didn't want to kill them. When those men murdered that poor old man and his wife it made us sick. And right after that it looked like all the Indians in the world were after us. I'd have made a run for it but I was afraid they'd kill me. They must have outnumbered us two to one. I've never been so scared in all my life."

I tried not to smile. "There were at most sixty Indians after you," I told him. He looked like he couldn't believe me.

"Sixty? Are you sure? I'd have sworn there was maybe five times as many." He stared at the ceiling for a moment. "Baylor sent Garland to Camp Cooper with half of his army. He'd been told there weren't many soldiers there, and they could easily capture all the guns and cannons. They were supposed to meet us when we got to the agency, but only one man came. He said there was some infantry there and they wouldn't surrender. When the soldiers got ready to fight everybody quit."

"Have you any idea what Baylor and the others will do now?" He shook his head. "Whatever they do they'll do it by theirselves. Everyone I know is shaggin' it for home. Wisht I was with 'em." He turned his head and closed his eyes as tears rolled down his cheeks.

I returned to the agency and told Captain Ross what I'd learned.

"The scouts say they went back to their camp on Rock Creek," he said. "The minute they got there a lot of them rolled up their blankets and hightailed it. We won't see any of them again, but there are still a bunch of horse thieves and desperadoes with Baylor. No telling what they might do, especially if they find a few Indians who can't defend themselves."

Lieutenant Holman rode in from Camp Cooper with a letter from the Major. The Captain read it and then handed it to me. "I arrived here yesterday and expected to come to your agency today, but owing to news of your victory over the enemy and they, threatening this reserve next, I concluded to wait here until I hear from you. Please write me all the particulars of your fight by return express and give me such other information as you have in regard to matters generally."

He went on to say he hoped the Captain would remain on the defensive, "but if those desperadoes again come on the reserve *try to wipe them out!* All intelligent citizens below sustain us, and as long as we can claim the defensive for the Indians we will be sustained." The Clear Fork Comanches were ready to fight, he added, and had expressed the determination to "give as good an account of themselves as you have done if they are attacked. I wonder what the governor is doing. Probably nothing. It is a disgrace both to him and the State that such outrages are allowed. I intend to have writs served on the leaders of those outlaws and have them taken before the United States Court in Austin after we have removed the Indians."

Major Thomas came to the agency several days later to see the Captain and check on the situation. "I just received a message from Van Dorn," he told the Captain. "He wiped out or captured an entire Comanche camp in southern Kansas. He said he never could have done it without the help of the Brazos Indians."

"I wish you'd send a cavalry company to Rock Creek and round up the leaders and those horse thieves with them," the Captain remarked.

"I wish I could, believe me, but my orders are not to send troops off the reserves. General Twiggs has informed the governor that this is a state affair, and that he should immediately take steps to arrest those men and bring them to justice. But if the army interferes in civil affairs we'll be in big trouble." He added that Twiggs had sent Van Dorn instructions to allow the Indian scouts to return to the Brazos Agency at once and then to send the cavalry companies as quickly as possible. "That will give us more than enough men to protect both reserves," he concluded.

The same day as the skirmish at Marlin's ranch the Waco *Southerner* published a letter from "A Good Citizen," which we saw the following week. Baylor had threatened army officers with civil trials and hanging if soldiers killed any of his men, the letter stated. He had also seized government supplies and stolen the Indians' horses and cattle, which we already knew. "Baylor publicly threatened to hang Captain S. P. Ross, Mr. Charles Barnard, and Major Neighbors, also threatens James Duff, U. S. Deputy Marshal, Harvey Mathews, William Marlin, Mr. Bandy the Sheriff of Young County, and others, all of whom are among the best citizens in the County. We think it is time that the State and General Government take notice of this offender against the law and rights of good people of the frontier of Texas," the letter concluded. We certainly agreed with that, but the governor failed to respond.

"All of this could have been prevented," the Major said when he read the letter, "if we had a governor who would do anything to prevent it except promulgate proclamations for popularity, which he never intended to carry out."

Runnels lamely claimed his delay in taking action was because he had been away from Austin. An editorial in the *Intelligencer* said that people in Austin were convinced that the governor and Lieutenant Governor Lubbock were both absent from the capital while blood flowed on the frontier because they didn't know what to do, with an election so near. They weren't equal to the emergency, the editor concluded.

J. H. Baker, a Palo Pinto teacher who had been with Baylor's force, wrote the papers complaining that the Indians were better armed than the Army of Defense and were "assisted and abetted by renegade white men." Neither was true. When they took the wounded to Belknap, Baker wrote, "we found plenty of enemies there and some friends, who were almost afraid to express themselves because of the government siding with the Indians."

William Pevelor, a frontier settler, explained to the Major why he had joined Baylor. "We were afraid if these Indians were turned loose they would wipe out everything, like Baylor said. We didn't think it was especially spite on his part in breaking up the reserves. He thought they were depredating. He is a man highly respected and a great Indian fighter."

"Don't believe it," the Major replied. "Until he was fired he knew and swore that none of the reserve Indians took part in the depredations. He still knows it, but now he wants revenge for being dismissed."

On June 5 one of the Belknap men told the Major he'd heard that Baylor and five hundred men had left the camp on Rock Creek to attack the Clear Fork Indians. "I doubt that," the Major said after the man had left. "He doesn't have anywhere near five hundred men, but just to be safe I'd better see about it." The Major and Lieutenant Eagle soon headed for Clear Fork with a cavalry company.

The report was a ruse, as the Major had suspected. Baylor had heard that Van Dorn's cavalry was coming after him, and he spread the rumor so the rest of his men could scatter before the troops caught them.

Two of Van Dorn's companies reached Camp Cooper a few days later. These and others that came to the Brazos reserve were enough to protect both agencies. Baylor's crowd, after robbing travelers and stealing more horses from ranchers and Indians, had scattered.

When he returned to the Brazos Agency the Major found a letter from his wife. During all the commotion his second son, Ross Simpson Neighbors, had been born. "I wonder when I'll ever get to see him," the Major said. None of us speculated about that.

Another man who'd been with Baylor stopped at the agency office. He came in sheepishly twisting his hat in his hands. "No man likes to admit his folly," he said, "but like a lot of others, I was taken in and I want to apologize." He drew a deep breath.

"What happened after you left Marlin's place?" the Major asked.

"We got a lot more speeches by Baylor and Nelson, but they'd lost their appeal, and no one was willing to listen to any more of them. Every man was feeling low enough to walk under a snake's belly with his hat on. The leader of the bunch from Palo Pinto quit and left, and most of his men went with him. The next day we got word Van Dorn's cavalry was coming after us, and that was enough for the rest. Baylor and Nelson ranted and raved, but we just saddled our ponies and hit the trail. I hope I never again do anything so foolish."

"You weren't alone," the Major assured him. "But after all their lies and blunders, it's hard to understand why anyone would follow them. The Northern Comanches are the ones you should be fighting, not these Indians. While you were coming here to attack these people, seventy-five of their best warriors were with the army after Comanches."

"You're right," the man admitted. "We also knew these Indians will soon leave the state and that all we had to do was wait a little. But Baylor and Nelson made it sound different. We finally figured out that they don't really want the Indians to leave. They want to kill them, and you, too. They've sent men to other counties for more recruits. I'm afraid you haven't heard the last of them."

A few days later we found that what he had said was true. Baylor and Nelson hadn't given up. They'd sent messengers to every settlement from Waco to Gainesville calling for all able-bodied men to help "wipe out the reservations even if it is necessary to fight the army."

Several Tawakoni warriors rode off one morning to look for some of their ponies that had strayed from around the agency. Half an hour later I heard gunshots in the distance, and rode toward the sound. I met a young Tawakoni coming on the run who slid his pony to a stop. "White men shoot Big Foot's brother," he gasped. I knew who he meant—George Washington, the one who'd adopted the Captain as his brother. Together we raced back the way he'd come.

We found the Tawakonis standing around the body of George Washington, and it took only a glance to tell he was dead. I remembered how he'd stuck close to the Captain and Sul, to protect them from danger.

"Where are the men who did it?" I asked. The Tawakonis pointed to a nearby hill that was covered with brush.

"Carry him back to the agency," I told them. "I'm goin' to find out who it was."

"You be careful—they kill you, too," one warned me. I nodded and circled the hill until I saw the tracks of two shod horses that had been running hard, like their riders had seen a ghost. I followed their trail, but was careful not to ride into an ambush. Like Tosche had taught me, I stayed in ravines when I could, after seeing the direction the tracks were heading. When I had to cross ridges I left my pony partway down and crawled to the top. All of this took a lot of time, so I had no hope of overtaking the men, much as I wanted to.

They tried to hide their trail, after they'd calmed down a bit, I guess. They rode into a little stream and waded their horses in it for half a mile, then left it by crossing a sandstone ledge, figuring their tracks wouldn't show. I had no trouble following their trail—Tosche's training sure came in handy.

Finally their tracks led to the road to Belknap, and I saw they'd headed for town. I followed their trail right to Dyches' saloon and stopped. There were half a dozen cow ponies standing at the hitching rack, but it was easy to tell the two that had just been ridden hard, for the sweat hadn't dried on them. I glanced at their brands. One belonged to Patrick Murphy, the other to Ed Cornett. I looked toward the door—both men were standing there, watching me, probably wondering if I was trailing them. I stared at them for a moment, then rode on to the general store, but didn't stay long.

I told the Major about it, and he had me write a statement and swear to it. "When I get the Indians safely out of Texas I'll give the courts enough to keep them and a bunch of lawyers busy for a while," he remarked, and his voice had a steely ring.

The next morning a letter from the Commissioner arrived, after being forwarded from San Antonio. The Major read it and smiled, one of the few times I'd seen him smile. "At last!" he said. "The Commissioner has instructed me to remove the Indians from Texas as quickly as it can be arranged! The Secretary of War has ordered the army to provide escorts. Now we must get to work, for there's much to be done and no time to lose."

NINE

When Governor Runnels finally took action it was to announce that he would appoint a peace commission to investigate the charges against the Indians and restore quiet around the reserves. "You may be assured that the board will be composed of men whose interests and sympathies are identified with the frontier," the governor stated, "and whose high standing and character will afford a guarantee to the citizens that their rights will be in safe hands."

The Major was at Fort Belknap when the stage from Dallas dropped off the mail bag containing the Austin paper with the governor's statement in it. While the Captain read his mail I scanned the paper and saw the announcement. "Look at this." I handed him the paper. He read the governor's statement twice.

"Translated, this means he's figured out a way to make it look like he's doing something and at the same time win himself votes on the frontier," the Captain observed. "I hope he puts Rip Ford on the commission, but that's not likely, for he knows Rip respects the Indians. My guess is he won't appoint anyone he can't count on to do exactly what he wants."

The next paper listed the commissioners—George Erath, J. M. Smith, Richard Coke, John Henry Brown, and Dr. J. M. Steiner. The Major and Captain Ross read over the names. "Steiner killed your friend Major Ripley Arnold at Fort Graham in '53," the Captain remarked, "and he's in the anti-Houston faction, which means he's no friend of the Indians. I don't know anything about Coke, but the others are opposed to the reservations, at least to some degree."

"Brown is working for Runnels' re-election, so we know where he stands," the Major said. "I think Erath and Smith will try to be fair. Let's hope the others will." Captain Ross rubbed his chin and looked dubious but said nothing.

In mid-June the commissioners came to the agency to see the Major and Captain Ross. Both politely shook hands with them, but it reminded me of someone petting a strange dog, not knowing if it would bite. As I watched the Major I was suddenly struck by something I hadn't noticed before—his hair was turning white and he looked tired and careworn, like he was in his sixties rather than early forties.

"You probably read in the papers about our appointment," Erath said in his German accent. The Major nodded.

"We're here to make an impartial investigation of the charges against the Indians," Brown added, but he didn't look at the Major.

"That's all we ask," the Major replied. "In case you didn't see the report of Hawkins' investigation, he disproved all of the charges against the Indians. Remember, too, the part these Indians have played in the three victories over the Comanches." The commissioners listened solemnly, but I couldn't tell from their expressions if his words made any impression on them.

"There is not on file any legal affidavit or other testimony," the Major continued, "to show that any Indian on either reserve has committed a single one of the many depredations charged to them, although the parties making the charges have been called on frequently to produce evidence. It must appear preposterous to attempt to impose such falsehoods upon the people of the frontier as 'the agents shielding the Indians in crime.' I assert, without fear of contradiction from any source whatever, that there has not been, within my knowledge, a single violation of the treaty between the Indians of the reserves and the United States."

"Then what, in your opinion, caused the recent disturbances?" Erath asked.

"I can only give it as my opinion that the causes are, first, the unbounded ambition of Nelson, Baylor, and others to obtain the offices held by Captain Ross, Colonel Leeper, and myself, and to get hold of the money appropriated for the support of the Indians. They have frequently said that 'the agents have a good time of it,' and J. R. Baylor is no doubt a good judge, because the government dismissed him from the service for 'having a good time of it' during the eighteen months he was in service. This his own accounts will show whenever anyone chooses to examine them."

"You should never have allowed the Indians to leave the reserves," Brown said. "Then they wouldn't have been accused of depredating."

The Major reminded them that the Indians were protected by a treaty with the government of the United States, and that treaties are the law of the land. "There are no provisions in that treaty by which these Indians are to be kept within the limits of the reserves; nor is there any law or rule that would compel the Indians to submit to it, as they all have the right to claim protection under the state laws, should they desire to do so. It is consequently only a police regulation between the chiefs, the United States Army, and the agents by which the Indians are confined as strictly to the reserves as possible, and for the last six or eight months they have not been permitted to go out, even to hunt their own stock, except in the company of some responsible white man. The troops have been equally vigilant in order to protect the Indians from being shot down by some lawless person, or of bringing about a collision with citizens."

He reminded them that the government intended to remove the Indians at the earliest practicable moment, and that this information had been published in state papers. The Indians had assured him they were willing to bury the past and to rely on the laws to redress their grievances. That, he said, was more than Baylor's party was willing to do—they had tried to massacre the wives and children of warriors who were still with Van Dorn in the service of their country.

"I will continue to do my best to prevent another clash between hostile whites and the Indians," he added. "I wish you gentlemen success in your mission to restore peace and quiet."

Shortly after the attack on the Brazos reserve a Dr. Worrall, who had recently moved to Jacksborough, wrote a letter to the Dallas *Herald* to justify Baylor's act as well as the murder of Fox. The Caddo Indian, he stated, was a notorious horse thief and killer of whites. Everyone knew the Brazos Indians had committed depredations for years, he said, adding more of the usual Baylor line. The lies about Fox infuriated all of us.

The Major wrote a long letter to the Dallas *Herald* refuting Dr. Worrall. He had known Fox for fifteen years, the Major said, and he was absolutely trustworthy and dependable. He had also served with Van Dorn on his Comanche campaign. With regard to the attack on the Brazos Indians, he referred them to Captain Plummer's report, which had been published in the papers, and which told the story straight.

"There is now an intelligent commission from the governor investigating this movement of our citizens," the Major continued, "and we are willing to rely upon their investigation for a vindication of the reserves. We are willing and anxious to meet any legal issue on this subject, but protest against a newspaper controversy or with a mob, such as Baylor's company, who attack this reserve," he concluded.

On the same day, as we learned a few days later, Smith and Erath had written the Major. "I would beg leave to inform you as a friend," Smith wrote, "that much complaint and proof of depredations, of a circumstantial character, strongly implicating your Indians, have been furnished by Patrick Murphy and Hamner as well as others. There is no doubt, also, that still another movement is on foot to attack the agency again, as soon as the troops leave and you can be caught off your guard. I am fully satisfied that the destruction of the reserves is determined on, and they had rather kill you two than the Indians. I have heard that sentiment from almost all. I make this statement to you as a friend. I fear the commissioners will not make as favorable a report as I hoped they would. In great haste, &c."

"Good God!" the Major exclaimed, putting down the letter and opening the one from Erath.

To prevent another rising against the Indians, Erath explained, Waco attorney Edward J. Gurley had recommended to the governor that the present state troops be disbanded and a hundred men be called up from Bell and McLennan counties, where there was no agitation against the Indians. The governor had accepted that advice, and the commissioners had recommended that Brown or Smith be named to command the new company. Its purpose would be to keep the Indians confined to the reserves so they wouldn't clash with settlers. The Major's hand trembled as he laid the letter down.

"The state not only refuses to protect the Indians from lawless men— it's taking sides against them," he said. "And I trusted those men to be impartial—I must be losing my mind." They had talked only to the most biased men they could find. Hamner was publisher of *The White Man.*

The commissioners' report to the governor was soon published, and it was worse than Smith had hinted. It followed the Baylor line about the agency Indians having committed depredations, claiming that stolen horses had frequently been found on both reserves. The agents, it said, appeared to be honest men who had done their best but were unable to control the Indians.

"That's a left-handed compliment if I ever saw one," the Captain remarked. "We tried but failed."

When it was known that the ranger companies recruited in frontier counties were to be disbanded and sent home there was a lot of squawking. Baylor called a big meeting in Weatherford, and it passed several resolutions. The first was to approve the attack on the Brazos reserve. The second was that they would resist the arrest of any man who had been involved in it. Another was to organize militia companies to remove or destroy the Indians altogether. The last one was: "Resolved, that we

regard the recommendation of the so-called peace commissioners in calling out one hundred troops from elsewhere for our protection as a gross
insult to our frontier citizens."

When it came down to it, Baylor found that few men were willing to
join him in another attack on the Indians. They'd heard how fifty or sixty
Indians had run off more than two hundred and fifty of Baylor's men,
and they also knew that Van Dorn's cavalry had been recalled to defend
the agencies.

Right after receiving instructions to remove the Indians as soon as
arrangements could be made, the Major had sent a message to Superintendent Elias Rector, asking him to prepare for receiving nearly fifteen
hundred Texas Indians. Rector, with headquarters at Fort Smith, Arkansas, was in charge of all tribes in Indian Territory. He suggested that the
Major come to Fort Arbuckle, where they could confer on the matter.
The Major replied that he would meet him there about July 1, and would
bring a party of chiefs and headmen.

They set out on June 26 for the 160-mile ride to Arbuckle, and returned two weeks later. They had held a council with the chiefs of the
tribes that would be their neighbors, the Major told us. José María,
Ketumse, Ah-ha-dot, and other chiefs had made eloquent speeches, and
the others had replied in a friendly fashion. He was encouraged by that.

The land that had been set aside for the Texas tribes was worthless
and unsuitable. "Rector and I selected a new location in the valley of the
False Washita and along the Canadian," the Major said. "The soil is
fertile and the grass is the thickest and finest we saw. The Indians should
do well in both places. The chiefs were all satisfied and expressed the
hope that at last they may have a home of their own where their families
can live in peace."

The governor announced that John Henry Brown would command the
new company, and published his instructions to Brown.

"As you are fully apprised of the existing difficulties," the statement
began, "and the complicated state of affairs demanding the exercise of
prudence, impartiality, and firmness, it is unnecessary to impress them
upon you further than to say that the object is to prevent another collision between the citizens, on the one side, and the Indians, their agents,
and the federal army on the other. For this purpose you are instructed
forthwith to repair with said force to the vicinity of the reserves, and act
as a police guard around them, to prevent Indians from leaving them
until they shall be finally removed; and while treating all Indians found

off the reserves, unaccompanied by an agent or some responsible white man, as hostile, at the same time preventing attacks upon the reserves."

"I can believe they'll shoot any Indians they find off the reservation, but preventing attacks on the reserves is something else again. That wouldn't win Runnels any votes," the Captain remarked after reading the orders to Brown. At least most frontier settlers seemed to be satisfied with the arrangement and willing to wait for the government to move the Indians out of Texas.

Not long after he returned from Arbuckle the Major received a letter from Brown. He'd set up camp at Caddo Spring between the upper and lower reserves, he said, and his men would patrol the boundaries of both to prevent Indians from leaving unless a white man accompanied them.

The Major discussed Brown's letter with Captain Plummer, then wrote a reply. He reminded Brown that he and Captain Plummer were both under specific orders from the general government to protect the Indians against hostile whites. "Should the 'police' you propose to exercise around the United States reserves lead to a collision with the Indians who will be sent out to gather their stock, you alone must be responsible for the consequences, and the State will have to settle with the general government whatever losses she may sustain by your operations, if any."

Captain Plummer added a note stating that his orders were to protect the Indians of the Brazos Agency from attacks by armed bands of citizens, and that he intended to assist Major Neighbors and Captain Ross in the execution of their duties.

Brown replied, saying he regretted that the Major would provoke a conflict by sending Indians out to look for stock. Again he claimed to be impartial, saying the interests of Texas were at stake. He offered to provide men to accompany the Indians, and asked the Major to inform Captain Ross and Colonel Leeper.

"It is not my wish to discuss the unfortunate state of affairs existing on this frontier," Brown wrote. "I can only say that the State had adopted this course as the only means within its power of restoring quiet and tranquility to the frontier."

"I can assure you that I have no desire to discuss with you the subject of our frontier difficulties," the Major replied. "When I did so before, when you were here as a commissioner, I was under the impression that you would act impartially in your investigation. I am sorry to see from the newspaper publication made by you and others that you had already prejudged the Indians on the reserves and accused them of having committed most if not all of the late depredations on this frontier. As I am not prepared to admit any such assertions, I, as superintendent of Indian affairs, do not feel authorized or justified in aiding you in the exercise of surveillance over them."

Although the Major refused to acknowledge Brown's right to interfere with Indians gathering stock off the reservation, as he had told the commissioners, one of us had gone with them at such times for some months. The Captain had always allowed ranchers to hunt for their strays on the reserve; it was only right that the Indians should have the same opportunity to recover theirs.

We soon learned that Lieutenant Nowlin, one of Brown's officers, had tried to arrest Comanche subchief Kaharaway and had a fight with the Indians at Clear Fork. Leeper had heard the shooting and rode between the two parties and stopped the fighting. By then one Comanche had been killed and another badly wounded. Two rangers had been hit. News of this attack greatly excited both the Comanches and the Brazos Indians, for they didn't know what might happen next. Since Brown's men had no authority to arrest an Indian or to be on the reservation without permission from Leeper, it sure looked like they were out to start a war before we could move the Indians out of Texas.

Major Thomas was outraged over the attack on the Clear Fork reserve, and asked me to deliver a letter to Brown immediately. I didn't see what was in the letter, but Brown frowned when I handed it to him, then turned pale when he read it.

"Nowlin acted on his own, without my knowledge," he stammered. "He said that settlers accused Kaharaway of stealing horses, and thought it was his duty to make the arrest. We don't want any trouble with the cavalry. I'll order Nowlin to keep his men back a mile or two from the boundary, like Major Thomas says. You can tell him that for me."

Right after that one of Captain Plummer's patrols reported seeing eight armed men prowling around on the Brazos reservation. The Major and Captain Ross had gone to Fort Belknap and were absent when John Henry Brown came to the agency. Captain Plummer confronted him.

"Allowing your men onto the reserve after you publicly stated your intention of attacking the Indians is outrageous," he said. "This is government land, and citizens may come on it only after reporting to the proper authorities, stating their purpose, and receiving permission. Men coming here illegally can only excite the Indians, after what Nowlin did at the upper reserve. I have no doubt you will unite with me in the hope that these Indians, many of whom have but recently returned from an expedition against the Comanches in which they fought in defense of the lives and property of the frontier settlers, may soon be permitted to leave the state unmolested." He stopped to catch his breath after all that.

"Those weren't my men scouting on the reserve," Brown hastily replied. "They were settlers who had complained to me that they had come to the agency to see about their cattle and could get no satisfaction. They asked me to intercede for them. None of my men were with them." He left for his camp in a hurry, before Captain Plummer could say anything else.

When the Major and Captain Ross returned Plummer told them what Brown had said about citizens not being allowed to hunt for their strays on the reservation. The Major and Captain Ross looked shocked, then angry. The Major wrote a short letter and handed it to me. "Read it, Chip, in case you lose it on the way. Take it to Brown and wait for a reply."

"The parties alluded to in your conversation with Capt. Plummer have misrepresented the facts, if nothing worse," the letter said, "and I should like to know their names. I shall return to the State in a short time and resume my duties as a citizen. Then those who appear determined to force unjust issues on me will have to meet them."

I rode to Brown's camp at Caddo Spring and handed him the letter. "He asked me to wait for a reply," I told him.

Brown wrote a note and handed it to me. In it he said he didn't know the names of the men, except that the one who seemed to be their leader was John Anderson.

When I got back to the agency a dozen ranchers and cowboys were there to ask permission to hunt for their cattle on the reserve. The Major told them what Brown had said, then read them his note.

"That's hogwash," John Dayton said. "The last grand jury indicted Anderson for rustling. Those men were after the Indians' cattle, or any of ours they found. I hear they've been selling Indian cattle at Jacksborough."

Robert Shaw, one of the ranchers, wrote a statement about their treatment when they came to the agency to see about their stock. They had been allowed to hunt freely and to inspect the pen where the Indians were holding their cattle, he said. All of the ranchers signed it.

"I'm sending you this so you will have no excuse for reporting false testimony," the Major wrote Brown. "You appear to be equally as fortunate in your sources of information, having accepted the statement of a man who was presented at the last Grand Jury of this county for cattle stealing, as you were when you were here as an impartial commissioner."

I took the note and the statement to Brown. He didn't look glad to see me.

"You again. You're always bad news. What is it this time?" He read the letter and statement, and his expression didn't get any pleasanter. In fact his face turned red.

"I'm not here to make trouble for the agents or the Indians," he said, swallowing hard. "I wish the Major could understand that. I have my orders from the governor. There have been lots of complaints about the agents and Indians, and he's only trying to do what's right by the settlers."

"What about the Indians?" I asked. "Don't they have rights? As you know, both Rip Ford and Major Van Dorn say they couldn't have found and defeated the Comanches without the help of the Brazos Indians. And yet you'll kill them just for leaving the reserve to round up their own stock."

"I've offered to provide men to accompany them. That offer is still good, and it's as far as I am allowed to go. Remind them of that. The governor's running for re-election, and there's a limit to what we can do. You can tell Major Neighbors that the story about Indians burning Baylor's ranch was sheer fabrication. I sent men to check on it. He's the one trying to make trouble, not me."

The Major was busy making preparations for the move, and had let contracts for supplying wagons for the trip north. Charles Barnard was also busily laying in supplies. When he had things under way at the Brazos Agency, the Major went to the upper reserve to see about arrangements for the Comanches.

John Dayton came by the agency one morning a few days later. "There's a bunch of Indian cattle along the river below the reserve," he told the Captain. "I thought you'd like to know. There's probably a couple hundred head, maybe more. If you don't get 'em pretty quick Anderson and that bunch are likely to find them."

"That's decent of you," the Captain said. "We appreciate it." He turned to me.

"Chip, get Tosche and some of his cowboys and gather all you can find. Better go by Brown's camp first and tell him, so his men won't have an excuse for attacking you."

We rode to Brown's camp. "Captain Ross sent us to gather some strays below the reserve and said to check in with you first," I told him. Having a chance to use his authority seemed to please him.

"Go ahead. I'll send one of the boys to alert the patrol in that area."

We rode down the river and combed the brush along both sides, rounding up nearly three hundred cows and calves. That meant we had nearly eight hundred head on the reserve. There were at least seven hundred more still missing, but most of them probably had already been stolen.

The Major wrote from the Clear Fork that Baylor was trying to round up men to attack us on the way north. "We have nothing to fear from him. Right now our worst enemy is probably John Henry Brown, for he's working for Runnels' re-election. I hear he intends to herd us and the troops all the way to the Red. It appears from his orders that Runnels is determined to give us a practical demonstration of his secession principles by making war on the United States forces. His endorsing Baylor's and Nelson's treason has complicated matters on our frontier ten times worse than Baylor alone did." Runnels' action, he added, had made it necessary to recall Van Dorn's cavalry just when they were making some headway against the Comanches. Runnels would, by his policy, the Major predicted, cause the breakup of the whole frontier. The Democrats had renominated him for governor, but Houston was running as an independent. "I have but one consolation, which is that Sam Houston will get almost a unanimous vote on the frontier and beat Runnels handily."

I'd had few chances to see Taka or even to think about the fact that she and the others would soon be leaving, never to return. Tosche and his Tonkawa cowboys were busy circling the reservation every day to prevent the cattle from straying off it, so I didn't see much of him. There were armed white men lurking around the reserve, and though some of them were Brown's rangers, others were probably Baylor men or rustlers, and I was worried they might kill Tosche.

Whenever I passed near the Tonkawa village I rode in and looked for Taka, but saw her only once. I gave her the signal, then rode down the trail and waited. I was taking a message to Ah-ha-dot, but that could wait.

She soon caught up with me and we headed for the spring and spread her robe on the ground. We clung to each other desperately for a few minutes. Later we lay back and watched a hawk circling overhead. It seemed like a peaceful time, but that was sure deceiving.

"Taka, the most important thing right now is getting all of you safely out of Texas before anything else happens."

"I know. Then I'll be far away and never see you again." A tear ran from the corner of her eye.

"No, that's not true. I'll have to come back here for a while, but I aim to see you again. I haven't figured it out yet, but one day I'll come for you.

It may be a year or two before I have my own ranch, but when I do I'm going to carry you off with me."

She smiled at that and kissed me. "That's what I wanted to hear. When you come I'll be ready." We clung to each other and made love again, then parted. I meant what I said about carrying her off.

The last week of July we made final preparations for the trip north. The eighty Mexican carts and wagons the Major had contracted for had arrived, and the Indians were gradually filling them with their possessions. A lot of them had no ponies because of Comanche raids, so those who had none and couldn't ride on one of the wagons would have to walk.

One of Brown's officers came by the agency and watched the preparations. " 'Bout ready to head out?" he asked Captain Ross.

"Far from it."

The man hung around awhile, then left. "If Brown thinks I'll tell him when we're goin' to leave so he can ride herd on us he's dead wrong," the Captain said.

The Major returned from Clear Fork. "They're about ready to move," he said. "They're missing a lot of stock, probably fifteen thousand dollars' worth. I've hired Ashley Marlin and John Battory to round up all of the strays they can find so we can sell them for the Indians when we get back."

"We're missin' a lot more than that," the Captain replied. "I figure we can put in a claim for them later."

The Major nodded. "Twiggs has ordered Major Thomas to accompany us with two companies of cavalry and one of infantry. Captain Gilbert will accompany Leeper and the Comanches."

In a heavy rain we all moved to a temporary camp on Scott Creek on the last day of July. Tosche and his Tonkawa cowboys brought the cattle herd and took turns guarding it all night.

"Not an auspicious beginning," the Major remarked, looking up at the dark clouds. "So far nothing much has favored these Indians. Like us, they're in the hands of Providence, and there's not much we can do but accept what comes."

"The greatest thing that ever happened to them is having you looking after them," Captain Ross replied. "But for you there wouldn't be many of them left. And look what it has cost you."

"It has been my destiny, I guess, to sacrifice myself for others. I wonder how much longer that will last."

TEN

Soon after daybreak the next morning Major Thomas and his troops slogged up the muddy road to the Indian camp. He and the Major talked briefly, then the march began. The women and children cried and the dogs howled, while the men were silent and impassive. It was so sad I felt like joining in the wailing. They'd done their best to be good citizens of Texas—no one could have tried harder or done better. They'd risked their lives fighting Comanches, and this was their reward. Seeing Taka and Tosche leaving made a lump rise in my throat.

The cavalry led the way, followed by the Major, Captain Ross, and a few others. Next came the Indians, and the eighty wagons and Mexican carts that Peter Ross had leased. Then came the infantry; Tosche and his cowboys brought up the rear with the cattle. When we got to open country, people and wagons spread out in a long line traveling abreast. In the August heat no one moved very fast; the animals just plodded along listlessly.

We traveled about ten miles to Judge Harmanson's ranch on Salt Creek, then made camp. The Major opened the polls there so all of the agency men and teamsters could vote absentee; I sure hoped every vote would be for Sam Houston. I rode through the camp hoping to see Taka alone, but she was with White Buffalo and his other wife. She gave me a quick smile, but we had no chance to speak. In the morning we headed for Cottonwood Spring, but when we got there all we saw were a few pools of brackish water—the spring was dry.

"The next water is the West Fork of the Trinity," Captain Ross reminded the Major.

"We'd best push on, then." We kept on traveling, although it was twenty-one miles from the Judge's ranch to the West Fork, a long haul for both cattle and teams, but we made it by dark. The following day it was just as far to the Little Wichita, but a cool rain in the afternoon gave us and the animals some relief. The Major looked over the cattle and teams —most stood with drooping heads. He announced that we'd lay over a day to rest, and that was welcome news to all.

"I'm sure by now Brown is on our trail," the Major remarked early the next morning. "I wish we knew how close he is, and if Baylor is out there somewhere. He bragged he'd attack us on the way, but after his fiasco at the agency I doubt many will follow him. They have a pretty good idea what would happen if they attacked us."

"Brown probably started after us as soon as he discovered we were gone," the Captain replied. "That may have delayed him a day or two. We need to know who's following us and how close they are, but we don't dare let any of the Indians out of sight of the column. Those men would like any excuse for killing a few friendly Indians."

"Tosche taught me to get around like a Tonkawa scout," I told them. "He even said I was almost as good as one of them. Let me check on them."

The Major and Captain Ross looked at each other.

"Brown knows me," I added, "and I don't think I'd be in any danger if I ran into his party. But I know I can avoid that, and I'll sure steer clear of any Baylor men."

"Go ahead, Chip," the Major said, "but don't take any unnecessary chances. Baylor's crowd would likely shoot you on sight, and I wouldn't trust some of that Brown bunch very far. Or him, for that matter."

I put some biscuits and dried beef in my saddlebags, then rolled up my blankets and tied them back of my saddle. When I rode past the Indian camp Taka saw me and walked toward me.

"Where are you going?" She looked worried, like she thought maybe I was leaving.

"To see if any men are following us." She looked relieved for a moment, then frowned.

"Watch out for them. I don't want anything to happen to you." She smiled, a bit sadly.

"I'll be all right. After all, Tosche taught me." She smiled happily at that.

I followed ravines and stayed in trees wherever I could, watching my pony's ears for signs that he heard or smelled strangers. Even so we made good time, and by late afternoon I was back at the West Fork of the Trinity. I tied my pony out of sight, climbed the highest hill, and watched the trail we'd followed from Fort Belknap.

A large party of horsemen appeared just before sundown, riding at a walk. I watched them ford the river and set up camp, but I was too far away to recognize anyone, so I wasn't sure if it was Brown's company or Baylor's. I returned to my pony and rode to about a quarter of a mile from their camp and tied him in a clump of red oaks. Then I stealthily approached the camp on foot. They had a big fire going and they hadn't posted any guards, so I crawled up to where I could see and hear them.

"If we wasn't gettin' paid for this I'd damn sure head for home," one said. "Why are we follerin' 'em Injuns anyways?"

"I aim to see to it they get outa Texas," Brown replied. "Major Neighbors is a Houston man, no friend of the governor. I'd like to catch him or them Indians doin' something that would cost Houston votes. Otherwise the governor's in big trouble. Anyway, I want to see Texas rid of the lot of 'em. That's what we're gettin' paid for."

"We ain't gittin' paid to be killed by no damn Injuns. I heard what happened to Baylor's army," another remarked, and that ended the palaver.

I slipped away and rode upriver a mile, hobbled my pony so he could graze, then rolled up in my blankets. An hour before dawn I ate a biscuit and some dried beef, wishing I had a tin cup of Arbuckle's coffee to wash it down. Then I saddled my pony and headed north. I caught up with the column at Frog Pond, where they'd made camp though it was only midafternoon.

"Brown's men are on our trail, but they're not travelin' much faster than we are," I told the Major and Captain Ross. "From what I heard 'em say they don't want to get much closer to us, at least his men don't. I figure they'll keep a safe distance from us. I didn't see any sign of Baylor."

"You're probably right about them not wanting to get close to us. They know if they bother us the troops and Indians will make it hot for them," the Major said.

They'd stopped at Frog Pond because there was no good water between it and the Red River. "Tomorrow's the Sabbath," the Major said. "It should be a day of rest, but we can do our resting when we get across the Red, out of Texas. Right now that must come first, for the sake of the Indians."

The next afternoon we camped at a spring near the Red and a couple of miles below the mouth of the Big Wichita. A few hours after we arrived Colonel Leeper, Captain Gilbert's infantry company, and Ketumse's Comanches appeared and set up camp.

Luckily for us the Red was low, so we forded it the next morning at Major Steen's crossing, near where we'd camped. Even though the river was fairly low it still took half a day to get all of the wagons and people and cattle across. When all were over, the Major sat on his horse and gazed back at the land we'd just left.

"We have this day crossed all Indians out the heathen land of Texas and we're now out of the country of the Philistines," he said. His voice sounded hollow and it seemed like he was talking to someone we couldn't see. My skin prickled as I listened. He looked at Peter and Robert Ross and me. "If you boys want a good description of our exodus from Texas," he told us, "read the Bible where the children of Israel crossed the Red Sea. You will find that we've had about the same show except our enemies didn't follow us to the Red River." His expression turned grim. "If they had, I suspect that our Indians would have sent them back without the interposition of Divine Providence."

We set up camp near a stream a few miles from the Red to rest for the afternoon. One of Brown's men forded the river and rode up to Major Thomas, who was talking to Captain Ross.

"Captain Brown said to tell you that when we were at Cottonwood Spring Patrick Murphy reported that the Indians had stolen five of his horses. Captain Brown protests your leaving without informing him and allowing him to look for stock belonging to private citizens."

Major Thomas coolly replied that Major Neighbors and Captain Ross were in the service of the U.S. government, not the state of Texas. They had, furthermore, given citizens every opportunity to look for their stock before we left the reservation, and all were satisfied that none of their animals was with those of the Indians. "Once we commenced our march," he added, "no Indian left the column. If Murphy's horses are missing, they must have strayed or been stolen by white thieves. You may so inform Captain Brown." The man left.

The Major sent a party of Caddos to alert Samuel Blain at the Wichita Agency that we were out of Texas and would soon arrive. When we traveled on, Captain Ross had scouts out in all directions, for we were now likely to run across Comanches, Kiowas, or even Kickapoos. The following day we were overtaken by a party of express riders from Fort Belknap with a message for Major Thomas.

He read the dispatch and frowned. "General Twiggs orders me to return at once with the cavalry," he told the Major. "The infantry companies are to remain until you reach your destination, then return immediately. I don't understand why he didn't order the infantry back instead of us. Since your scouts have seen Indian sign I'll chance staying one more day, but then I'll have to leave you. Unfortunately, it seems you may not be much safer here than in Texas."

"Knowing the Comanches and Kiowas hate these Indians," the Major replied, "I'm also surprised that he'd cut us loose like this. I'd feel a whole lot safer if you were with us." Major Thomas just shook his head, for there was nothing more he could do for us.

We rode on the next day and camped, and in the morning unhappily watched the cavalry trot away. When we reached the Wichita Agency a few days later we learned why the Caddo messengers had failed to return. They'd been surrounded by a big Kiowa war party. After threatening to kill them, the Kiowas just took their ponies and let them go. Even though we were in danger of attack, the infantry had to leave us and march back to Fort Belknap.

After we'd rested a few days, the Major, Captain Ross, and several others of us, along with the chiefs and headmen, set out to select locations for the different villages in the area the Major had selected earlier, a three days' ride or more away. When I saw White Buffalo in the party I wished I'd stayed behind, for I'd been able to see Taka alone only once and I knew we'd soon be on our way back to Texas.

We traveled slowly the first day and a half, when the scouts reported a lot of Comanche sign around us, but saw that they had moved on. The Major looked thoughtful. "I should have asked Blain to request Major Emory to set up a base camp near our villages until the army finishes building Fort Cobb. Otherwise they'll likely be exposed to constant harassment."

I saw my chance. "I'll take a message to Mr. Blain," I said. The Major wrote a note to Blain, tore out the leaf, and handed it to me. I folded it and put it in my shirt pocket, trying to conceal how eager I was to go.

"Thanks, Chip. I should have thought of this before. Sorry to trouble you. For heaven's sake, watch out for Comanches."

"Yes, sir. In a few hours it'll be dark and I figure my pony can get there by morning. No danger of running into Comanches at night."

My pony trotted and loped, and we made good time, reaching the Wichita Agency around sunup. I delivered the note to Blain, ate breakfast at the agency, then rode through the Indian camp until I saw Taka. She smiled broadly when she saw me and hurried after her mare. I rode down toward the creek with a heavy growth of timber along its banks, where Taka caught up with me. We tied our ponies where they could graze, spread out her robe, and sat on it. I crushed her in my arms.

"Let's meet here every day until they get back," I said. She smiled and kissed me.

"I can't bear the thought of not seeing you," she whispered. "If you don't come back I'll just die."

"I'll come back for sure," I promised. "I don't know how or when, but I'll find a way as soon as I can and come for you. Life without you is empty." She snuggled happily in my arms. Even though I'd ridden all night to get there, being with her gave me new life.

We had seven glorious days together before the Major's party returned. "You're sure you can stand being all alone with me on a ranch far from your people?" I asked her while we rested. She smiled happily and threw her arms around me.

"Maybe we won't always be alone," she whispered. I wondered right then if I'd been wise to return early, for after a week with her I didn't see how I could bear not seeing her every day.

Some of the men who came with us had made plans to stay with the Indians. John Shirley was setting up a trading post of his own and he would also serve the government as an interpreter. Now I wondered why I hadn't drawn my pay and gotten some appointment for myself. But that would have been foolish and probably would have led to trouble with White Buffalo. Sturm told me he intended to stay with Deer Woman and the Caddos, but his situation was different.

"I want to keep in touch with Tosche and Taka," I told him. "I'll write you when there's news of either of them," he assured me. "And you can send me any message for them and I'll see that they get it."

The Major formally turned the Indians over to Agent Blain. "I am now at last free of government service and the cares of the Indians, and leave them in good hands," he told us. "I've sent in my resignation as superintendent, to take effect as soon as my accounts are settled. If I live to get home and keep my senses I will never hold another Indian appointment." He stood there a moment, hat in hand, his white hair blowing in the wind, his lips quivering. He looked weary and careworn. He cleared his throat.

"I guess I'm just plain tired and miss my family," he continued. "I'd like an appointment as agency farmer and to move my family here. Then I could help these people become self-supporting."

There were only twenty of us in the party returning to Texas, including the Major, Captain Ross, his sons Peter and Robert, his son-in-law Frank Harris, Colonel Leeper, and some Tejano and Anglo employees. We had one wagon and two army ambulances.

"Luckily, most of us are well armed," the Captain said. "If a big war party spots us we'll have the scrap of our lives, and maybe our last one. I can't see how Twiggs could leave us without at least a cavalry troop to see that we made it back."

Most of us had a Sharps carbine and a Navy .36 Colt like the Second Cavalry used, but a few had only shotguns. We weren't hunting birds, but shotguns were good at close range if loaded with buckshot.

It might have been better if we'd slipped away at night, for taking leave of the Indians was the saddest thing I'd ever seen. They were devoted to both the Major and Captain Ross, and the two men shook hands with all the chiefs and warriors. A woman started wailing, and that sound spread quickly through the whole crowd, gradually rising in intensity until the air seemed to vibrate. When the Major shook hands with Plácido the old chief cried uncontrollably. Some of the men threw themselves to the ground with grief, while others clung to the Major's clothing and tried to keep him from leaving. I had a big lump in my throat when Tosche came to shake hands with me.

"Taka and I will both miss you," he said. "You'll come back one day. I know."

"I'll come back, my friend. We'll meet again for sure."

We rode off to the sound of wailing, and I still imagined I could hear it when we were miles away. There was a lot of clearing of throats as we rode, and everyone looked straight ahead. Finally Captain Ross called to me.

"You and Peter ride ahead and keep your eyes peeled for Indian sign," he said hoarsely. "Stay in sight of us and watch out you don't stumble into a trap."

Peter and I rode ahead, on opposite sides of the trail. On the second day just before noon I spotted pony tracks and knew that Indians had been watching us. I signaled to Captain Ross, and he rode up to me.

"A rider was watching us from the knoll over there," I told him. "He must have left just as we came in sight, for the tracks are fresh. They're probably watching us right now."

"I don't like the looks of it," Captain Ross said. When we stopped at noon he ordered the teamsters to unhitch their mule teams. "Tie them to the wagons and feed them some corn," he told them. "The Indians would rather steal mules than horses. Tie the horses with short ropes where the grass is good and guard them. Don't take your eyes off the animals."

Even with these precautions, several Indians were able to crawl through the tall grass and to untie Colonel Leeper's fine horse and two others before the guards saw them and shouted a warning. Colonel Leeper, with shotgun in hand, ran to save his horse but was shot in the stomach, leg, and wrist while an Indian leaped on his horse and dashed away. Other Indians ran up to finish Leeper off, but one of the Tejano hands rushed to his rescue and saved his life. More Indians galloped up and shot at us.

Peter Ross and I slipped into a ravine and ran until we got behind the Indians and opened fire on them with our Colts. That panicked them and the survivors fled, leaving a number dead on the ground. It happened so fast we didn't have time to think about what we were doing or to know for sure if either of us had hit any of the Indians; the rest of our party was also shooting at them.

"That one I shot don't look like any Indian I ever saw," Frank Harris remarked. "His hair is too short. I'm going to wash the paint off his face and see if he isn't an old acquaintance of ours." He got a wet rag and scrubbed some of the paint off. Sure enough the dead Indian was a red-haired white man. None of us recognized him, but we figured he must have been the one who directed the killing of the Masons and Camerons. Those Indians and renegade whites had badly wounded Colonel Leeper and stolen three horses, but seven of them had been on their last raid. We figured we'd come out lucky not to lose anyone.

The Captain dressed Leeper's wounds and we lifted him into one of the army ambulances and moved on. We camped that night in a ravine off the trail and took turns guarding the stock. A cold rain fell, but we didn't try to build a fire, for the smoke might bring us more visitors. Leeper suffered terribly, but there was little anyone could do to ease his pain.

When we reached the Red it was flooding over its banks, so we had to build a raft of cottonwood logs to get the wagon and ambulances and people across, and this took most of a day. The Little Wichita and other streams were also high, so we didn't make good time.

The Brazos was also at flood stage when we reached it late on the afternoon of September 13. The Major had planned to go to Camp Cooper, but we couldn't cross the river, so we made camp. A farmer rode by in a wagon and stopped when he recognized the Major.

"I hope you ain't figurin' on goin' into Belknap, sir," he said to the Major. "Most folks there will be glad to see you, but there're a few bad characters around and they've threatened your life if you ever return. Reckon they're afraid of bein' arrested. I wouldn't go there at all if I was you."

"Thanks," the Major replied. "I'll keep that in mind."

Word got around fast that the Major had returned after we took Colonel Leeper to the army hospital at Fort Belknap next morning.

"What are your plans?" Major Thomas asked.

"I've got to spend a few hours at the county clerk's office settling accounts," the Major replied.

"Let me assign a few men as an escort. Your life may be in danger. The men you left to guard the agency have been threatened more than once."

"No, thanks. I don't think there's any need of that."

Major Thomas looked like he was going to insist, but he glanced at the Captain and me, then shrugged and left. Captain Ross and I accompanied the Major to the county clerk's office, intending to keep watch over him, but we figured wrong.

"You two check on the government property at the agency and see that it's secure and that the men are still guarding it. I should be through here by the time you get back."

The Captain and I looked at each other helplessly. "Come on, Chip, we'd best get moving," the Captain said. "I don't like leavin' him alone here for one minute. We better be back here by the time he finishes." We headed for the agency at a lope. Several men were watching us leave town, and that didn't make me feel any better.

It took us nearly an hour to get to the agency, and we spent about fifteen minutes making a hasty inspection and letting our ponies rest. "Every time there's a raid anywhere around here someone accuses us of bein' responsible for it," Dykes said. We didn't have anything comforting to say about that.

We turned our ponies toward Belknap at a fast lope, both of us staring grimly ahead. Just as we hit the edge of the little town we heard a shotgun blast in the distance and saw men running toward a figure in a black coat lying in the street.

"My God!" Captain Ross exclaimed. "It's the Major!" We were too far away to recognize him—the Captain just sensed somehow that it was the Major. Unfortunately, he was right.

I was even more stunned than when I saw Choctaw Tom's people lying riddled in their blankets. Sheriff Ed Woolfforth was leaning over the Major trying to talk to him when we got there, but it was too late for that. County Clerk Bill Burkett and a man named McKay ran up, both white-faced.

"How did this happen?" the sheriff asked.

"He'd finished settling his accounts," Burkett stammered. "Then he said, 'I am now free of all responsibility to the government at last, and I'm going to return to my wife and children. I'll never leave them again until death takes me. My second son will soon be three months old, and I haven't even seen him. I'd give everything I own to be with them this minute.'

"Then he and McKay left to visit Colonel Leeper at the fort. A minute or two later McKay ran in shouting that Major Neighbors had been killed."

The sheriff turned to McKay.

"We hadn't gone fifty paces when Patrick Murphy stepped around the corner of that house with his gun in his hand." He pointed to the house next to the one where the Major was lying. " 'Neighbors,' Murphy said, 'I understand that you said I'm a horse thief. Is that so?' " McKay explained.

" 'No, sir, I never did,' the Major replied. Just then Ed Cornett stepped from behind this chimney here with a double-barreled shotgun. He held it close to the Major's back and fired both barrels. The Major said, 'Oh, Lord,' and fell to the ground. Then Cornett and Murphy mounted their horses and galloped out of town."

There's no way to describe my feeling of emptiness when I saw the Major lying there, his back riddled with buckshot. He'd wondered when he'd get to see his new son. Now he never would. Then I thought of that yellow-bellied Ed Cornett and his sneaky friend Murphy, and burned with rage. If it was the last thing I ever did I'd see that they got what they deserved.

The sheriff assembled a coroner's jury and held an inquest; McKay repeated what he'd said before. No matter how many times I heard it, I still couldn't believe it had happened to the Major.

"I'll write Mrs. Neighbors and tell her," Burkett told the Captain.

"Thanks. I don't think I could bear to tell her."

When he heard about it Major Thomas came at once to see Captain Ross. "While you're here I insist that all of you stay at the fort," he said, "and that you have an army escort whenever you leave it. I wish I hadn't let Major Neighbors talk me out of giving him an escort, but I thought you two would be with him. You're still a government official, and it's my duty to protect you."

An army ambulance carried the Major's body to the fort, and we silently followed. Major Thomas sent some soldiers to our camp to bring the rest of our party and our gear to the fort. While waiting for them I wrote Sturm a letter telling him the bad news.

The next day the Major was given a military funeral. After they lowered him into the grave and fired several volleys over it I heard uncontrollable sobbing, and some of it came from me.

It was lucky for us we stayed at the fort. Some Baylorites held a meeting in Belknap, threatening to kill the rest of us just because we'd worked on the reservations. The ones who knew they were likely to be indicted for crimes against the Indians wanted all of us out of the way so we couldn't testify against them. But from what we heard no one was willing to join them in any more killings.

I saw Lieutenant Burnet at the fort a few days later. "The Baylor party finally murdered Major Neighbors like they wanted to," he said. "I suppose they still have plans to kill Captain Ross and maybe you and others." I figured he was right about that.

"I've felt guilty at times for the part I took against these people," Burnet continued, "but this murder puts it beyond all question. My only regret is that I didn't go ahead and wipe them all out at Marlin's."

The Dallas *Herald* reported the murder. "Thus has the spirit of human envy and hatred found its fruition," the editor wrote, "not alone in the woes of unoffending Indians, but also in the untimely taking of as gallant a knight as any who ever balanced a lance or drew a broadsword in behalf of the oppressed." That, I thought, was a fitting epitaph for the Major.

ELEVEN

We stayed at the fort, waiting for things to quiet down. The only good news was that Sam Houston had beaten Runnels by nine thousand votes; I wished the Major could have known that. It caused a lot of speculating, for Runnels was an out and out secessionist while Houston was a staunch Union man.

"You figure that Houston's winnin' means most Texans are against seceding?" I asked Captain Ross.

"I suspect that many Texans, and Southerners, too, for that matter, don't want to leave the Union, but now that the Whigs have folded there's no organized support for the Union here or anywhere in the South. That's what makes it look like most folks favor secession."

"How do you account for Houston's victory?"

"Sam's still popular and trusted, and folks haven't forgotten San Jacinto. That's part of it. Add to that the fact that the Democrats didn't help Runnels much and the frontier was solid against him for not protecting settlers. But I doubt that secession figured in it. We'll know soon."

Even after I no longer worked for the Indian service I stayed on at the fort, working for sutler J. T. Ward. I hadn't drawn much of my salary and wasn't even sure how much I had coming. The Major had raised my pay to $25 a month in January '58—I felt rich when I collected just over $1,100. The sutler kept it locked up for me. Now if I could find some way to get Taka away from the reservation, I was all set.

A letter from Sturm came one day. When he got mine and told the Indians about the Major, they wailed for a week. He had a hard time keeping them from sending a revenge party. "Let me know what they do about Cornett and Murphy," he added. "Both of them deserve to hang."

We waited to hear that Sheriff Woolfforth had arrested Ed Cornett, for he swore he'd bring him in, even though the grand jury hadn't met to indict him for murder. Cornett was lying low, and the sheriff couldn't find him. In June Cornett had married Margaret Murphy, so he and Patrick Murphy were in-laws. Folks figured that Cornett was hiding somewhere near Belknap and the Murphys were keeping him in grub. I was impatient to run off with Taka, but I couldn't even think much about that while Cornett was still on the loose. I could never leave until the score had been settled.

One night in November Murphy's stage station was burned to the ground. Half a dozen horses and Margaret Cornett disappeared the same night, so everyone figured it was the work of Indians. A party of men followed the trail of the thieves a day or two but couldn't overtake them. Some in the party, no doubt Baylor men, swore the raiders were Caddos and maybe Anadarkos. I talked to A. J. Woolfolk, who'd been with the posse.

"Do you really think they were Caddos?" I asked.

"Not a chance of it. Those men were riding shod horses; they weren't even Indians. If you want my opinion, it was a put-up job and she went along by choice. Probably couldn't stand bein' hitched to that blustering, murdering drunkard."

A man named Page had a ruckus with a couple of hard characters near the Clear Fork and they left him where he fell. A cavalry patrol came upon his body the next day and found a letter in his coat pocket. They sent it to Major Thomas, who read it and showed it to Captain Ross. The Captain read it and handed it to me.

"Dear Chum," it began.

"Yours of the 25th ult. has been duly received and we are happy to know your party succeeded so well in getting the last drove of horses, etc., from Belknap and that you so completely fixed the affair on the Indians; but I am now becoming apprehensive, as the animals or the proceeds have not come to hand or been heard from in this quarter; there are traitors in camp; be careful. I am sorry to hear that Gabb Y. and Wooten had a difficulty, or rather falling out; and I think if you can quietly get rid of them both, it would be all the better, as one talks too much and the other is liable to get drunk and make disclosures that would implicate themselves and us. Neither have I much confidence in Wms; he acted badly in Kansas you know; also Gary and the five others you spoke of in your last letter. I think *our friend near Camp Cooper* is asking too much compensation for the burning down of his stable, particularly as he has not succeeded in making that haul on Camp Cooper; let me know if they have moved to the Stone Ranch above the latter place yet. I am a little afraid to take in friend W——'s brother-in-law as they were kind of Indian men heretofore; be careful in informing me on this last as we are anxious to dispatch the next party by that way. Also inform me if the *Captain* has as yet gotten back from Austin, and what he has done towards raising the Regiment of Rangers, which is of all importance to us. Should he succeed in getting them up, you will of course instruct him when we are likely to pass, that he may know in what quarter not to scout with his rangers.

"I was not aware that you and Murphy was on bad terms when we concocted the arrangement in regard to his sister, or I would not have had anything to do with it, as I fear it will end badly should he come to find out; for it will not do to let him, or even offer to take him, among our party as I think he has too much mistaken pride, and in that case it will answer a better part to keep him in ignorance. Tell our friend of the *Whiteman,* above all things, to keep up the Indian excitement, as it must be kept up until spring for there cannot be much done this bad weather; also acquaint our friends of Belknap particularly that it will be necessary to keep the matter up; even if we have to kill or shoot at some fellow there; there are a great many emigrants passing through here on their way to Texas. It will be well to keep them scared out of the upper part of the state as much as possible; but such as do come, keep your eye on them, as they have some excellent mules and horses. Try and encourage our friends to play them that you spoke of to us; it will help to keep the excitement up. This is actually necessary as we have got to go further down the country to get a better stock of animals, as the last drove were inferior. Everything is quiet here at the present except some little grumbling about the last division, as some you know got too much, but this was policy, as for the others, we can scare them into terms. Yours, etc., etc., O. L. M.

"N. B. Tell friend Howell that the parties here are not agreed to enter on his proposals regarding the cattle matter, as the drive is too far and some men cannot be trusted; I think it best to confine our operations this winter to horses etc., etc., I send you this by Page, our faithful guide, as he is at present acquainted with your whereabouts, and particularly as he has a small matter to settle with a couple of fellows on the Clear Fork; and I have told him that you would render all the assistance possible."

"What do you think of it?" Major Thomas asked us.

"There's a big horse-stealing ring like we all figured," the Captain replied, reaching for the letter and reading it again, "and they have local help in stealing stock and blaming it on the Indians. I wonder who their friend near Camp Cooper is, and who is trying to raise a regiment of rangers. Obviously he's in cahoots with them. The Stone Ranch belongs to Givens, unless he sold it." He read some more.

"We know who Murphy is, but not who he's on bad terms with. That's probably most everyone who knows him. It's clear they helped his sister get away. Their friend of *The White Man* has to be Hamner."

"That's about what I reckoned," Major Thomas said.

I told them what Woolfolk had said about the tracks of shod horses when Margaret Cornett disappeared.

"That figures," Captain Ross said.

The Commissioner of Indian Affairs wrote asking the Captain to go to San Antonio and complete settling the Major's accounts. I hated to see him go, for I was afraid he might never come to the Belknap area again, even though he had a few cattle on the range.

"Chip," he said when we shook hands, "don't ever let your guard down as long as you stay around here. It's possible some of those skunks will try to bushwhack you. I'll be back to check on my cattle now and then until I sell them, so we'll meet again."

In the early fall large numbers of Comanches and Kiowas camped between the Arkansas and Canadian rivers, and sent big war parties to hit the frontier in many places south of us. They killed so many settlers and burned so many cabins that everyone living along the Llano gave up and left. Comanches and Kiowas destroyed a whole settlement about twenty-five miles from Fredericksburg. We soon felt their fury.

The Captain had been gone only a few days when the biggest Comanche party ever terrorized the Parker County folks and then swept into Palo Pinto County. Some figured there were at least a hundred and fifty warriors. They wiped out several families and carried off some children as well as all the saddle stock and mules they could find. They took their time, like they were daring the army or the settlers to attack them. It was like the big raids they used to make in Mexico, where they'd stay for months, helping themselves to whatever they wanted.

Major Thomas ordered Captain Bradfute to take three cavalry troops and try to rescue the children and recover the stolen stock. While the troops were assembling, I stood near the two officers.

"I wish we had some Tonkawa scouts," Major Thomas remarked. "They're invaluable when you're following Indian trails. That war party probably outnumbers you by two to one, and if you stumble into an ambush you'll have heavy casualties. Your only hope is to surprise them, and without Tonkawa scouts that won't be easy."

"I know, sir. I wish we had some scouts, too. We'll just have to be extra careful," Bradfute replied. "But that will slow us down."

"Sir, a Tonkawa scout trained me, and he said I can follow tracks and get around about as good as one of them," I told Major Thomas. He looked at me in surprise.

"How old are you, Chip?"

"I'm fixin' to turn twenty-three, sir."

"Good. You're hired. Get your gear and go with them."

The last we'd heard of the raiders was that they were moving slowly through Palo Pinto County, like they weren't afraid of anyone coming after them. All the families had forted up when they heard the raiders had hit Parker County.

"When they're ready to head for home they usually go through Baker's Gap," I told Captain Bradfute when we moved out. He nodded.

"Let's head there and see if we can surprise them," he said.

I led the way at a lope, for it was twenty miles or more to Baker's Gap. As we neared it I saw the tracks of maybe three hundred horses and knew we were too late. We pulled up and looked for signs of the Indians, but saw none. The cavalry horses stopped in their tracks, sides heaving, while the troopers waited.

"If they figured they might be followed they'd get the stock through the hills and come back," I told Captain Bradfute. "Not seeing any of them don't mean a thing."

"What had we best do?"

"I'll circle around and check. If they've gone on, I'll fire three shots and you can come on through."

It was hard going for my cow pony and took most of an hour to be sure the Comanches hadn't laid an ambush. They'd gone on, still figuring no one would dare follow such a big war party. I rode to the top of the gap and fired three shots. Pretty quick I heard the cavalry coming.

We followed the trail, and I could tell from the tracks the raiders still weren't in a hurry. Then I saw they'd killed several buffalo cows.

"They'll gorge themselves and sleep good tonight," I told Bradfute. "If I can locate their camp in time we should be able to surround it before morning. You follow their trail while I go on ahead. I'll come back as quick as I find it."

"Make sure they don't find you first," he warned me.

I hurried on a few miles as the sun neared the horizon. Ahead was a little valley I'd seen before, and a dozen spirals of smoke were rising from it. That was all I needed to know, so I headed back. It was dark when I met the cavalry. We ate hardtack and dried beef while the horses rested.

When it was time to move on, Captain Bradfute gave orders. "We must all be in position before daybreak, and without arousing them. At first light the bugler will sound 'charge,' and every man will cut loose on them. Don't anyone fire a shot before that." He gave the lieutenants and sergeants their special instructions.

We split up, half going to one side, half going to the other, and rode as quietly as we could, taking most of the night to get into position. I stayed with Captain Bradfute and his unit. As it began to grow light the troopers checked their Navy Colts and carbines, then at the Captain's signal, moved quietly to the rim of the valley.

When the sound of the bugle rang out in the early morning stillness, echoing and re-echoing across the valley, I remembered the campaign with Van Dorn. That bugle blast had really stirred my blood and put me in a mood for a scrap. I nearly joined the headlong charge down the slope but checked my pony in time.

My orders were to get the troops where they could attack, and then keep out of their way and let them do the fighting. If I saw a chance to run off the stolen horses and mules, that was all right. Otherwise, Captain Bradfute had told me, I was strictly a noncombatant, not paid to fight.

At the sound of the bugle the Comanches abandoned everything but their weapons and ran for their ponies. In a moment they were mounted and heading for the brush while the cavalry carbines barked and the warriors whooped their war cries. In the early morning mist and smoke it was hard to see what was going on, but it looked like the Indians were probing the line for a place to break through it. As the shots and sounds of pursuit grew fainter, I rode down the slope to where the stolen horses were milling around in fright, and started them back down the trail.

I'd just gotten them started when an arrow plowed a furrow in my right side. I pulled my carbine from the scabbard and slipped off the left side of my pony all in one motion, as another arrow whished over my head. Kneeling, I raised my carbine and looked, but saw nothing. "He's in that brush yonder," I heard a boy shout, and thought I recognized his voice.

Crouching, carbine ready, I moved slowly toward the brush, watching for any movement. I heard a rustling sound and another arrow sped over me. I fired three shots in that direction, then waited. I couldn't tell if I had gotten him or if he was playing possum. After maybe ten minutes I backed away, keeping my eyes in the brush. No more arrows, so I figured he was either dead or on his way to Comanche country.

I caught my pony and led him to where the boy was standing. He was Johnny Parsons, a ten-year-old towhead I'd gotten to know when he and his pa delivered oats and corn to the sutler. With him were three younger children, two girls and a boy, who cowered behind Johnny, afraid I was a Comanche.

"Hi, Johnny," I called. "Tell them it's all right."

He turned and talked to them, but they stared at me, wide-eyed. They were a pitiful sight, snatched from their folks by a lot of terrifying Comanches, and maybe having to watch as their mothers were raped and murdered. I noticed some roasted buffalo meat on sticks around the ashes of one of the campfires.

"I'll bet you're hungry," I said, pulling up four of the sticks. "Did they give you anything to eat?" Johnny shook his head.

I handed him the sticks and he gave one to each child. They really tore into that meat; I got a piece of meat and joined them. By then they'd concluded I wasn't a Comanche and relaxed a little, but they still glanced around, scared-like.

"How'd it happen?" I asked Johnny. "Did your folks, I mean the Indians . . . ?" There wasn't any good way to ask him if his folks were killed.

"I was in the field hoein' corn," he said. "When they came along I ran for the woods, but one snatched me up on his horse. I don't know about the folks." His voice quavered. The Parsons were good people, and I sure hoped they'd escaped.

It was about an hour before the cavalry returned. A couple of soldiers had stopped arrows, but they could still ride, and they all seemed to be feeling pretty good.

"We killed at least a dozen, and I don't know how many more are carryin' lead," Captain Bradfute told me. "We'd have done better if all the men had gotten into position before we attacked, but at least we punished them this time. I'd say you're about as helpful as a Tonk."

"Or maybe lucky," I said.

He looked around. "Where are the horses?"

"I shucked 'em down the trail. We'd better get after 'em before the Comanches try to recover 'em. But first, a Comanche shot a couple of arrows at me from over there." I pointed to the brush. "Nicked me here." I showed him the bloody tear in my shirt. "I fired a few shots where I figured he was hiding, but didn't go in to see if I got him."

"That was wise." He called a sergeant, who sent a squad of troopers to check. They cautiously approached the brush.. "Dead Comanche!" one shouted.

"That's one more that didn't get away," the Captain remarked.

When we got back to the fort Major Thomas sent word to the ranchers to come for their stock, and to the families or relatives of the children. I took Johnny Parsons up behind me and headed for his place, for I had to know about his folks. When we got there we saw nothing but the charred remains of the cabin and the swollen body of a black dog with an arrow in it.

"Shep!" Johnny called. "Come, Shep!"

"He can't hear you, Johnny. He's dead. I'm sure sorry."

We headed for the nearest neighbor, whose farm was down the road about a mile away. Behind me I heard Johnny's muffled sobs. There was smoke coming from the cabin chimney, so I loped my pony until we reached the yard. Johnny stayed on my pony, afraid of what he might learn. "Anybody home?" I called.

John Parsons came to the door. "Rachel!" he shouted. "It's Johnny! He's alive! He's alive!"

After they got through a tearful family reunion I told them about our fight with the Comanches and rescuing the children. Then they told me how they'd seen the Indians coming when their dog started barking wildly, and had hastily forted up with their neighbors, hoping Johnny would be able to hide. After the Indians had gone they went to the field and saw the pony tracks, and figured they'd never see Johnny again. Before I could leave I had to shake hands with everybody twice, and Johnny's mom kissed me on the cheek.

While we'd been away after the Comanches there'd been another meeting in Belknap. The Baylor men who called it claimed the raiders were former Brazos reserve Indians, and they tried to talk the crowd into going with them to kill the men guarding the agency, swearing they encouraged the Indians to get revenge. Even though men who'd seen the raiders swore they were Comanches, those Baylor men refused to admit it. That bunch still had it in for the army for protecting the Indians, but the ranchers were mighty happy to get their cow ponies back. And the families whose children we'd rescued couldn't have been more grateful.

That scrap with the Comanches ended the raids for a while, for they'd lost a bunch of warriors, and anyway the weather was bad. I rode on some cavalry patrols and did some scouting on my own without seeing any Indian sign. Cornett was still on the loose, and no one had seen him, except maybe the Murphys. Whenever I had time to myself I scouted the country around Belknap looking for him. There were lots of good hiding places, and it was sort of a hopeless task for one man, but I couldn't rest until he was found.

The slowdown in raids also gave me a chance to follow the newspapers and try to figure out where the country was heading. The thing that really got a lot of Southern editors pushing their pencils was John Brown's raid on the federal arsenal at Harper's Ferry in Virginia. The editors were already furious about what Northern abolitionists were saying about the South. Now Brown and other abolitionists had gone beyond insults in a harebrained attempt to arm the slaves. Nothing could have strengthened the secessionists' hand more than that. When Brown was hanged early in December there was a lot of rejoicing. The movement toward secession seemed stronger than ever.

In January '60 the papers mentioned a letter from the governor of South Carolina to Sam Houston inviting Texas to join other slave states in preparing for what he called an emergency. Houston sent the letter to the legislature along with reasons why seceding was a mistake. He also pleaded with the legislators to deny the right of secession and to reject the invitation to send delegates to the convention.

The state senate agreed to defend the Constitution, but maintained that freeing the slaves was unconstitutional and that all states had the right to leave the Union. The house took a more threatening stand. It upheld the right of any state to secede, vowed not to submit to Black Republican rule, and pledged to cooperate with other Southern states.

In February the raids broke out again, and a number of big war parties hit settlements many miles apart at the same time all along the frontier. It was more dangerous for frontier settlers than ever before, and a lot of families pulled up stakes and headed for safer country. They took everything they could load on their wagons, but they had to abandon a lot of their possessions along with their hopes. On one scout I stopped at a ranch in Young County near the Palo Pinto line and talked to the rancher, a man named Easton. He'd come to Texas with the Peters Colony folks; like most of them he was from one of the border states and had never owned a slave.

"With all the Indian troubles and talk of secession, I'm about convinced this is no place for us," he told me. "I'm thinking of packing up my family and heading for California before it's too late. I've got title to five thousand acres of some of the best grazing land I've ever seen—good grass, good water, and enough timber. I guess I should have sold it when there were still buyers. With so many leaving, we'll probably have to abandon it and lose everything."

I'd crossed his range before and knew what he said was true. He'd built a snug, double-log cabin with squared logs that fit tightly together, not like the ones built of round logs. A lot of those just slowed up the wind a bit as it blew between the logs where the chinks had fallen out. He'd also built a stable, sheds, a couple of round-pole corrals, and a horse pasture. I'd always admired his place—it was what a well-kept ranch should look like.

"If you decide to sell," I told him, "I'll be interested if I can meet your price."

He laughed, a dry, bitter laugh. "Thanks to the Comanches and the secessionists," he replied, "my price ain't near what this place is worth. Where can I find you?"

"I'm scouting for the army, and will be either at the fort or on patrol."

"You think you could raise some cash in a hurry? Won't do us any good to sell it on credit."

"Yes, sir. I'm sure of it."

"Good. That may help me make up my mind. I sure hate to part with this place, but no use stayin' and having the secessionists run me off."

I rode back to the fort, thinking about Easton's place. I sure didn't wish him any bad luck, but I liked his ranch as much as any I'd ever seen. If he decided to sell, I sure was ready to buy. Indian raids kept us so busy after that I soon forgot about it.

There were only two things men talked about in the spring of '60— Indian troubles and the April Democratic Party convention in Charleston, South Carolina, to nominate candidates for President and Vice President. If Texas seceded, that would mean the Second Cavalry would have to leave, and the frontier would be in even worse trouble. Near as I could tell there weren't many secessionists in our part of the frontier. I was only interested in what the grand jury was going to do about Cornett; I couldn't stand the thought of him still on the loose.

On one patrol Major Thomas came along in command of the troopers. We'd made a big swing around the area, and on the fourth day were heading back to Fort Belknap from the northwest when we crossed a fresh trail heading west. I looked over the tracks for a few minutes.

"There's about ten warriors driving forty to fifty horses," I reported to Major Thomas.

He looked dubious. "You sure it's not a big war party? That's what it looks like to me."

"Yes, sir, I'm sure. If we had time I'd show you how I know, but if we hope to catch 'em we'd best not waste any time. They're movin' pretty fast, which means there aren't enough of them to make a stand."

He ordered immediate pursuit, and we followed the tracks toward the Double Mountains of the upper Brazos. By mid-afternoon we could see their dust, and we gained steadily. When we got close they abandoned the stolen horses and whipped their ponies. Thomas looked at them with his binoculars.

"I've got to hand it to you," he said. "Either you really know how to read tracks or you're plain lucky. I count eleven."

The trail wound through a narrow pass between two rocky hills, and when Major Thomas and the leading troopers and I reached it we pulled up in a hurry. An old Comanche warrior had planted himself behind some rocks squarely in our way. He crouched there, bow strung and a fist full of arrows. He looked plenty fierce.

"Tell him to surrender. I don't want to kill him."

I called on the old warrior in Spanish, telling him he wouldn't be killed if he surrendered. His reply was a shower of arrows that came so fast it looked like a whole bunch of Comanches were shooting at us. He nicked Major Thomas in the ribs and winged a trooper in the shoulder before we got back out of range.

"I've heard the old ones throw themselves away so the others can escape," I told Major Thomas. "This is the first time I've seen it done."

"I'd heard the same thing, but I never wanted to see it for myself. I hate to kill the old fellow, but I guess there's no other way. He'd probably be disappointed now if we didn't." He nodded to the sergeant, who spread out his men and ordered them to fire. That old Comanche dodged around and kept sending arrows our way, so it took half an hour and about twenty shots to bring him down. But he'd done his job. The rest of his party were miles away and the sun would soon set. We recovered most of the stolen horses, but the raiders had escaped.

Because of the increased raiding, Governor Houston ordered ranger companies organized for the frontier, and the state furnished rifles to families who needed them. In March Houston authorized Colonel Middleton T. Johnson of Fort Worth to raise five ranger companies from McLennan, Dallas, Fannin, Collin, and Tarrant counties. Captain J. M. Smith recruited the Waco company, and Sul Ross was elected first lieutenant. The five companies all came to Fort Belknap in April. They were dressed in whatever they owned, and their guns ranged from squirrel rifles to double-barreled shotguns and Colt revolvers. Most were mounted on half-broken mustangs, and you couldn't tell by looking at them who were officers and who were privates. At Fort Belknap Captain Smith was elected lieutenant colonel of the regiment and Sul Ross replaced him as captain.

They made a lot of patrols and pursuits, and I visited Sul whenever we were both at the fort. "There's still a lot of hostility toward me because my father was Brazos agent," he told me. "We were following an Indian trail and stopped at a cabin to get a drink from the well. One of the men told her we were after Indians. 'Whose company is it?' she asked. 'Captain Ross of Waco,' the man replied. 'I wish the Injuns may scalp the last one o' you!' she screeched. It made no difference that we were there to protect her and others like her. The men just laughed at her, but that's what we face in many places."

Every paper I saw was full of political talk, mostly about abolition and secession. According to what I read, the Democratic convention was badly split—the slave state delegates refused to accept Stephen A. Douglas as candidate and walked out. Before either group took action, the Constitutional Union Party met at Baltimore and chose John Bell over Sam Houston, and a week later the Republicans nominated Abraham Lincoln. Except for Houston, these were all just names to me.

"I'm confused by all this, sir," I mentioned to Major Thomas. "What does it all mean?"

"It looks bad for the country and I fear our worst years are ahead. The Democrats have split into two, no, three, branches and can't agree on a candidate. The Republicans are a sectional party, so there won't be any party left that represents the whole nation. By their intransigence the Democrats might just allow Lincoln to win. He will anyway, if he carries all of the Northern states, for that would give him enough electoral votes." He paused.

"Even though the Republicans are a sectional party, their platform was astutely designed to contain something that appeals to every part of the country," he continued. "They really did a masterful job, and it's likely to pay off where it counts. Listen to this: their platform starts by reaffirming the principles of the Declaration of Independence. Who can quarrel with that? Next it upholds the Wilmot Proviso, which passed the House but not the Senate." He noticed that I looked a bit puzzled.

"The Proviso was to exclude slavery from land ceded by Mexico after the war," he explained. "The Republicans also have a plank that asserts the right of each state to control its domestic institutions. They support internal improvements, which should also appeal to everyone, a railroad to the Pacific, a homestead law, and a liberal immigration policy. The railroad and homestead law are aimed at the Midwest and California; the immigration policy is for those who want cheap labor. They also call for a protective tariff, and that will win votes in Pennsylvania and New Jersey. They deny the authority of Congress or a territorial legislature to legalize slavery in the territories, and the whole North will like that. I've got to hand it to them—even if the Democrats weren't split they offer nothing to the big states with the most electoral votes as long as they talk only of slavery and the right to secede." He stopped to catch his breath.

"Though Mr. Lincoln admits there's no legal way he could end slavery, everyone is convinced that's what he'll do, and I'm afraid they won't wait to see what happens. If there's a blowup between the North and South I suspect that most of the officers and men of this regiment will go with the South. Most of us are Southerners." He paused again and looked at me.

"You're wondering what I'll do in that case, aren't you?" I guess my expression gave me away, for that's exactly what I was curious about. I nodded.

"I'll probably do some soul-searching because I'm from Virginia, but I can't see regional loyalty or anything else taking precedence over the oath I took to support the Constitution of the United States."

The Young County grand jury finally met and indicted Cornett for the murder of Major Neighbors and for an attempt to kill his father-in-law, Dennis Murphy. His trial was set for May 24, but he didn't appear. A lawyer representing him claimed that he had been mentally deranged because Indians had abducted his wife. He knew the Major had defended the Indians, and that is why he killed him. That was nonsense, of course —his wife disappeared about six weeks after he'd murdered the Major.

Now that Cornett had been indicted for murder I had to find him. I tried to remember places where he might easily hide, places no one was likely to visit. I thought so much about it I had trouble sleeping at nights. Then one night it came to me—the place where Jake and Skinny hid the stolen ponies! If he'd been in cahoots with that bunch of horse thieves he'd know about that place.

The next morning I had to go out with a cavalry patrol but we got back at noon. I found Major Thomas in his office; as usual, he looked ready to stand inspection.

"Sir," I told him, "I think I've finally figured out where Cornett may be hiding. If you can spare me I'd sure like to see."

"I hope you're right," he replied, "but watch out for him. He's poison."

I ate with the soldiers, then headed for the lower end of the reserve, where Tosche and I had gone to check on the cattle, and got there late afternoon. On the trail along the creek I saw tracks of a shod horse that looked two or three days old. He probably had to meet Murphy once a week for grub. Seeing the tracks made me extra cautious.

Hiding my pony, I took my carbine and slipped along to the ridge where Jake had been hiding. I climbed it and crawled along until I could see the horse trap. There was a horse in it! Hopes rising, I slithered along until I could see the lean-to.

Cornett came out and looked at the setting sun. Then he got a jug and squatted down, taking a swig now and then as he got a fire going and started frying a slab of bacon. I raised my Sharps. His back was toward me—he'd shot the Major in the back, so that would be paying him back with his own coin. I drew a bead right between his shoulders, but couldn't bring myself even to cock my carbine.

When he finished eating it was almost dark. He caught his horse and tied it to a tree near the shanty. When he picked up the jug and went into the lean-to, I crawled closer and waited. Soon I heard him snoring.

I walked quietly to his horse. Scared, it snorted and pulled back a little. Stroking its neck, I calmed it, then untied the rope. Remembering what Tosche had told me about stealing horses from enemy camps, I led it a step or two at a time until we were out of hearing. I got my pony and led Cornett's horse toward Murphy's stage station, then turned it loose, figuring it would go on to where it had been fed before. By the time I got to the fort it was almost dawn, but I couldn't have slept anyway.

After breakfast I told Major Thomas, then rode to Belknap and stopped at Sheriff Woolfforth's office. "If you want to catch Ed Cornett I can lead you to him," I told him. "I turned his horse loose last night so he can't get far."

The sheriff hopped to his feet. "Let me round up a posse and we'll go get him."

He returned with five men, and I led the way to Cornett's camp. When we were half a mile from it we dismounted and went on foot. At the ridge we spread out in a circle to surround him.

"Ed Cornett!" the sheriff yelled. "Surrender in the name of the law."

We heard cursing and a bullet whined over the sheriff's head. I was about fifty yards from him and crawling forward. The others in the posse fired now and then, but none of them had a target. I crawled faster—I didn't want one of them to beat me to him.

Cornett was behind a big log, with his rifle over it. The other posse men weren't closing in very fast, but the sheriff got off a shot that knocked some bark off the log. I lay there with my carbine cocked and aimed where Cornett's head would appear. He held up his hat on a stick, but no one fired at it. Then he slowly raised up and aimed his rifle at the sheriff. I got his head square in my sights, then squeezed the trigger, and heard several more shots at the same time—close enough so no one could swear whose shot had done the trick. Cornett's rifle flew up and he went over backward, arms flailing. I knew I'd gotten him.

I waited, gun ready, while the sheriff cautiously approached the log. "You can come in, boys," he called. "He's one dead sumbich."

TWELVE

Right after word spread that the sheriff's posse had shot Ed Cornett, Patrick Murphy quit the country. I guess he figured he might be next, and that's what I had in mind, but things were happening so fast no one but me gave him much thought, what with Indian raids and talk of secession.

In June Colonel Johnson and his ranger regiment left for Camp Radziminski to launch their Comanche campaign. When they got there they found the whole prairie between the Arkansas and the Red burned over, so there was nothing for them to do but return empty-handed to Fort Belknap. There had been no letup in the raids while they were gone, which caused a lot of grumbling about the rangers as well as the army.

Baylor took advantage of the complaints to call a protest meeting in Weatherford. The crowd passed his resolution stating that the protection the state government gave frontier settlers "is a humbug and deserves the condemnation of all honest men." They claimed that Baylor and his men had shot all of the Indians killed in Texas since the rangers were organized. They blamed Governor Houston for the rangers' failure, calling him "an Indian lover who never had the most remote intention of punishing the Indians."

Baylor, who had become Hamner's partner in publishing *The White Man*, wrote that Colonel Johnson's ranger regiment was "the most stupendous sell ever practiced on a frontier people." Its failure, he said, "emboldened our enemies by demonstrating that the rangers are perfectly harmless." He swore that he and his followers would hang any ranger they caught. He blamed the Caddos and others on the new reservation for the raids, and tried to talk men into going with him to destroy them. After another raid in Palo Pinto County, Baylor wrote, "This is the way Houston protects the bleeding frontier." Since Houston was a Union man and Baylor a secessionist, it was his way of trying to discredit the governor.

All of the newspapers I saw were full of talk about secession, and the Texas editors were doing their best to whip up enthusiasm for it. "The great question that is agitating the public mind," one wrote, "is what shall be done if Lincoln is elected? The general sentiment in Texas is against submission to the Black Republicans. Such submission involves the loss of everything and will end in the prostration of the Southern states." Houston, Throckmorton, and others did their best to counteract the secessionist talk, but they were outnumbered and shouted down.

All of the talk of secession made my prospects for getting to Indian Territory seem pretty slim. The Comanches and Kiowas were on a rampage, and the only safe way to get there was with troops or rangers. I hated all the talk about secession and war. In the first place it was foolishness; in the second it was interfering with my plans.

By the end of October the whole state was in an uproar, for the election was November 8—everyone was waiting to see who'd be President. When the news finally came that Lincoln had won, the editors went wild. We hardly had time to think about it, for the Comanches figured it was a great time to depopulate the whole frontier.

Late in November Comanche Chief Peta Nocona led the biggest raid ever to hit Jack and Parker counties. They struck the settlers around Jacksborough first, killing most of the members of several families. Early the next morning a Jack County man headed for Weatherford to get help. He stopped at settler John Brown's cabin to warn him that Comanches were coming.

Brown gave him his fastest horse, then saddled another so he could alert his neighbors. Before he mounted he asked his wife if she'd read the paper that came from Dallas the previous afternoon, and if there was any news about the South.

"Yes," she replied. "It says that South Carolina is getting ready to secede."

"Our country is ruined, then," Brown said. "I wouldn't turn in my tracks between life and death." He mounted and rode off without his gun, while his worried wife watched him. Indians soon approached the cabin. Mrs. Brown leveled a rifle out the window. The Comanches saw the gun and rode on.

Brown didn't return that night, and it snowed for a few hours. In the morning a search party found his body half a mile from his cabin, riddled with arrows and covered with snow.

The Peta Nocona war party struck Parker County next. Several of them rode up to the Shermans' cabin on Rock Creek as the family was eating supper. Scowling warriors entered the cabin and ordered the family to "vamoose." The terrified Shermans started on foot for a neighbor's house, but the Indians soon followed them. Mrs. Sherman, who was with child, clung to her husband, but a big warrior grabbed her by the hair and dragged her back to the cabin. Sherman tried to follow, but several Comanches threatened to run him through with their lances.

After the Indians left, Sherman and his neighbors hurried through the rain to search for his wife. As they approached the cabin they saw that the Comanches had set fire to it, but the rain had kept it from burning. Inside they found the body of Mrs. Sherman—raped, stabbed to death, and scalped. The only thing missing from the cabin was her Bible.

This killing shocked folks as much as the murders of the Masons and Camerons. Two days after news of the brutal slaying reached Palo Pinto there was a mile-long line of wagons filled with frightened families leaving the county. Still others were preparing to flee, and families who were determined to remain began building cabins and stockades where a bunch of them could fort up together. They figured that when things were quiet they could slip out and look after their farms and stock.

Immediately after disbanding Johnson's ranger regiment in August, Governor Houston had asked Sul Ross to raise a company of sixty rangers to serve in the Fort Belknap area. Sul had recruited the company in Waco and arrived at the fort in mid-October. A few days earlier there'd been a barbecue in Palo Pinto in honor of Baylor's men. They'd heard the new company was on its way, and they passed a resolution requesting Captain Sul Ross to resign and leave the frontier; eighty men signed it. Baylor had convinced them that the raiders were the former Brazos Agency Indians. He also told them that Sul was a friend of those Indians. That much was true. One man remarked, "I hope the Captain may accomplish some good, but if he does it will be an agreeable surprise to the frontier people." The old hatreds still weren't far from the surface.

Right after the Peta Nocona raid, Jack Cureton, an early settler in Palo Pinto County, organized a volunteer company to go after the raiders; C. C. Slaughter and I both joined it. When he had learned of the raid Governor Houston ordered two companies of twenty-five men each raised to join Sul's force for a Comanche campaign. A Parker County posse had trailed the raiders to their winter camp on the Pease River, but the camp was too large for the small force to attack, so they returned.

Sul was ready to march, but this news convinced him he needed more men. He requested help from Camp Cooper; Captain Evans sent him Sergeant John Spangler and twenty Second Cavalry troopers. Cureton had sixty-eight volunteers, but he also needed more.

"Why don't we throw in with Sul Ross?" I asked. "That would give us enough men to take on Peta Nocona's band."

"No!" one of Cureton's men yelled. "He's the son of that Indian lover Captain Ross." Most of the rest of them glowered at me and agreed with him.

"We need more men," Cureton said calmly. "I'm goin' to talk to him." While he was gone his men stood around grumbling and scowling at me. They were volunteers who could quit if they wanted to, and no one could stop them. But it was foolish for two separate forces to go after Comanches when neither was large enough to do the job.

Cureton returned a short time later. His men stopped talking and sullenly waited to hear what he had to say.

"You all know that we can't let the Comanches come here and murder women without being made to pay," he told them. They mumbled something that indicated agreement. "Our only chance of really punishing them is to send the biggest force possible. That's why Ross and I have agreed on a joint campaign—it's the only sensible thing we could do. You're all volunteers, so I can't stop you from leaving. But before you do, think of what happened to Mrs. Sherman and the others."

Some of them had turned as if they were leaving, but when he said that they stopped and glumly remained. We set out the next day with Antonio Martínez as guide. He'd been a captive of Peta Nocona's band and knew their country.

Cureton was a good bit older than Sul, and his men figured he should be commander. But we were just citizen volunteers, while Sul and his men were official state troops, and that meant he should be in command. Cureton accepted this; Sul tactfully consulted him frequently. Most of the volunteers were cool toward Sul and not overly friendly to me; they hardly spoke to the soldiers, just because they'd been ordered to protect the agency Indians earlier. We were an odd, divided bunch to be heading for a showdown with a lot of Comanches.

If relations among us were cool, the December weather was downright frigid, and a lot of the time we plodded along in heavy rain or sleet. It was hard on the men but even worse on the horses, for the grass was poor and the going was hard. Most of Cureton's men were poorly mounted to begin with—Comanches or Kickapoos had made off with the best horses in Palo Pinto County. The nags they left simply weren't up to a hard campaign.

Late one afternoon we came onto a fresh trail; Martínez and I figured it had been made by a Comanche hunting party.

"What do you reckon we'd better do?" Sul politely asked Cureton. "I think we ought to follow as fast as we can."

Cureton scratched the stubble on his chin and looked over his men's mounts before replying. He frowned. "Our ponies are wore out—they couldn't run if a cougar was after 'em. If we don't rest 'em they'll give out for sure and we'll all be on foot. You go on; we'll follow best we can."

C. C. Slaughter was well mounted and my pony was in good shape, and we sure wanted to go on with Sul and the cavalry. But if we did Cureton's men would never get over it, so we had to stay and watch Sul and the others ride ahead.

In the morning we pushed on, but the horses were still too weak to move very fast. We'd ridden about an hour when one of Sul's men loped up.

"They spotted a camp up ahead on Mule Creek," he told Cureton. "The Injuns are taking down their tipis and fixin' to move, so you best hustle." He turned and loped away.

We slogged along in the mud, strung out in a long line with those of us on the strongest horses well in the lead. Finally we rode over a hill and saw the Comanche camp in a little valley along Mule Creek. Dead Indians were scattered around—the battle was already over. Cureton and a few of his men congratulated Sul and the others on their good fortune. Not one of them had even been scratched, and they'd killed some Comanches and captured a woman and her daughter as well as a big bunch of branded horses and Indian ponies.

"I'm sorry we couldn't wait for you," Sul said to Cureton. "As you can see, they were breaking camp and all would have been gone if we'd waited. Some had already left when we struck 'em."

"I understand," Cureton replied. "You had to move fast. I'd have done the same thing in your place. I'm just glad you caught 'em."

We searched through the camp for trophies, and I found a well-tanned buffalo robe. It reminded me of Taka's; I thought of the times we'd wrapped up in it and wondered when we would again. One of the men found Mrs. Sherman's Bible.

"You sure hit the right camp," Cureton told Sul when he saw it. "I hope you killed the ones that did it. Tell us about the scrap."

"I spotted the camp from that hill." Sul pointed to the one we'd crossed. "Dust was blowing, so they didn't see me. The women were taking down the tipis and packing the ponies, so I knew we had to be quick or lose 'em. The cavalry circled around to cut them off while we charged the camp. The warriors fought like demons so that the women and children could escape. They always do."

He went on to say that he and Tom Kelliher had followed some fleeing Comanches. He'd been after a pair riding double and shot one who pulled the other off. "I thought they were both men, but the one I shot was a woman." Sul continued. "The man hit my horse in the neck with an arrow, and I thought he'd throw me before I got him under control. Then I shot at the man and broke his right arm. He couldn't use his bow then, but he tried to lance me with his other hand. Finally he just ignored me and sang his death chant, so I quit shooting. It was weird."

Antonio Martínez had ridden up. He told Sul the Comanches had massacred his family and taken him captive, and he begged Sul to let him shoot the warrior. The man wouldn't surrender and Sul didn't want to kill him, so he let Martínez do it.

Tom Kelliher had captured the other rider, Sul told us, and was mighty disgusted when he found he'd run his horse so hard after "a damn squaw and her daughter." The woman looked like any Comanche from a distance, but Sul noticed that her eyes were blue and knew she was white. She was sullen and downcast and wouldn't even look at us until Martínez surprised her by asking questions in Comanche. She was worried about her sons, she told him, afraid they'd been killed. He assured her that they must have escaped, for no boys had been killed or captured. She told him there was a big Comanche band camped not far away. Later we captured a nine-year-old boy hiding near camp, but he wasn't one of her sons.

We stayed that night on Mule Creek, and tried to figure out who the white woman was. Sul thought she might be Cynthia Ann Parker, who'd been captured by the Comanches back in '36 when she was a young girl. All attempts to ransom her had failed.

By morning Cureton's men were grumbling because Sul hadn't waited for them, even though they knew that all the Comanches would have escaped. What they really wanted were some of the captured horses. When Sul said that he and the troops were returning to Fort Belknap, Cureton's volunteers insisted on staying and hunting for the big camp the woman had mentioned. Sul took her and the two children, the only captives.

We stayed a few days looking for the other camp, but when we found it the Indians were gone, and that was probably lucky for us. The horses were still weak, so we had to give up and head for home. When we finally got back we learned that the captured woman was the missing Cynthia Ann. Her uncle, Isaac Parker, soon came for her and her daughter and took them to Birdville. She'd been with the Comanches so long she was more Indian than white; she wanted only to return to her husband, Peta Nocona, and her sons. She had a wild look and it didn't seem like she'd ever settle down and live like a white woman. It was kind of sad.

Everywhere but on the frontier all that men talked about was war with the Yankees—the Comanches and Kiowas gave us enough to talk about without worrying about abolitionists. We heard that General Twiggs had sent in his resignation from the army so he could retire and go back to Georgia, and was impatiently waiting for his replacement. Most of the Second Cavalry officers had done the same thing. It was like the troops weren't even there, for they stopped sending out patrols or pursuing raiding parties. They were just waiting to see what would happen.

After South Carolina seceded, Texas secessionists called for delegates to a convention in Austin in late January, and by the time it met five more Southern states had left the Union. The convention ordered a statewide vote on February 23. If the voters favored secession, and the delegates were sure they would, it was to take place on March 2, the same day Texas had declared independence from Mexico twenty-five years earlier. Without waiting to see how Texans would vote, the convention sent delegates to Alabama requesting the admission of Texas into the Confederacy.

"You better make plans to take charge of your money," sutler Ward told me. "There's no tellin' what may happen, and quickly. You don't want to chance losin' it."

"I'll get it the next day or two," I told him. That same day Easton came looking for me. I'd almost forgotten him.

"Do you still want to buy my place?" he asked.

"Yes, sir, if I can afford to."

"Can you give me five hundred dollars for the ranch and brand? That's one fifth of what I paid for the land. I'll throw in livestock and improvements."

He waited while I went to the sutler's office and counted out $500 in gold coins. Easton handed me a deed to his place and a bill of sale for his brand, the bar diamond bar.

"Have the Indians given you trouble lately?" I asked.

"Some, but that's not why we're pullin' out. Like Sam Houston I'm a Union man, and I can see a time comin' when that won't be healthy here.

We're headin' for California; the wagon is loaded and the family is waiting in Belknap."

"About how many head you figure I'm likely to find?"

"Should be about five hundred cows and steers, twenty-five mares and
a good stallion, and maybe fifteen cow ponies. There's also a buckboard
and a team of little Mexican mules. My wife isn't up to handlin' them or
we wouldn't leave 'em. They're real boogery until they get warmed up;
then they settle down."

"Good luck, sir. I'll take good care of the place, and if the Indians don't
clean me out I'll be in good shape."

"Good luck to you, son. I'm glad you're the one takin' over, and I know
you'll do well with it. This money's a real godsend—we can make a fresh
start in California. But for you we'd be in hard times like the others who
are pulling out." We shook hands and parted.

Just like that I'd become a rancher. The first thing I did was to write
Sturm so he could get word to Taka and Tosche. Then I headed for the
county clerk's office to file the deed and bill of sale. Next I put the rest of
my money in a canvas bag and rode to my new ranch to hide it.

"It looks like we're headin' for war and there's no way to avoid it,"
Sheriff Woolfforth said when I met him at the general store in Belknap a
week later. "Unless it's over in six months or a year at most there's no
way the South can win. Better lay in a supply of powder and lead and salt
and anything else you may need in case it drags on for several years.
That's what I'm doing. Some things are likely to get real scarce."

The next morning I headed for my ranch and rounded up the two
little mules. They were spooky rascals, but I got them harnessed and
hitched without getting kicked. When we started out they took off like
Indians were after them, but after they'd run a few miles they slowed
down and were easy to handle. It reminded me of when the stagecoaches
changed teams, and I understood why Mrs. Easton didn't care to drive
them all the way to California. I headed for the general store in Palo
Pinto.

Before the convention had adjourned until after the statewide secession vote on February 23, it appointed a Committee of Public Safety to
act for it. Even though it wasn't a legal body, the committee practically
ran the state, and the legislature didn't object. Major Thomas sent for me
the moment he heard about the committee. He got right to the point.

"Chip," he said, "I've got to get a message to headquarters and things
are happening so fast a military courier might be stopped and searched.

They may even open military mail. But first I need to ask you a personal question. Do you mind?"

"No, sir."

"How do you stand on secession? You know my feelings about it."

"I'm a Houston man, sir, and I think seceding would be a mistake. But I was born here, and I won't do anything to hurt Texas. It's still my state."

"Good answer. I trust you and I know you can get through. Will you deliver this letter to General Twiggs and bring me his reply as soon as possible? Hand it to him personally if you can, or to his aide, Colonel Wilson."

"If you want it done, sir, I'll do it."

He gave me a sealed envelope. "Better put it inside your shirt in case someone goes through your saddlebags. It wouldn't do for those hotheads to find it."

I packed my saddlebags with hard biscuits and dried meat at the sutler's in case I had to camp out on the way, then rolled up my blankets and tied them to my saddle. The paymaster gave me money enough for food, lodging, and corn for my pony whenever I found a place that took in travelers. Then I headed south on the military road.

My mustang cow pony was a good traveler, and we made it to San Antonio late afternoon on February 14, just over a week on the road. I stabled him, then found a place to stay with a German family not far from army headquarters. When I asked for General Twiggs or Colonel Wilson the orderly told me that both were meeting with Texas commissioners; I should come back in the morning.

When we ate supper that night I told the Germans I'd been on the road for over a week and hadn't heard any news. The men looked at me like they wondered if I was a secessionist spy before they opened up. They were Unionists to a man.

"The Committee of Public Safety asked Sam Maverick and three others to serve as civil commissioners and negotiate with General Twiggs for surrender of all federal forts and property," one said. "They thought because he's a Georgian he'd hand over everything they wanted. They're tryin' to keep it secret, but everyone knows whatever they say. Twiggs refuses to do anything before Texas secedes. When it does he insists that his men be allowed to march out under arms."

There was more talk about the old general, not all of it favorable. Some were sure he was conspiring with the commissioners to sell out his country. There was no doubt his sympathies were with the South, but he was no firebrand. According to what the men had heard, he'd told the commissioners he was against Black Republicans, but he was also opposed to Texas seceding. It cost the federal government over a million dollars a year to keep troops on the frontier. Texas couldn't afford to take on that burden, he told them.

The next morning I went to army headquarters and was shown into Colonel Wilson's office. "I have a message from Major Thomas to General Twiggs," I told him, handing him the envelope. He opened it and read the letter. At that moment General Twiggs burst in, waving a dispatch in his hand. He looked real old to be in the army; his face was lined and he had puffy circles under his eyes, but he was smiling.

"At last!" he exclaimed. "Here's what I've been waiting for! Colonel Waite has been ordered to relieve me!"

Colonel Wilson, who'd risen to his feet when the general came in—I was already standing—congratulated him and handed him the letter.

"It's from Major Thomas, sir."

"Thomas? What does he want?"

"He wants instructions as to what he should do when Texas secedes. Should he march his companies to Indian Territory before it's too late?"

"He wants instructions? How many times have I requested instructions from the War Department?" the general asked himself. "And what were the replies? Nothing. Absolutely nothing. They just left me here in limbo —there's not one word in army regulations about what to do in cases of secession. What Thomas wants I can't even get myself. As soon as Waite gets here from Camp Verde, he can figure out what to tell Thomas. It's out of my hands."

Colonel Wilson told me to come back every morning; he should have a message for Major Thomas in a day or two at most.

I knew Major Thomas wanted an answer as quickly as possible, but there was nothing I could do until Colonel Waite took over. I walked around town, listening to the talk.

"I heard Sam Maverick talkin' to the commissioners," a man told others who were standing in front of a saloon. "He was pretty excited when he heard that Colonel Waite is replacing Twiggs. He said the time for talkin' is over—he sent word for Ben McCulloch to bring his rangers here without delay. They're camped down on Salado Crick, maybe five miles outa town. Waite's a Union man, you know—won't be so easy to deal with."

They all looked pleased at the prospect of a fight, so I knew they were secessionists. I spent the rest of the day loafing around and listening to more talk. I heard that Twiggs had only 160 men at headquarters, along with the Eighth Infantry regimental band. I gathered that McCulloch had 400 or 500 men, and that a bunch more from San Antonio planned to join him. A little before sunset I saw eagle-eyed men with long rifles walking into town and climbing to the roofs of buildings around army headquarters and the San Antonio Barracks. I figured McCulloch had sent them ahead as sharpshooters.

I was out at daybreak next morning, and found people already in the streets. Pretty soon we heard shouting, and McCulloch and his rangers swarmed into the main plaza. They'd been camping out a week or more in cold weather and looked like they'd welcome a scrap just to get warmed up.

About six o'clock General Twiggs came through the plaza on his way to headquarters. The rangers stopped his carriage and loudly demanded that he surrender all government property. McCulloch made his way through the crowd and spoke to Twiggs, but I couldn't hear what they said above the shouting. I guess McCulloch also demanded surrender, for I saw Twiggs shake his head. He looked a pretty forlorn old man, and I sure felt sorry for him. The rangers finally released his carriage, and the driver took him on to headquarters.

A little later I heard one of the rangers telling others that Twiggs had refused to surrender and that McCulloch had given him six hours to reconsider. Around noon there was a lot of shouting in the plaza, so I hurried there. McCulloch and the commissioners had just announced that Twiggs had surrendered all military posts and supplies on the condition the troops be allowed to march away with their arms and possessions. He'd insisted that the eight field pieces be considered the arms of the artillery companies. Some men grumbled about that to Maverick.

"He's an honorable old soldier," Maverick replied. "His sympathies are with the South, but he swore he'd sacrifice his life before he'd allow his men to be disgraced by being deprived of their guns. It's a matter of honor with all of them. Would you rather see the old gentleman die?" No one answered.

I went to headquarters to see Colonel Wilson, who had his office staff making copies of Twiggs' General Order Number 5.

"You're the one waiting for a reply to Major Thomas," he said when he saw me. "Here it is." He handed me two envelopes. "One is for Captain Carpenter at Camp Cooper," he said. "I'll appreciate it if you'll deliver these to Major Thomas right away."

A little over a week later I handed the envelopes to Major Thomas at

Fort Belknap. He read the order aloud: "All post commanders in Texas are to turn over possession of their forts to the Texas commissioners or their representatives. As soon as preparations can be made for transporting provisions, medical supplies, and personal property, you are to evacuate the posts and march to Indianola, where transports will be waiting. In the meantime, the troops in San Antonio, except for the headquarters staff and regimental band, will camp outside of the town until they leave for the coast."

Major Thomas shook his head. "The commissioners blocked us from marching to New Mexico or Indian Territory," he said. "Can't say I blame them. We could still make it to Fort Arbuckle, but orders are orders. If we did that now it would look like treachery on the part of General Twiggs. We waited too long, but then things moved too fast."

"One is for Captain Carpenter," I told him.

"Ha!" he said. "No need for that now. Hamner and a bunch of men from Parker County tried to force him to surrender—wanted to loot the place, no doubt. When Carpenter prepared to fight they backed off in a hurry. But just then Colonel Dalrymple arrived with four companies of state troops. That made the odds about two hundred and fifty to thirty-five against Carpenter, and since they were official state troops he surrendered and marched off to Fort Chadbourne. Sent me a note saying he was sure that's what General Twiggs would have done rather than start a war. Looks like he was right about that."

When Texans voted on February 23, all of the counties north of us were opposed to secession, but in Palo Pinto the vote was unanimous for seceding. A bunch of firebrands had sworn they'd hang anyone who voted nay. Most men stayed home that day.

Like Baylor and some of his other friends, Hamner figured he was above the law, and he got pretty high-handed with Union men. When word had gotten around that he was helping white horse thieves blame their thefts on Indians, some men started watching his movements. They were mighty quiet about it, so I never learned the details. An unsigned letter in the Dallas *Herald* said that "his conduct was so odiferous that the element whose business it was to purify the social atmosphere of the frontier town, saw fit to 'elevate' Mr. Hamner to a cottonwood limb, thus separating the editor and *The White Man* definitely." I had to admit I enjoyed reading that letter. Hamner sure had it coming to him.

THIRTEEN

In late December '60 Governor Houston had named Buck Barry to raise one of the ranger companies to cooperate with Sul Ross. About two months after the company assembled at Fort Belknap the Committee of Public Safety ordered Barry to raise a hundred men and assist Colonel Henry McCulloch in taking over the federal forts.

I was at Fort Belknap the day Barry received the order. He assembled his company. "Men," he said, "I've been ordered to disband this company and raise a hundred men for a new one." He paused.

"What's it fer?" one asked. "To fight Comanches?"

Barry cleared his throat. "You've heard that Colonel McCulloch is raising a regiment to take over the federal posts north of Chadbourne," he said. "The new company is for that purpose. It's to help him and then maybe to hold one of the posts, probably Cooper. I'll be glad for any of you to re-enlist."

There was a lot of palaver, then the men separated into two groups, about half in each. "We'll sign on," a man in one group said.

"What about you men?" Barry asked the others.

One of them stepped forward. "No thanks, Mr. Barry," he said. "None of us is willin' to fight our own government."

Barry's headquarters were at Camp Cooper, but he came to Fort Belknap frequently. He was a typical frontiersman, slender and of medium height, with dark curly hair that reached his shoulders, and a low voice. Like many on the frontier, he always wore buckskin shirts and pants.

I still resented him trying to get Allison Nelson in the Major's place as Indian superintendent, but when I got to know him I found him straightforward and honest. Nelson was a friend and he believed what his friends told him, and he had no use for any Indians except Tonkawas. "They're the only ones I trust," he said. "They've been allies of the whites for years, and there are no better scouts." I agreed with that.

Barry was as active as any man could be in defending the settlers and punishing raiders and thieves, red or white. With a few men he'd followed two white thieves who'd stolen his neighbor's horses, tracking them to San Antonio, then back to Waco, and finally to Meridian. After three weeks on the trail they caught the two and strung them up with their own lariats. By the time Barry got back to his ranch, Comanches or Kickapoos had run off half a dozen of his horses.

In February the legislature authorized each of the frontier counties to organize forty-member minuteman companies for their defense. I joined the Young County company under Sheriff Woolfforth. He'd been a sergeant in the Second Cavalry, and he really knew how to boss a campaign. We didn't make patrols except when Indians were seen in the county or nearby, but we had to be ready to ride at any time. Although the legislature promised to provide powder and lead and grub, we had to furnish our own horses and guns. Most of the time, in fact, we had to furnish everything we needed, for it wasn't often that the state sent us anything, and it paid us only for the days we were in the saddle.

Henry McCulloch's cavalry regiment was supposed to take over frontier defense, but after it was inducted into the Confederate service it was sent off to meet Union armies threatening Arkansas. That left only the minuteman companies to protect settlers and punish raiders.

Between raids I rode around my range, pushing bar diamond bar stock back on it and other brands off, but I couldn't do much by myself—I needed help. I had fifty big steers ready for market but nowhere to sell them even if I could round them up.

In May Confederate colonels William Young and James Throckmorton raised a volunteer cavalry regiment in North Texas. Throckmorton had been one of the eight voting nay at the secession convention, but once the decision to secede was made, he joined the Confederate Army. The federal troops who'd served in Texas forts had been sent out of the state by sea so they couldn't reinforce Union garrisons in Indian Territory and New Mexico. Now the governor figured we'd better take over forts Washita, Arbuckle, and Cobb before the Yankees used them to build up a big force and invade Texas from the north. I heard that Baylor, who was in Rip Ford's regiment, was marching toward El Paso, on his way to seize the federal forts in New Mexico.

Soon after I learned that the Young-Throckmorton regiment was to take over the federal forts in Indian Territory, one of their recruiting officers came to Belknap.

"I'll be glad to hire on as a civilian guide," I told him. I figured that after we got to Fort Cobb I could quit and make off with Taka, but of course I didn't tell him that. He looked me up and down before replying. Becoming an officer all of a sudden must have made him feel pretty important.

"You look able-bodied to me," he said. "What we need are privates, not civilian guides. Most of them are no account anyway. If you want to help us, you'll enlist in the ranks where you belong."

"I'll think about it." I must admit I was tempted to, because I couldn't see any other way to get to Fort Cobb and the Tonkawas. But after that I'd have to desert if I was going to run away with Taka, and the idea of being branded a deserter didn't appeal to me at all. Anyway, if I didn't check on my cattle now and then they'd stray or be stolen. Either way I'd lose them.

The cavalry regiment rode off without me, and they found that the federals had abandoned all three forts just before they got to them. The Wichitas and most of the other tribes around Fort Cobb were pro-Union or at least anti-Texas, and when they learned that Texas troops were coming they lit out for Kansas. Only the Tonkawas and a few Caddos remained around the agency, where Colonel Leeper was now Confederate Indian agent.

The regiment soon returned to Texas and was sworn into the Confederate Army. It was supposed to go back to Indian Territory and garrison the three forts, but it was needed more in Louisiana and went there instead. When I heard that I was sure relieved I hadn't enlisted.

Although the secessionist hotheads had repeatedly sworn that there'd never be a need for Texans to fight east of the Mississippi, in late summer the Confederate government asked the state to raise twenty infantry companies for service in Virginia. About every young man who could be spared from home enlisted; thirty-two, not twenty, companies were quickly filled, but there weren't enough guns for them.

Peter Ross recruited a cavalry company in Waco to join Colonel Warren Stone's regiment in Dallas. Sul married Lizzie, then joined Pete's company, and in Dallas he was elected major before the regiment rode off to Missouri. When I heard that I felt guilty for not joining him, but about that time we had a scrap with Comanches and Kiowas. If some of us didn't stay and fight Indians, the frontier would be pushed back to East Texas.

In the early fall of '61 a small party of Tonkawas appeared at Barry's headquarters and asked for an escort to the Red River, for they feared Comanches would attack them. I never found out why they were in

Texas, but Barry sent ten men to get them back to the Red safely. On their return the escort ran into fifty Comanche warriors in open country about ten miles south of the ranger camp at Willow Spring. The Comanches surrounded them and they had to fight their way through the Indian line twelve times before they got to Fish Creek, where a scout squad was stationed. By then three of the escort were badly wounded and the Comanches were closing in for the kill. Luckily the scout squad heard the shooting and rushed to the rescue.

I talked to Barry afterward. He said he'd sent word to Colonel Leeper asking for a bunch of Tonkawa scouts.

"Do you think that's a good idea?" I asked. "Your friends used to claim that all agency Indians were guilty, and they killed some right after they'd served with Van Dorn."

"I know," he admitted. "We maybe listened too much to Baylor. But nobody around here has anything against Tonks living in Texas, and we damn sure need them. Bad."

I was glad to hear him say that, for it made me feel better about bringing Taka back. I aimed to anyway, but it would be a lot easier if folks were friendly to her. Right after the Tonkawa scouts came to Cooper, Barry told me later, Colonel McCord asked him to send four of them. "I feel their service to my regiment will be equal to that of two or three companies," he said.

By the end of '61 it was clear that frontier defense would remain a Texas problem, for the minuteman companies were the only forces available. The Confederate government and the army had the Yankees to worry about, so the legislature created the Frontier Regiment, and Barry's company became part of it. In January '62 Governor Lubbock named Colonel James Norris regimental commander.

They set up a chain of camps or posts a day's ride apart from the Red to the Rio Grande, with fifty or sixty men in each. The companies sent out two patrols daily to cover half the distance to the camps above and below them. That helped some, but Comanche raiding parties soon learned to wait until a patrol had passed, then cross the line behind it. Several hours or more would pass before the patrol returned and discovered the tracks. By then the raiders had a pretty good head start, and that's when the minutemen got busy.

Even so, the men of the Frontier Regiment did about as well as the Second Cavalry had in protecting the settlers and punishing raiders. Life in those camps was miserable and dangerous, for they were short of everything they needed and always exposed to attack by large war parties.

Some men were poorly armed, and they had no medical supplies or commissary. If they had tents for shelter and even poor food to eat they considered themselves lucky, and a lot of them were sick both summer and winter. The gunpowder the state furnished them was often so bad they swore a bullet wouldn't kill a man ten paces from the gun's muzzle. They also had to furnish their own mounts, and good saddle horses were scarce.

Somehow those Frontier Regiment men hung on to their posts and on three occasions fought off war parties of several hundred screeching warriors. Sick or well, they stayed in the saddle and made their patrols. Luckily for them there weren't many big raids in the spring of '62, but I still figured the state owed them a lot more than anyone realized. The papers were full of war news, but the Frontier Regiment was seldom mentioned.

To add to their troubles, Colonel Norris suddenly insisted on following army regulations. That made discipline a serious problem—they were independent cusses.

In April '62, the Confederate government passed a conscription act making all men between eighteen and thirty-five subject to military service. Just about every young man whose family could survive without him had already enlisted voluntarily. The conscription officers were high-handed—they had to raise a certain number of men, I guess, and they didn't much care how they did it. When they ordered anyone into the army he had to go, even though his wife and children might starve.

By now the war was no longer popular—the early enthusiasm for it had vanished, to be replaced by grumbling. Those of us in the minute-man companies were badly needed on the frontier, so we weren't subject to conscription. We got a lot more volunteers because of that, and we heard that a lot of men who'd been forced into the Confederate Army had deserted at the first opportunity.

Oliver Loving began buying steers for the Confederate Army and trailing them to Arkansas or Louisiana. That gave me a chance to sell my big steers for Confederate scrip, and Loving's men helped me gather them. The price wasn't much, but it was enough to buy a couple of small herds from men who were giving up and willing to accept anything they could get. The Slaughters were determined to stay on their ranch, and they also bought cattle from families who were leaving for safer country.

I wrote Sturm, telling him what was happening around Belknap and asking for news of Taka and Tosche. I finally got a reply early in September. He told me about the pro-Union Indians fleeing to Kansas, which I already knew. He was worried about Leeper and other men at the agency, he said, and especially for the Tonkawas. He kept hearing rumors from the Caddos in Kansas that a big bunch of pro-Union Delawares, Shawnees, and others were coming to wipe out the agency and the pro-Texas Indians. That meant the Tonkawas.

"I went to see Taka and Tosche," he wrote. "Taka and her son are with Tosche and his wife—you can probably guess why. I told them that if they heard shooting or anything to join us immediately. We'll hide them and see that they get to Fort Arbuckle somehow. Then maybe they can make it back to Texas from there."

It took a few moments for this to sink in. Taka and her son! Those words hit me like a blood-chilling blue norther. I couldn't guess why they were living with Tosche and his wife, unless White Buffalo had died. She'd bring his son with her! For the rest of my life I'd be reminded that White Buffalo had . . . I choked on the thought. The prospect of seeing his son every day was more than I could stand. No man should have to bear that burden.

I forgot about the war and tried to figure out what I should do if Taka came to Texas with White Buffalo's son. I was really torn, for I'd see her sad little face and remember our times together until I was ready to burst with love for her. Then I'd see White Buffalo crawling onto her robe and pushing her legs apart and I'd go mad.

Comanche raiders were reported, so I hastily met Sheriff Woolfforth's company and we beat them to Baker's Gap and hid. A dozen warriors appeared with a herd of stolen stock; when they were about even with us we charged. I was so worked up over White Buffalo's son I tore after the Comanches and tried to kill every last one of them, but those who didn't stop a bullet scattered fast and disappeared. When we rode back to round up the stolen horses, Sheriff Woolfforth was staring at me.

"You acted like you were tryin' to get yourself killed," he said.

I hadn't thought about that, but I figured maybe he was right. "I just got carried away, I guess," I told him.

"Don't do it again," he said friendly-like. "We need every man."

What he said got me to doing some cold figuring. In a way I did want to get myself killed, only I hadn't even realized it before. Now things got clearer. If Taka and Tosche came to Fort Belknap I'd go see them one last time. Then I'd say goodbye and join the Confederate cavalry, maybe Terry's Texas Rangers. They'd been in so many fights and had suffered so many casualties there were few of the original men left—even Terry had been killed. The chances of surviving the war in that outfit were slim, and that suited me. Better to stop a Yankee bullet, I thought, than . . . What made me even more miserable was remembering that if I had only followed my own plans and not listened to Dr. Stern, Taka and I would be raising our own children and I'd have been spared all the agony. Knowing it had been my own foolishness that got me into this mess made me all the more bitter and determined. I'd been stupid and deserved whatever I got.

Once I had it figured out I calmed down and even quit thrashing around nights and slept for a change. I wrote Sturm to thank him for looking after Taka and Tosche, but I didn't have much more to say. The Confederacy's mail system was chancy at best, but the letters usually got through eventually. His last letter had taken about a month to reach me.

Early in November I was surprised to see John Shirley at Fort Belknap when our minuteman company returned from a two-day run after Comanches.

"What are you doing here?" I asked.

"Saving my life," he replied. "A big bunch of Delawares and Shawnees and I don't know what others came down from Kansas and attacked the agency the night of October 23. Leeper had just returned from moving his family out of harm's way, and just in time. He and Horace Jones and Phil McCusker managed to escape somehow and warned me, so we headed for Arbuckle in a hurry. The rest of the men at the agency were killed."

"What about the Tonkawas?" I asked, my fears rising.

"They lived along the Washita just south of the agency, and when they heard the shooting they fled east. When they figured they were safely away they stopped and camped, but some of those Indians were on their trail. They surrounded the camp in the dark and attacked at sunup." He paused.

I stared at him, dreading what he might say next.

"It was awful," he continued, "a slaughter of men and women. Plácido and many other good men were killed. About a hundred made it to Arbuckle; they're being escorted here and should arrive soon."

I got my bedroll and stayed in one of the fort's empty barracks, sleeping on the floor, worrying over the next news I might hear. I was terrified at the thought that Taka and Tosche were among those killed. At night I thrashed about on the hard floor, grinding my teeth and groaning like I had the ague. During the days I moped around just killing time; I had no appetite and found it hard even to swallow food. Waiting and not knowing was agony.

I did a lot of thinking about Taka, and I realized she meant even more to me than I'd ever imagined. I was so worried about her I knew now that her safety was all that really mattered. If only she escaped I'd leave her my ranch when I went off to war.

A week passed, and no sign of them. Maybe the Comanches had cut them off; they hated the Tonkawas and would kill every one they could. Finally I rode to the Belknap post office to see if a letter from Sturm might be there—he should know if Taka and Tosche had survived the massacre, and I was sure he'd let me know. While in Belknap I saw Sheriff Woolfforth.

"You look mighty grim, Chip," he said. "War news bad?"

"Reckon so. I haven't heard any good news in a spell. Have you?"

"Not much. We haven't lost yet, but the North gets stronger every day, and that looks bad. Whoever thought the Yankees can't or won't fight is an idiot. After McClellan fought Lee to a draw at Antietam the British and French backed off tryin' to stop the war, figurin' the smart thing for them to do is stay out of it. I reckon they're right about that, but they maybe could have saved a lot of lives if they'd stepped in."

I headed back to the fort, and from a distance I saw a big crowd of people around the gate. The Tonkawas had arrived! I loosened the reins and my pony broke into a fast lope. When he slid to a stop I hopped off and dropped the reins, looking frantically for Taka in the crowd, but couldn't see her. I broke out in a cold sweat.

"Here I am," she called. I practically flew to her side and crushed her in my arms. I didn't even see the others, and didn't care if White Buffalo was watching.

"I was so worried I'd never see you again," I blurted out. "I won't join the cavalry. I really didn't want to, anyway. And I'll treat him like my own."

"You talk funny. I don't know what you mean. Don't you want to say hello to Tosche?"

There he was, a few feet away, with his pretty little Tonkawa wife standing beside him holding a small boy by the hand.

"Tosche! It's great to see you again!" We shook hands, and he actually smiled.

"My wife," he said proudly, nodding toward the Tonkawa girl, who was shyly looking at her moccasins.

"Don't you want to say hello to your son?" Taka asked, kneeling by the little boy.

"My . . . son?" I gasped, and squatted down beside her. He was scared of me and buried his face in her shoulder.

"He'll get to know his father soon," she said softly, patting me.

It was like I'd been lost in a cave in total blackness and suddenly saw a light. Now I knew what Sturm meant when he said I could probably guess why she was living with Tosche and his wife. I arose. "Get your things," I told them. "I've got a double-log cabin, big enough for two families—one for you two, the other for us. And I've been needing a partner to help me run the ranch."

ABOUT THE AUTHOR

Don Worcester is a professor emeritus of history at Texas Christian University, and winner of the 1988 Western Writers of America Saddleman Award. He lives in Aledo, Texas, where he raises Arabian horses. His previous Double D Western is *The War in the Nueces Strip*.